The Orphan

Clarence E. Mulford

AFFECTIONATELY DEDICATED TO
MY MOTHER

CONTENTS

THE ORPHAN

CHAPTER I
THE SHERIFF RIDES TO WAR

Many men swore that The Orphan was bad, and many swore profanely and with wonderful command of epithets because he was bad, but for obvious reasons that was as far as the majority went to show their displeasure. Those of the minority who had gone farther and who had shown their hatred by rash actions only proved their foolishness; for they had indeed gone far and would return no more.

Tradition had it that The Orphan was a mongrel, a half-breed, asserting that his mother had been a Sioux with negro blood in her veins. It also asserted that his father had been nominated and unanimously elected, by a posse, to an elevated position under a tree; and further, that The Orphan himself had been born during a cloudburst at midnight on the thirteenth of the month. The latter was from the Mexicans, who found great delight in making such terrifying combinations of ill luck.

But tradition was strongly questioned as to his mother, for how could the son of such a mother be possessed of the dare-devil courage and grit which had made his name a synonym of terror? This contention was well stated and is borne out, for it can be authoritatively said that the mother of The Orphan was white, and had neither Indian nor negro blood in her veins, but on the contrary came from a family of gentlefolk. Thus I start aright by refuting slander. The Orphan was white, his profanity blue, and his anger red, and having started aright, I will continue with the events which led to the discovery of his innate better qualities and their final ascendency over the savagely hard nature which circumstances had bred in him. These events began on the day when James Shields, for reasons hereinafter set forth, became actively interested in his career.

Shields, by common consent Keeper of the Law over a territory as large as the State of New Jersey and whom out of courtesy I will call sheriff, was no coward, and neither was he a fool; and when word came to him that The Orphan had made a mess of two sheep herders near the U Bend of the Limping Water Creek, he did not forthwith pace the street and inform the citizens of Ford's Station that he was about to start on a journey which had for its object the congratulation of The Orphan at long range. Upon occasions his taciturnity became oppressive, especially when grave dangers or tense situations demanded concentration of thought. The more he thought the less he talked, the one notable exception being when stirred to righteous anger by personal insults, in which case his words flowed smoothly along one channel while his thoughts gripped a single idea. To his acquaintances he varied as the mood directed, often saying practically nothing for hours, and at other times discoursing volubly. One thing, a word of his, had become proverbial–when Shields said "Hell!" he was in no mood for pleasantries, and the third repetition of the word meant red, red anger. He was a man of strong personality, who loved his friends in staunch, unswerving loyalty; and he tolerated his enemies until the last ditch had been reached.

He, like The Orphan, was essentially a humorist in the finest definition of the term, inasmuch as he could find humor in the worst possible situations. He was even now forcibly struck with the humor of his contemplated ride, for The Orphan would be so very much surprised to see him. He could picture the expression of weary toleration which would grace the outlaw's face over the sights, and he chuckled inwardly as he thought of how The Orphan would swear. He did his shooting as an unavoidable duty, a business, a stern necessity; and he took great delight in its accuracy. When he shot at a man he did it with becoming gravity, but nevertheless he radiated pride and cheerfulness when he hit the man's nose or eye or Adam's apple at a hundred yards. All the time he knew that the man ought to die, that it was a case of necessity, and this explains why he was so pleased about the eye or nose or Adam's apple.

With The Orphan popular opinion said it was far different; that his humor was ghastly, malevolent, murderous; that he shot to kill with the same gravity, but that it was that of icy determination, chilling ferocity. He was said to be methodical in the taking of innocent life, even more accurate than the sheriff, wily and shrewd as the leader of a wolf-pack, and equally relentless. The Orphan was looked upon as an abnormal development of the idea of destruction; the sheriff, a corrective force, and almost as strong as the evil he would endeavor to overcome. The two came as near to the scientists' little joke of the irresistible force meeting the immovable body as can be found in human agents.

So Shields, upon hearing of The Orphan's latest manifestation of humor, appreciated the joke to the fullest extent and made up his mind to play a similar one on the frisky outlaw. He could not help but sympathize with The Orphan, because every man knew what pests the sheepmen were, and Shields, at one time a cowman, was naturally prejudiced against sheep. He was exceedingly weary of having to guard herds of bleating grass-shavers which so often passed across his domain, and he regarded the sheep-raising industry as an unnecessary evil which should by all rights be deported. But he could not excuse The Orphan's crude and savage idea of deportation. The sheriff was really kind-hearted, and he became angry when he thought of the outlaw driving two thousand sheep over the steep bank of the Limping Water to a pitiful death by drowning; The Orphan should have been satisfied in messing up the anatomy of the herders. He did not like a glutton, and he would tell the outlaw so in his own way.

He walked briskly through his yard and called to his wife as he passed the house, telling her that he was going to be gone for an indefinite period, not revealing the object of his journey, as he did not wish to worry her. Accustomed as she was to have him face danger, she had a loving wife's fear for his safety, and lost many hours' sleep while he was away. He took his rifle from where it leaned against the porch and continued on his way to the small corral in the rear of the yard, where two horses whisked flies and sought the shade. Leading one of them outside, he deftly slung a saddle to its back, secured the cinches and put on a light bridle. Dropping the Winchester into its saddle holster, he mounted and fought the animal for a few minutes just as he always had to fight it. He spun the cylinders of his .45 Colts and ran his fingers along the under side of his belt for assurance as to ammunition. Seeing that the black leather case which was slung from the pommel of the saddle contained his field glass and that his canteen was full of water, he rode to the back door of his house, where his wife gave him a bag of food. Promising her that he would take good care of himself and to return as speedily as possible, he cantered through the gate and down the street toward the "Oasis," the door of which was always open. Two dogs were stretched out in the doorway, lazily snapping at flies. As the sheriff drew rein he heard snores which wheezed from the barroom.

"Say, Dan!" he cried loudly. "Dan!"

"Shout it out, Sheriff," came the response from within the darkened room, and the bartender appeared at the door.

"If anybody wants me, they may find me at Brent's; I'm going out that way," the sheriff said, as he loosened the reins. "Bite, d——n you," he growled at his horse.

"All right, Jim," sleepily replied the bartender, watching the peace officer as he cantered briskly down the street. He yawned, stretched and returned to his chair, there to doze lightly as long as he might.

Shields usually left word at the Oasis as to where he might be found in case he should be badly needed, but in this instance he had left word where he could not be found if needed. He cantered out of the town over the trail which led to Brent's ranch and held to it until he had put great enough distance behind to assure him that he was out of sight of any curious citizen of Ford's Station. Then he wheeled abruptly as he reached the bottom of an arroyo and swung sharply to the northeast at a right angle to his former course and pushed his mount at a lope around the chaparrals and cacti, all the time riding more to the east and in the direction of the U Bend of the Limping Water. He frowned slightly and grumbled as he estimated that The Orphan would have nearly three hours' start of him by the time he reached his objective, which meant a long chase in the pursuit of such a man.

To a tenderfoot the heat would have been very oppressive, even dangerous, but the sheriff thought it an ideal temperature for hunting. He smiled pleasantly at his surroundings and was pleased by the playful vim of his belligerent pinto, whose actions were not in the least intended to be playful. When the animal suddenly turned its head and nipped hard and quick at the sheriff's legs, getting a mouthful of nasty leather and seasoned ash for its reward, he gleefully kicked the pony in the eye when it let go, and then rowelled a streak of perforations in its ugly hide with his spurs as an encouragement. The ensuing bucking was joy to his heart, and he feared that he might eventually grow to like the animal.

When he arrived at the U Bend he put in half an hour burying the human butts of The Orphan's joke, for the perpetrator liked to leave his trophies where they could be seen and appreciated. Shields looked sadly at the dead sheep, said "Hell" twice and forded the stream, picked up the outlaw's trail on the further side and cantered along it. The trail was very plain to him, straight as a chalk line, and it led toward the northeast, which suited the sheriff, because there was a goodly sized water hole twenty miles further on in that direction. Perhaps he would find The Orphan fortified there, for it would be just like that person to monopolize the only drinking water within twenty miles and force his humorous adversary to either take the hole or go back to the Limping Water for a drink. Anyway, The Orphan would get awful soiled wallowing about in the mud and water, and he would not hurt the water much unless he lacked the decency to bleed on the bank. Having decided to take the hole in preference to riding back to the creek, the sheriff immediately dismissed that phase of the game from his mind and fell to musing about the rumors which had persistently reiterated that the Apaches were out.

Practical joking with The Orphan and interfering with the traveling of Apache war parties were much the same in results, so the sheriff made up his mind to attend to the lesser matter, if need be, after he had quieted the man he was following. Everybody knew that Apaches were very bad, but that The Orphan was worse; and, besides, the latter would be laughing derisively about that matter concerning a drink. The sheriff grinned and rode happily forward, taking pains, however, to circle around all chaparrals and covers of every nature, for he did not know but that his playful enemy might have tired of riding before the water hole had been reached and decided to camp out under cover. While the sheriff was unafraid, he had befitting respect for the quality of The Orphan's marksmanship, which was reputed as being above reproach; and he was not expected to determine offhand whether the outlaw was above lying in ambush. So he used his field glass constantly in sweeping covers and rode forward toward the water hole.

CHAPTER II
CONCERNING AN ARROW

The bleak foreground of gray soil, covered with drifts of alkali and sand, was studded with clumps of mesquite and cacti and occasional tufts of sun-burned grass, dusty and somber, while a few sagebrush blended their leaves to the predominating color. Back of this was a near horizon to the north and east, brought near by the skyline of a low, undulating range of sand hills rising from the desert to meet a faded sky. The morning glow brought this skyline into sharp definition as the dividing line between the darkness of the plain in the shadow of the range and the fast increasing morning light. To the south and west the plain blended into the sky, and there was no horizon.

Two trails met and crossed near a sand-buffeted bowlder of lava stone, which was huge, grotesque and forbidding in its bulky indistinctness. The first of the trails ran north and south and was faint but plainly discernible, being beaten a trifle below the level of the desert and forming a depression which the winds alternately filled and emptied of dust; and its arrow-like directness, swerving neither to the right nor left, bespoke of the haste which urged the unfortunate traveler to have done with it as speedily as possible, since there was nothing alluring along its heat-cursed course to bid him tarry in his riding. There was yet another reason for haste, for the water holes were over fifty miles apart, and in that country water holes were more or less uncertain and doubtful as to being free from mineral poisons. On the occasions when the Apaches awoke to find that many of their young men were missing, and a proved warrior or two, this trail become weighted with possibilities, for this desert was the playground of war parties, an unlimited ante-room for the preliminaries to predatory pilgrimages; and the northern trail then partook of the nature of a huge wire over which played an alternating current, the potentials of which were the ranges at one end and the savagery and war spirit of the painted tribes at the other: and the voltage was frequently deadly.

The other trail, crossing the first at right angles, led eastward to the fertile valleys of the Canadian and the Cimarron; westward it spread out like the sticks of a fan to anywhere and nowhere, gradually resolving itself into the fainter and still more faint individual paths which fed it as single strands feed a rope. It lacked the directness of its intersector because of the impenetrable chaparrals which forced it to wander hither and yon. Neither was it as plain to the eye, for preference, except in cases of urgent necessity, foreswore its saving of miles and journeyed by the more circuitous southern trail which wound beneath cottonwoods and mottes of live oak and frequently dipped beneath the waters of sluggish streams, the banks of which were fringed with willows.

As a lean coyote loped past the point of intersection a moving object suddenly topped the skyline of the southern end of the sandhills to the east and sprang into sharp silhouette, paused for an instant on the edge of the range and then, plunging down into the shadows at its base, rode rapidly toward the bowlder.

He was an Apache, and was magnificent in his proportions and the easy erectness of his poise. He glanced sharply about him, letting his gaze finally settle on the southern trail and then, leaning over, he placed an object on the highest point of the rock. Wheeling abruptly, he galloped back over his trail, the rising wind setting diligently at work to cover the hoofprints of his pony. He had no sooner dropped from sight over the hills than another figure began to be defined in the dim light, this time from the north.

The newcomer rode at an easy canter and found small pleasure in the cloud of alkali dust which the wind kept at pace with him. His hat, the first visible sign of his calling, proclaimed him to be a cowboy, and when he had stopped at the bowlder his every possession endorsed the silent testimony of the hat.

He was bronzed and self-reliant, some reason for the latter being suggested by the long-barreled rifle which swung from his right saddle skirt and the pair of Colt's which lay along his thighs. He wore the usual blue flannel shirt, open at the throat, the regular silk kerchief about his neck, and the indispensable chaps, which were of angora goatskin. His boots were tight fitting, with high heels, and huge brass spurs projected therefrom. A forty-foot coil of rawhide hung from the pommel of his "rocking-chair" saddle and a slicker was strapped behind the cantle.

He glanced behind him as he drew rein, wondering when the sheriff would show himself, for he was being followed, of that he was certain. That was why he had ridden through so many chaparrals and doubled on his trail. He was now riding to describe a circle, the object being to get behind his pursuer and to do some hunting on his own account. As he started to continue on his way his quick eyes espied something on the bowlder which made him suddenly draw rein again. Glancing to the ground he saw the tracks made by the Apache, and he peered intently along the eastern trail with his hand shading his eyes. The eyes were of a grayish blue, hard and steely and cruel. They were calculating eyes, and never missed anything worth seeing. The fierce glare of the semi-tropical sun which for many years had daily assaulted them made it imperative that he squint from half-closed lids, and had given his face a malevolent look. And the characteristics promised by the eyes were endorsed by his jaw, which was square and firm set, underlying thin, straight lips. But about his lips were graven lines so cynical and yet so humorous as to baffle an observer.

Raising his canteen to his lips he counted seven swallows and then, letting it fall to his side, he picked up the object which had made him pause. There was no surprise in his face, for he never was surprised at anything.

As he looked at the object he remembered the rumors of the Apache war dances and of fast-riding, paint-bedaubed "hunting parties." What had been rumor he now knew to be a fact, and his face became even more cruel as he realized that he was playing tag with the sheriff in the very heart of the Apache playground, where death might lurk in any of the thorny covers which surrounded him on all sides.

"Apache war arrow," he grunted. "Now it shore beats the devil that me and the sheriff can't have a free rein to settle up our accounts. Somebody is always sticking their nose in my business," he grumbled. Then he frowned at the arrow in his hand. "That red on the head is blood," he murmured, noticing the salient points of the weapon, "and that yellow hair means good scalping. The thong of leather spells plunder, and it was pointing to the east. The buck that brought it went back again, so this is to show his friends which way to ride. He was in a hurry, too, judging from the way he threw sand, and from them toe-prints."

He hated Apaches vindictively, malevolently, with a single purpose and instinct, because of a little score he owed them. Once when he had managed to rustle together a big herd of horses and was within a day's ride of a ready market, a party of Apaches had ridden up in the night and made off with not only the stolen animals, but also with his own horse. This had lost him a neat sum and had forced him to carry a forty-pound saddle, a bridle and a rifle for two days under a merciless sun before he reached civilization. He did not thank them for not killing him, which they for some reason neglected to do. Apache stock was down very low with him, and he now had an opportunity to even the score. Then he thought of the sheriff, and swore. Finally he decided that he would just shoot that worthy as soon as he came within range, and so be free to play his lone hand against the race that had stolen his horses. His eyes twinkled at the game he was about to play, and he regarded the silent message and guide with a smile.

"If it's all the same to you, I'll just polish you up a bit"–and when he replaced it on the bowlder its former owner would not have known it to be the same weapon, for its head was not red, but as bright as the friction of a handful of sand could make it. This destroyed its message of plentiful slaughter and, he knew, would grieve his enemies. He touched it gently with his hand and it swung at right angles to its former position and now pointed northward and in the direction from which he expected the sheriff.

"It was d—d nice of that Apache leaving me this, but I reckon I'll switch them reinforcements–the sheriff will be some pleased to meet them," he said, grinning at the novelty of the situation. "Nobody will even suspect how a lone puncher"–for he regarded himself as a cowman–"squaring up a couple of scores went and saved the eastern valleys from more devilment. If the war-whoops are out along the Cimarron and Canadian they are shore havin' fun enough to give me a little. But I would like to see the sheriff' s face when he bumps into the little party I'm sending his way. Wonder how many he will get before he goes under?"

Then he again took up the arrow and carefully removed the hair and thong of leather, chuckling at the tale of woe the denuded weapon would tell, after which he placed it as before, wishing he knew how to indicate that the Apaches had been wiped out.

He rode to a chaparral which lay three hundred yards to the southeast of him and thence around it to the far side, where he dismounted and fastened his horse to the empty air by simply allowing the reins to hang down in front of the animal's eyes. The pony knew many things about ropes and straps, and what it knew it knew well; nothing short of dynamite would have moved it while the reins dangled before its eyes.

Its master slowly returned to the bowlder, where he set to work to cover his tracks with dust, for although the shifting sand was doing this for him, it was not doing it fast enough to suit him. When he had assured himself that he had performed his task in a thoroughly workmanlike manner he returned to his horse, and finally found a snug place of concealment for it and himself. First bandaging its eyes so that it would not whinny at the approach of other horses, he searched his pockets and finally brought to light a pack of greasy playing cards, with which he amused himself at solitaire, diligently keeping his eyes on both ends of the heavier trail.

His intermittent scrutiny was finally rewarded by a cloud of dust which steadily grew larger on the southern horizon and soon revealed the character of the riders who made it. As they drew nearer to him his implacable hatred caused him to pick up his rifle, but he let it slide from him as he counted the number of the approaching party, before which was being driven a herd of horses which were intended to be placed as relays for the main force.

"Two, five, eight, eleven, sixteen, twenty, twenty-four, twenty-seven," he muttered, carefully settling himself more comfortably. He could distinguish the war paint on the reddish-brown colored bodies, and he smiled at what was in store for them.

"I reckon I won't get gay with no twenty-seven Apaches," he muttered. "I can wait, all right."

Upon reaching the rock the leaders of the band glanced at the arrow, excitedly exchanged monosyllables and set off to the north at a hard gallop, being followed by the others. As he expected, they were Apaches, which meant that of all red raiders they were the most proficient. They were human hyenas with rare intelligence for war and a most aggravating way of not being where one would expect them to be, as army officers will testify. Besides, an Apache war party did not appear to have stomachs, and so traveled faster and farther than the cavalry which so often pursued them.

The watcher chuckled softly at the success of his stratagem and, suddenly arising, went carefully around the chaparral until he could see the fast-vanishing braves. Waiting until they had disappeared over the northern end of the crescent-shaped range of hills, he hurried to the bowlder and again picked up the arrow.

"Huh! Didn't take it with them, eh?" he soliloquized. "Well, that means that there's more coming, so I'll just send the next batch plumb west–they'll be some pleased to explore this God-forsaken desert some extensive."

Grinning joyously, he replaced the weapon with its head pointing westward and then looked anxiously at the tracks of the party which had just passed. Deciding that the wind would effectually cover them in an hour at most, he returned to his hiding place, taking care to cover his own tracks. Taking a chance on the second contingent going north was all right, but he didn't care to run the risk of having them ride to him for explanations. Picking up the cards again he shuffled them and suffered defeat after defeat, and finally announced his displeasure at the luck he was having.

"I never saw nothing like it!" he grumbled petulantly. "Reckon I'll hit up the Old Thirteen a few," beginning a new game. He had whiled away an hour and a half, and as he stretched himself his uneasy eyes discovered another cloud on the southern horizon, which was smaller than the first. He placed the six of hearts on the five of hearts, ruffled the pack and then put the cards down and took up his rifle, watching the cloud closely. He was soon able to count seven warriors who were driving another "cavvieyeh" of horses.

"Huh! Only seven!" he grunted, shifting his rifle for action. The fighting lust swept over him, but he choked it down and idly fingered the hammer of the gun. "Nope, I reckon not–seven husky Apaches are too much for one man to go out of his way to fight. Now, if the sheriff was only with me," and he grinned at the humor of it, "we might cut loose and heave lead. But since he ain't, this is where I don't chip in–I'll wait a while, for they'll shore come back."

The seven warriors went through almost the same actions which their predecessors had gone through and great excitement prevailed among them. The leaders pointed to the very faint tracks which led northward and debated vehemently. But the two small stones which held the arrow securely in its position against the possibility of the wind shifting it could not be doubted, and after a few minutes had passed they rode as bidden, leaving one of their number on guard at the bowlder. Soon the other six were lost to sight among the chaparrals to the west and the guard sat stolidly under the blazing sun.

The dispatcher noted the position of a shadow thrown on the sand by a cactus and laughed silently as he fingered his rifle. He could not think out the game. Try as he would, he could find no really good excuse for the placing of the guard, although many presented themselves, to be finally cast aside. But the fact was enough, and when the moving shadow gave assurance that nearly an hour had passed since the departure of the guard's companions, the man with the grudge cautiously arose on one knee.

After examining the contents of his rifle, he brought it slowly to his shoulder. A quick, calculating glance told him that the range was slightly over three hundred yards, and he altered the elevation of the rear sights accordingly. After a pause, during which he gauged the strength and velocity of the northern wind, he dropped his cheek against the walnut stock of the weapon. The echoless report rang out flatly and a sudden gust of hot wind whipped the ragged, gray smoke cloud into the chaparral, where it lay close to the ground and spread out like a miniature fog. As the smoke cleared away a second cartridge, inserted deftly and quickly, sent another cloud of smoke into the chaparral and the marksman arose to his feet, mechanically reloading his gun. The second shot was for the guard's horse, for it would be unnecessarily perilous to risk its rejoining the departed braves, which it very probably would do if allowed to escape.

Dropping his rifle into the hollow of his arm he walked swiftly toward the fallen Indian, hoping that there would be no more war parties, for he had now made signs which the most stupid Apache could not fail to note and understand. The dead guard could be hidden, and by the use of his own horse and rope he could drag the carcass of the animal into the chaparral and out of sight. But the trail which would be left in the loose sand would be too deep and wide to be covered. He had crossed the Rubicon, and must stand or fall by the step.

The Indian had fallen forward against the bowlder and had slid down its side, landing on his head and shoulders, in which grotesque position the rock supported him. One glance assured the "cowman" that his aim had been good, and another told him that he had to fear the arrival of no more war parties, for the arrow was gone. He was not satisfied, however, until he had made a good search for it, thinking that it might have been displaced by the fall of the Apache. He lifted the body of the dead warrior in his arms and flung it across the apex of the bowlder, face up and balanced nicely, the head pointing to the north. Then he looked for the arrow on the sand where the body had rested, but it was not to be found. A sardonic grin flitted across his face as he secured the weapons of the late guard, which were a heavy Colt's revolver and a late pattern Winchester repeater. Taking the cartridges from his body, he stood up triumphant. He now had what he needed to meet the smaller body of Indians on their return, ten shots in one rifle and a spare Colt's.

"One for my cavvieyeh!" he muttered savagely as he thought of the loss of his horse herd. "There'll be more, too, before I get through, or my name's not"– he paused abruptly, hearing hoofbeats made by a galloping horse over a stretch of hard soil which lay to the east of him. Leaping quickly behind the bowlder, he leveled his own rifle across the body of the guard and peered intently toward the east, wondering if the advancing horseman would be the sheriff or another Apache. The hoofbeats came rapidly nearer and another courier turned the corner of the chaparral and went no further. Again a second shot took care of the horse and the marksman strode to his second victim, from whose body and horse he took another Winchester and Colt.

"Now I am in for it!" he muttered as he looked down at the warrior. "This is shore getting warm and it'll be a d—n sight warmer if his friends get anxious about him and hunt him up."

Glancing around the horizon and seeing no signs of an interruption, he slung the body across his shoulders and staggered with it to the bowlder, where he heaved and pushed it across the body of the first Apache.

"Might as well make a good showing and make them mad, for I can't very well hide you and the cayuses–I ain't no graveyard," he said, stepping back to look at his work. He felt no remorse, for that was a sensation not yet awakened in his consciousness. He was elated at his success, joyous in catering to his love for fighting, for he would rather die fighting than live the round of years heavily monotonous with peace, and his only regret was having won by ambush. But in this, he told himself, there was need, for his hatred ordered him to kill as many as he could, and in any way possible. Knowing that he was, single-handed, attempting to outwit wily chiefs and that he had before him a carnival of fighting, he would not have hesitated to make use of traps if they were at hand and could be used. Perhaps it was old Geronimo whose plans he was defeating and, if so, no precautions nor means were unjustifiable and too mean to make use of, for Geronimo was half-brother to the devil and a genius for warfare and slaughter, with a ferocity and cruelty cold-blooded and consummate.

He had yet time to escape from his perilous position and meet the sheriff, if that worthy had eluded the first war party. But his elation had the upper hand and his brute courage was now blind to caution. He savagely decided that his matter with the sheriff could wait and that he would take care of the war parties first, since there was more honor in fighting against odds. The two Winchesters and his own Sharps, not to consider the four Colt's, gave him many shots without having to waste time in reloading, and he drew assurance from the past that he placed his shots quickly and with precision. He could put up a magnificent fight in the chaparral, shifting his position after each shot, and he could hug the ground where the trunks of the vegetation were thickest and would prove an effective barrier against random shots. His wits were keen, his legs nimble, his eyesight and accuracy above doubt, and he had no cause to believe that his strategy was inferior to that of his foes. There would be no moon for two nights, and he could escape in the darkness if hunger and thirst should drive him out. Here he had struck, and here he would strike again and again, and, if he fell, he would leave behind him such a tale of fighting as had seldom been known before; and it pleased his vanity to think of the amazement the story would call forth as it was recounted around the campfires and across the bars of a country larger than Europe. He did not realize that such a tale would die if he died and would never be known. His was the joy of a master of the game, a virile, fearless fighting machine, a man who had never failed in the playing of the many hands he had held in desperate games with death. He was not going to die; he was going to win and leave dying for others.

CHAPTER III
THE SHERIFF FINDS THE ORPHAN

The day dragged wearily along for the man in the chaparral, and when the sun showed that it was still two hours from the meridian he leaped to his feet, rifle in hand, and peered intently to the west, where he had seen a fast-riding horseman flit between two chaparrals which stood far down on the western end of the Cimarron Trail. Without pausing, he made his way out of cover and ran rapidly along the edge of the thicket until he had gained its northwestern extremity, where he plunged into it, unmindful of the cuts and slashes from the interlocked thorns. Using the rifle as a club, he hammered and pushed until he was screened from the view of any one passing along the trail, but where he could see all who approached. As he turned and faced the west he saw the horseman suddenly emerge from the shelter of the last chaparral in his course and ride straight for the intersection of the trails, his horse flattened to the earth by the speed it was making. Waiting until the rider was within fifty yards of him, he pushed his way out to the trail, the rifle leaping to his shoulder as he stepped into the open. The newcomer was looking back at half a dozen Apaches who had burst into view by the chaparral he had just quitted, and when he turned he was stopped by a hail and the sight of an unwavering rifle held by the man on foot.

"A truce!" shouted The Orphan from behind the sights, having an idea and wishing to share it.

"Hell, yes!" cried the astonished sheriff in reply, slowing down and mechanically following the already running outlaw to the place where the latter had spent the last few hours.

By keeping close to the edge of the chaparral, which receded from the trail, The Orphan had not been seen by the Apaches, and as he turned into his hiding place a yell reached his ears. His trophies on the bowlder were not to be unmourned.

As he wormed his way into the thicket, closely followed by the sheriff, he tersely explained the situation, and Shields, feeling somewhat under obligation to the man who had refrained from killing him, nodded and smiled in good nature. The sheriff thought it was a fine joke and enthusiastically slapped his enemy on the back to show his appreciation, for the time forgetting that they very probably would try to kill each other later on, after the Apaches had been taken care of.

As they reached a point which gave them a clear view of the bowlder, The Orphan kicked his companion on the shin, pointing to the Apaches grouped around their dead.

"It's a little over three hundred, Sheriff," he said. "You shoot first and I'll follow you, so they'll think you shot twice–there's no use letting them think that there's two of us, that is, not yet."

"Good idea," replied the sheriff, nodding and throwing his rifle to his shoulder. "Right end for me," he said, calling his shot so as to be sure that the same brave would not receive all the attention. As he fired his companion covered the second warrior, using one of his captured Winchesters, and a second later the rifle spun flame. Both warriors dropped and the remaining four hastily postponed their mourning and tumbled helter skelter behind the bowlder, the sheriff's second shot becoming a part of the last one to find cover.

"Fine!" exulted the sheriff, delighted at the score. "Best game I ever took a hand in, d—d if it ain't! We'll have them guessing so hard that they'll get brain fever."

"Three shots in as many seconds will make them think that they are facing a Winchester in the hands of a crack shot," remarked The Orphan, smiling with pleasure at the sheriff's appreciation. "They'll think that if they can back off from the bowlder and keep it between them and you that they can get out of range in a few hundred yards more. That is where I come in again. You sling a little lead to let them know that you haven't moved a whole lot, but stop in a couple of minutes, while I go down the line a ways. The chaparral sweeps to the north quite a little, and mebby I can drop a slug behind their fort from down there. That'll make them think you are a jack rabbit at covering ground and will bother them. If they rush, which they won't after tasting that kind of shooting, you whistle good and loud and we'll make them plumb disgusted. I'll take a Winchester along with me, so they won't have any cause to suspect that you are an arsenal. So long."

The sheriff glanced up as his companion departed and was pleased at the outlaw's command of the situation. He had a good chance to wipe out the man, but that he would not do, for The Orphan trusted him, and Shields was one who respected a thing like that.

The outlaw finally stopped about a hundred yards down the trail and looked out, using his glasses. A brown shoulder showed under the overhanging side of the bowlder and he smiled, readjusting the sights on the Winchester as he waited. Soon the shoulder raised from the ground and pushed out farther into sight. Then a poll of black hair showed itself and slowly raised. The Orphan took deliberate aim and pulled the trigger. The head dropped to the sand and the shoulder heaved convulsively once or twice and then lay quiet. Leaping up, the marksman hastened back to the side of the sheriff, who did not trouble himself to look up.

"I got him, Sheriff," he said. "Work up to the other end and I'll go back to where I came from. They have got all the fighting they have any use for and will be backing away purty soon now. The range from the point where I held you is some closer than it is from here, so you ought to get in a shot when they get far enough back."

"All right," pleasantly responded Shields, vigorously attacking the thorns as he began his journey to the western end of the thicket. "Ouch!" he exclaimed as he felt the pricks. Then he stopped and slowly turned and saw The Orphan smiling at him, and grinned:

"Say," he began, "why can't I go around?" he asked, indicating with a sweep of his arm the southern edge of the chaparral, and intimating that it would be far more pleasant to skirt the thorns than to buck against them. "These d——d thorns ain't no joke!" he added emphatically.

The outlaw's smile enlarged and he glanced quickly at the bowlder to see that all was as it should be.

"You can go around in one day afoot," he replied. "By that time they"–pointing to the Apaches–"will have made a day's journey on cayuses. And we simply mustn't let them get the best of us that way."

Shields grinned and turned half-way around again: "It's a whole lot dry out here," he said, "and my canteen is on my cayuse."

"Here, pardner," replied The Orphan, holding out his canteen and watching the effect of the familiarity. "Seven swallows is the dose."

The sheriff faced him, took the vessel, counted seven swallows and returned it.

"I'm some moist now," he remarked, as he returned to the thorns. "It's too d—n bad you're bad," he grumbled. "You'd make a blamed good cow-puncher."

The Orphan, still smiling, placed his hands on hips and watched the rapidly disappearing arm of the law.

"He's all right–too bad he'll make me shoot him," he soliloquized, turning toward his post. As he crawled through a particularly badly matted bit of chaparral he stopped to release himself and laughed outright. "How in thunder did he get so far west? My trail was as plain as day, too." When he had reached his destination and had settled down to watch the bowlder he laughed again and muttered: "Mebby he figured it out that I was doubling back and was laying for me to show up. And that's just the way I would have gone, too. He ain't any fool, all right."

He thought of the sheriff at the far end of the chaparral and of the repeater he carried, and an inexplicable impulse of generosity surged over him. The sheriff would be pleased to do the rest himself, he thought, and the thought was father to the act. He picked up the Winchester he had brought with him and fired at the bowlder, only wishing to let the Apaches know his position so that they would think the way clear to the northwest, and so innocently give the sheriff a shot at them as they retreated. Dropping the Winchester he took up his Sharps, his pet rifle, with which he had done wonderful shooting, and arose to one knee, supporting his left elbow on the other; between the fingers of his left hand he held a cartridge in order that no time should be lost in reloading. The range was now five hundred yards, and when The Orphan knew the exact range he swore with rage if he missed.

His shot had the effect he hoped it would have, for suddenly there was movement behind the bowlder. A pony's hip showed for an instant and then leaped from sight as the outlaw reloaded. A cloud of dust arose to the northwest of and behind the bowlder, and a series of close reports sounded from the direction of the sheriff. The Orphan leaped to his feet and dashed out on the plain to where his sight would not be obstructed and saw an Apache, who hung down on the far side of his horse, sweep northward and gallop along the northern trail. He fired, but the range was too great, and the warrior soon dropped from sight over the range of hills. As The Orphan made his way toward the bowlder the sheriff emerged from his shelter and pointed to the west. A pony lay on its side and not far away was the huddled body of its rider.

As they neared each other the outlaw noticed something peculiar about the sheriff's ear, and his look of inquiry was rewarded. "Stung," remarked Shields, grinning apologetically. "Just as I shot," he added in explanation of the Apache's escape. "Wonder what my wife'll say?" he mused, nursing the swelling.

The Orphan's eyes opened a trifle at the sheriff's last words, and he thought of the war party he had sent north. His decision was immediate: no married man had any business to run risks, and he was glad that he refrained from shooting on sight.

"Sheriff, you vamoose. Clear out now, while you have the chance. Ride west for an hour, and then strike north for Ford's Station. That buck that got away is due to run into twenty-seven of his friends and relatives that I sent north to meet you. And they won't waste any time in getting back, neither."

Shields felt of his ear and laughed softly. He had a sudden, strong liking for his humorous, clever enemy, for he recognized qualities which he had always held in high esteem. While he had waited in the chaparral for the Apaches to break cover he had wondered if the Indians which The Orphan had sent north had been sent for the purpose of meeting him, and now he had the answer. Instead of embittering him against his companion, it increased his respect for that individual's strategy, and he felt only admiration.

"I saw your reception committee in time to duck," the sheriff said, laughing. "If they kept on going as they were when I saw them they must have crossed my trail about three hours later. When they hit that it is a safe bet that at least some of them took it up. So if it's all the same to you, I'll leave both the north and the west alone and take another route home. I have shot up all the war-whoops I care about, so I am well satisfied."

He suddenly reached down toward his belt, and then looked squarely into The Orphan's gun, which rested easily on that person's hip. His hand kept on, however, but more slowly and with but two fingers extended, and disappeared into his chap's pocket, from which it slowly and gingerly brought forth a package of tobacco and some rice paper. The Orphan looked embarrassed for a second and then laughed softly.

"You're a square man, Sheriff, but I wasn't sure," he said in apology. "So long."

"That's all right," cried the sheriff heartily. "I was a big fool to make a play like that!"

The Orphan smiled and turned squarely around and walked away in the direction of his horse. Shields stared at his back and then rolled a cigarette and grinned: "By George!" he ejaculated at the confidence displayed by his companion, and he slowly followed.

After they had mounted in silence the sheriff suddenly turned and looked his companion squarely in the eyes and received a steady, frank look in return.

"What the devil made you ventilate them sheep herders that way?" he asked. "And go and drive all of them sheep over the bank?"

The Orphan frowned momentarily, but answered without reserve.

"Those sheep herders reckoned they'd get a reputation!" he answered. "And they would have gotten it, too, only I beat them on the draw. As for the idiotic muttons, they went plumb loco at the shooting and pushed each other over the bank. To hell with the herders–they only got what they was trying to hand me. But I'm a whole lot sorry about the sheep, although I can't say I'm dead stuck on range-killers of any kind."

The sheriff reflectively eyed his companion's gun and remembered its celerity into getting into action, which persuaded him that The Orphan was telling the truth, and swept aside the last chance for fair warfare between the two for the day.

"Yes, it is too bad, all them innocent sheep drowned that way," he slowly replied. "But they are shore awful skittish at times. Well, do we part?" he asked, suddenly holding out his hand.

"I reckon we do, Sheriff, and I'm blamed glad to have met you," replied the outlaw as he shook hands with no uncertain grip. "Keep away from them Apaches, and so long."

"Thanks, I will," responded the arm of the law. "And I'm glad to have met you, too. So long!"

CHAPTER IV
THE SECOND OFFENSE

Bill Howland emerged from the six-by-six office of the F. S. and S. Stage Company and strolled down the street to where his Concord stood. He hitched up and, after examining the harness, gained his seat, gathered up the lines and yelled. There was a lurch and a rumble, and Bill turned the corner on two wheels to the gratification of sundry stray dogs, whose gratification turned to yelps of surprise and pain as the driver neatly flecked bits of hair from their bodies with his sixteen foot "blacksnake." Twice each week Bill drove his Concord around the same corner on the same two wheels and flecked bits of hair from stray dogs with the same whip. He would have been deeply grieved if the supply of new stray dogs gave out, for no dogs were ever known to get close enough to be skinned the second time; once was enough, and those which had felt the sting of Bill's leather were content to stand across the street and create the necessary excitement to urge the new arrivals forward. The local wit is reported as saying: "Dogs may come and dogs may go, but Bill goes on forever," which saying pleased Bill greatly.

As he threw the mail bag on the seat the sheriff came up and watched him, his eyes a-twinkle with humor.

"Well, Sheriff, how's the boy?" genially asked Bill, who could talk all day on anything and two days on nothing without fatigue.

"All right, Bill, thank you," the sheriff replied. "I hope you are able to take something more than liquid nourishment," he added.

"Oh, you trust me for that, Sheriff. When my appetite gives out I'll be ready to plant. I see your ear is some smaller. Blamed funny how they do swell sometimes," remarked the driver, loosening his collar.

The sheriff knew what that action meant and hurried to break the thread of the conversation.

"New wheel?" he asked, eying what he knew to be old.

"Nope, painted, that's all," the driver replied, grinning. "But she shore does look new, don't she? You see, Dick put in two new spokes yesterday, and when I saw 'em I says, says I, 'Dick, that new wheel don't look good thataway,' says I. 'It'll look like a limp, them new spokes coming 'round all alone like,' says I. So we paints it, but we didn't have time to paint the others, but they won't make much difference, anyhow. Funny how a little paint will change things, now ain't it? Why, I can remember when–___"

"Much mail nowadays?" interposed the sheriff calmly.

"Nope. Folks out here ain't a-helpin' Uncle Sam much. Postmaster says he only sold ten stamps this week. What he wants, as I told him, is women. Then everybody'll be sendin' letters and presents and things. Now, I knows what I'm talking about, because—-"

"The Apaches are out," jabbed the sheriff, hopefully.

"Yes, I heard that you had a soiree with them. But they won't get so far north as this. No, siree, they won't. They knows too much, Apaches do. Ain't they smart cusses, though? Now, there's old Geronimo–been raising the devil for years. The cavalry goes out for him regular, and shore thinks he's caught, but he ain't. When he's found he's home smoking his pipe and counting his wives, which are shore numerous, they say. Now, I've got a bully scheme for getting him, Sheriff—"

"Hey, you," came from the office. "Do you reckon that train is going to tie up and wait for you, hey? Do you think you are so d—d important that they won't pull out unless you're on hand? Why in h–l don't you quit chinning and get started?"

"Oh, you choke up!" cried Bill, clambering up to his seat. "Who's running this, anyhow!" he grumbled under his breath. Then he took up the reins and carefully sorted them, after which he looked down at Shields, whose face wore a smile of amusement.

"Bill Howland ain't none a-scared because a lot of calamity howlers get a hunch. Not on your life! I've reached the high C of rollicking progress too many times to be airy scairt at rumors. Show me the feather-dusters in war paint, and then I'll take some stock in raids. You get up a bet on me Sheriff, make a little easy money. Back Bill Howland to be right here in seventy-two hours, right side up and smiling, and you'll win. You just bet you'll—"

"Well, you won't get here in a year unless you starts, you pest! For God's sake get a-going and give the sheriff a rest!" came explosively from the office, accompanied by a sound as if a chair had dropped to its four legs. A tall, angular man stood in the doorway and shook his fist at the huge cloud of dust which rolled down the street, muttering savagely. Bill Howland had started on his eighty-mile trip to Sagetown.

"Damnedest talker on two laigs," asserted the clerk. "He'll drive me loco some day with his eternal jabber, jabber. Why do you waste time with him? Tell him to close his yap and go to h–l. Beat him over the head, anything to shut him up!"

Shields smiled: "Oh, he can't help it. He don't do anybody any harm."

The clerk shook his head in doubt and started to return to his chair, and then stopped.

"I hear you expect some women out purty soon," he suggested.

"Yes. Sisters and a friend," Shields replied shortly.

"Ain't you a little leary about letting 'em come out here while the Apaches are out?"

"Not very much–I'll be on hand when they arrive," the sheriff assured him.

"How soon are they due to land?"

"Next trip if nothing hinders them."

"Jim Hawes is comin' out next trip," volunteered the clerk.

"Good," responded the sheriff, turning to go. "Every gun counts, and Jim is a good man."

"Say," the agent was lonesome, "I heard down at the Oasis last night that The Orphant was seen out near the Cross Bar-8 yesterday. He ought to get shot, d—n him! But that's a purty big contract, I reckon. They say he can shoot like the very devil."

"They're right, he can," Shields replied. "Everybody knows that.

"Charley seems to be in a hurry," remarked the agent, looking down the street at a cowboy, a friend of the sheriff, who was coming at a dead gallop. The sheriff looked and Charley waved his arm. As he came within hailing distance he shouted:

"The Orphan killed Jimmy Ford this morning on Twenty Mile Trail! His pardner got away by shootin' The Orphan's horse and taking to the trail through Little Arroyo. But he's shot, just the same, 'though not bad. The rest of the Cross Bar-8 outfit are going out for him; they've been out, but they can't follow his trail."

"Hell!" cried the sheriff, running toward his corral. "Wait!" he shouted over his shoulder as he turned the corner. In less than five minutes he was back again, and on his best horse, and following the impatient cowboy, swung down the street at a gallop in the direction of Twenty Mile Trail.

As they left the town behind and swung through the arroyo leading to the Limping Water, through which the stage route lay, Charley began to speak again:

"Jimmy and Pete Carson were taking a rest in the shade of the chaparral and playin' old sledge, when they looked up and saw The Orphan looking down at them. They're rather easy-going, and so they asked him to take a hand. He said he would, and got off his cayuse and sat down with them. Jimmy started a new deal, but The Orphan objected to old sledge and wanted poker, at the same time throwing a bag of dust down in front of him. Jimmy looked at Pete, who nodded, and put his wealth in front of him. Well, they played along for a while, and The Orphan began to have great luck. When he had won five straight jack pots it was more than Jimmy could stand, him being young and hasty. He saw his new Cheyenne saddle, what he was going to buy, getting further away all the time, and he yelled 'Cheat!' grabbing for his gun, what was plumb crazy for him to do.

"The Orphan fired from his hip quick as a wink, and Jimmy fell back just as Pete drew. The Orphan swung on him and ordered him to drop his gun, which same Pete did, being sick at the stomach at Jimmy's passing. Then The Orphan told him to take his dirty money and his cheap life and go back to his mamma. Pete didn't stop none to argue, but mounted and rode away. But the fool wasn't satisfied at having a whole skin after a run-in with The Orphan, and when he got off about four hundred yards and right on the edge of Little Arroyo, where he could get cover in one jump, he up and let drive, killing The Orphan's horse. Pete got two holes in his shoulder before he could get out of sight, and he remembered that his shot had hardly left his gun before he had 'em, too. Pete says he wonders how in h–l The Orphan could shoot twice so quick, when his gun's a Sharp's single shot."

Shields was pleased with the knowledge that it was not a plain murder this time, and fell to wondering if the other killings in which The Orphan had figured had not in a measure been justified. Hearsay cried "Murderer," but his own personal experience denied the term. Did not The Orphan know that Shields was after him, and that the sheriff was no man to be taken lightly when he had shown mercy near the big bowlder? The outlaw must be fair and square, reasoned the sheriff, else he would not have looked for those qualities in another, and least of all in an enemy. The outlaw had given him plenty of chances to kill and had thought nothing of it, time and time again turning his back without hesitation. True, The Orphan had covered him when his hand had streaked for his tobacco; but the sheriff would have done the same, because the movement was decidedly hostile, and he had been fortunate in not having paid dearly for his rash action. The Orphan had taken a chance when he refrained from pulling the trigger.

Charley continued: "Jimmy's outfit swear they'll have a lynchin' bee to square things for the Kid. They are plumb crazy about it. Jimmy was a whole lot liked by them, and the foreman is going to give them a week off with no questions asked. They are getting things ready now."

The sheriff turned to his companion, his hazel eyes aflame with anger at this threat of lynching when he had given plain warning that such lawlessness would not for one minute be tolerated by him.

"We'll call on the Cross Bar-8 first, Charley, and find out when this lynching bee is due to come off," he said, turning toward the northwest. Charley looked surprised at the sudden change in the plans, but followed without comment, secretly glad that trouble was in store for the ranch he had no use for.

After an hour of fast riding they rode up to the corral of the Cross Bar-8, and Shields, seeing a cowboy busily engaged in cleaning a rifle, asked for Sneed, at the same time making a mental note of the preparations which were going on about him.

The foreman, as if in answer to the sheriff's words, walked into sight around the corral wall and stepped forward eagerly when he saw who the caller was.

"I see that you know all about it, Sheriff," he began, hastily. "I've just told the boys that they can go out for him," he continued. "They're getting ready now, and will soon be on his trail."

"Yes?" coldly inquired the sheriff.

"They'll get him if you don't," assured the foreman, who had about as much tact as a mule.

"I'll shoot the first man who tries it," the sheriff said, as he flecked a bit of dust from his arm.

"What!" cried Sneed in astonishment. "By God, Sheriff, that's a d—d hard assertion to make!"

"And I hold you responsible," continued the sheriff, leaning forward as if to give weight to his words.

The cowboy stopped cleaning his rifle and stood up, covering the sheriff, a sneer on his face and anger in his eyes.

"If you're a-scared, we ain't, by God!" he cried. "The Orphan has got away too many times already, and here is where he gets stopped for good! When we gets through with him he won't shoot no more friends of ourn, nor nobody else's!"

Shields looked him squarely in the eyes: "If you don't drop that gun I'll drop you, Bucknell," he said pleasantly, and his eyes proclaimed that he meant what he said.

Sneed sprang forward and knocked the gun aside; "You d—n fool!" he cried. "You ornery, silly fool! Get back to the bunk house or I'll make you wish you had never seen that gun! Go on, get the h–l out of here before you join Jimmy!"

Then the foreman turned to Shields, feeling that he had lost much through the rashness of his man.

"Don't pay any attention to that crazy yearling, Sheriff," he said earnestly. "He's only feeling his oats. But we only wanted to round him up," he continued on the main topic. "We meant to turn him over to you after we'd got him. He's a blasted, thieving, murdering dog, that's what he is, and he oughtn't get away this time!"

"You keep out of this, and keep your men out of it, too," responded Shields, turning away. "I mean what I say. Jimmy started the mess and got the worst of it. I'll get The Orphan, or nobody will. As long as I'm sheriff of this county I'll take care of my job without any lynching parties. Come on, Charley."

"Deputize some of my boys, Sheriff!" he begged. "Let 'em think they're doing something. The Orphan is a bad man to go after alone. The boys are so mad that they'll get him if they have to ride through hell after him. Swear them in and let them get him lawfully."

"Yes?" retorted Shields cynically. "And have to shoot them to keep them from shooting him?"

"By God, Sheriff," cried Sneed, losing control of his temper, "this is our fight, and we're going to see it through! We'll get that cur, sheriff or no sheriff, and when we do, he'll stretch rope! And anybody who tries to stop us will get hurt! I ain't making any threats, Sheriff; only telling plain facts, that's all."

"Then I'll be a wreck," responded Shields, still smiling. "For I'll stop it, even if I have to shoot you first, which are also plain facts."

Sneed's men had been coming up while they talked and were freely voicing their opinions of sheriffs. Sneed stepped close to the peace officer and laughed, his face flushed with foolish elation at his strength.

"Do you see 'em?" he asked, ironically, indicating his men by a sweep of his arm. "Do you think you could shoot me?"

The reply was instantaneous. The last word had hardly left his lips before he peered blankly into the cold, unreasoning muzzle of a Colt, and the sheriff's voice softly laughed up above him. The cowboys stood as if turned to stone, not daring to risk their foreman's life by a move, for they did not understand the sheriff's methods of arguments, never having become thoroughly acquainted with him.

"You know me better now, Sneed," Shields remarked quietly as he slipped his Colt into its holster. "I'm running the law end of the game and I'll keep right on running it as I d—d please while I'm called sheriff, understand?"

Sneed was a brave man, and he thoroughly appreciated the clean-cut courage which had directed the sheriff's act, and he knew, then, that Shields would keep his word. He involuntarily stepped back and intently regarded the face above him, seeing a not unpleasant countenance, although it was tanned by the suns and beaten by the weather of fifty years. The hazel eyes twinkled and the thin lips twitched in that quiet humor for which the man was famed; yet underlying the humor was stern, unyielding determination.

"You're shore nervy, Sheriff," at length remarked the foreman. "The boys are loco, but I'll try to hold them."

"You'll hold them, or bury them," responded the sheriff, and turning to his companion he said: "Now I'm with you, Charley. So long, Sneed," he pleasantly called over his shoulder as if there had been no unpleasant disagreement.

"So long, Sheriff," replied the foreman, looking after the departing pair and hardly free from his astonishment. Then he turned to his men: "You heard what he said, and you saw what he did. You keep out of this, or I'll make you d—d sorry, if he don't. If The Orphan comes your way, all right and good. But you let his trail religiously alone, do you hear?"

CHAPTER V
BILL JUSTIFIES HIS CREATION

Bill Howland careened along the stage route, rapidly leaving Ford's Station in his rear. He rolled through the arroyo on alternate pairs of wheels, splashed through the Limping Water, leaving it roiled and muddy, and shot up the opposite bank with a rush. Before him was a stretch of a dozen miles, level as a billiard table, and then the route traversed a country rocky and uneven and wound through cuts and defiles and around rocky buttes of strange formation. This continued for ten miles, and the last defile cut through a ridge of rock, called the Backbone, which ranged in height from twenty to forty feet, smooth, unbroken and perpendicular on its eastern face. This ridge wound and twisted from the big chaparral twenty miles below the defile to a branch of the Limping Water, fifteen miles above. And in all the thirty-five miles there was but a single opening, the one used by Bill and the stage.

In crossing the level plain Bill could see for miles to either side of him, but when once in the rough country his view was restricted to yards, and more often to feet. It was here that he expected trouble if at all, and he usually went through it with a speed which was reckless, to say the least.

He had just dismissed the possibility of meeting with Apaches as he turned into the last long defile, which he was pleased to call a cañon. As he made the first turn he nearly fell from his seat in astonishment at what he saw. Squarely in the center of the trail ahead of him was a horseman, who rode the horse which had formerly belonged to Jimmy of the Cross Bar-8, and across the cut lay a heavy piece of timber, one of the dead trees which were found occasionally at that altitude, and it effectively barred the passing of the stage. The horseman wore his sombrero far back on his head and a rifle lay across his saddle, while two repeating Winchesters were slung on either side of his horse. One startled look revealed the worst to the driver–The Orphan, the terrible Orphan faced him!

"Don't choke–I'm not going to eat you," assured the horseman with a smile. "But I'm going to smoke half of your tobacco–and you can bring me a half pound when you come back from Sagetown. Just throw it up yonder," pointing to a rocky ledge, "and keep going right ahead."

Bill looked very much relieved, and hastily fumbled in his hip pocket, which was a most suicidal thing to do in a hurry; but The Orphan didn't even move at the play, having judged the man before him and having faith in his judgment. The hand came out again with a pouch of tobacco, which its owner flung to the outlaw. After putting half of it in his own pouch and enclosing a coin to pay for his half pound, The Orphan tossed it back again and then moved the tree trunk until it fell to the road, when he dismounted and rolled it aside.

"You forget right now that you have seen me or you'll have heart disease some day in this place," warned the horseman, moving aside. Bill swore earnestly that at times his memory was too short to even remember his own name, and he enthusiastically lashed his cayuse sextet. As he swung out on the plain again he glanced furtively over his shoulder and breathed a deep breath of relief when he found that the outlaw was not in sight. He then tied a knot in his handkerchief so as to be sure to remember to get a half-pound package of tobacco. A new responsibility, and one which he had never borne before, weighed upon him. He must keep silent–and what a rich subject for endless conversations! Talking material which would last him for years must be sealed tightly within his memory on penalty of death if he failed to keep it secret.

After an uneventful trip across the open plain, which passed so rapidly because of his intent thoughts that he hardly realized it, he ripped into Sagetown with a burst of speed and flung the mail bag at the station agent, after which he hastened to float the dust down his throat.

When he met his Sagetown friends he had fairly to choke down his secret, and his aching desire to create a sensation pained and worried him.

"You made her faster than usual, Bill," remarked the bartender casually. "Yore half-an-hour ahead of time," he added in a congratulatory tone as he placed a bottle and glass before the new arrival.

"Yes, and I had to stop, too," Bill replied, and then hastily gulped down his liquor to save himself.

"That so?" asked old Pop Westley, an habitué of the saloon. Pop Westley had fought through the Civil War and never forgot to tell of his experiences, which must have been unusually numerous, even for four years of hard campaigning, if one may judge from the fact that he never had to repeat, and yet used them as his coup d'état in many conversational bouts. "What was it, Injuns?" he asked, winking at the bartender as if in prophecy as to what the driver would choose for his next lie.

"Oh, no," replied Bill, groping for an idea to get him out of trouble. "Nope, just had to lose twenty minutes rollin' rocks out of the cañon–they must have been a little landslide since I went through her the last time. Some of 'em was purty big, too."

"I thought you might a had to kill some Injuns, like you did when they broke out four years ago," responded the bartender gravely. "Tell us about that time you licked them dozen mad Apache warriors, Bill," he requested. "That was a blamed good scrap from what I can remember."

"Oh, I've told you about that scrap so much I'm ashamed to tell it again," replied the driver, wishing that he could remember just what he had said about it, and sorry that his memory was so inferior to his imagination.

"Bet you get scalped goin' back," pleasantly remarked Johnny Sands, who had not fought in the Civil War, but who often ferociously wished he had when old Pop Westley was telling of how Mead took Vicksburg, or some other such bit of history. Pop must have been connected to a flying regiment, for he had fought under every general on the Union side.

"You're on for the drinks, Johnny," answered Bill promptly, feeling that it would be a double joy to win. "The war-whoops never lived who could scalp Bill Howland, and don't forget it, neither," he boastfully averred as he made for the door, very anxious to get away from that awful gnawing temptation to open their eyes wide about his recent experience.

"Then The Orphan will get you, shore," came from Pop Westley. Bill jumped and slammed the door so hard that it shook the building.

He saw that his sextet was being properly fed and watered for the return trip, which would not take place until the next day. But a trifle like twenty-four hours had no effect on Bill under his present stress of excitement, and he fooled about the coach as if it was his dearest possession, inspecting the king-bolt, running-gear and whiffletrees with anxious eyes. He wanted no break-down, because the Apaches might be farther north than was their custom. That done he took his rifle apart and thoroughly cleaned and oiled it, seeing that the magazine was full to the end. Then he had his supper and went straight therefrom to bed, not daring to again meet his friends for fear of breaking his promise to The Orphan.

At dawn he drew up beside the small station and waited for the arrival of the train, which even then was a speck at the meeting place of the rails on the horizon.

The station agent sauntered over to him and grinned.

"I guess I will get that telegraph line after all, Bill," he remarked happily. "I heard that the division superintendent wanted to get word to me in a hurry the other day, and raised the devil when he couldn't. I've been fighting for a wire to civilization for three years, and now I reckon she'll come."

"I always said you ought to have a telegraph line out here," Bill replied. "Suppose that train should run off the track some day, what would they do, hey?"

"Huh, that train never goes fast enough to run off of anything," retorted the station agent. "She'd stop dead if she hit a coyote–by gosh! Here she comes now! What do you think of that, eh? Half-an-hour ahead of time, too! Must be trying to hit up a better average than she's had for the last year. She's usually due three hours late," he added in bewilderment. "She owes the world about a month–must have left the day before by mistake."

"Johnny Sands says he raced her once for ten miles, and beat it a mile," replied Bill, crossing his legs and yawning. Then he began one of his endless talks, and the agent hastily departed and left him to himself.

When the train finally stopped at its destination, after running past the station and having to back to the platform, three women alighted and looked around. Seeing the stage, they ordered their baggage transferred to it and gave Bill a shock by their appearance.

"Is this the stage which runs to Ford's Station?" the eldest asked of Bill.

Bill fumbled at his sombrero and tore it from his head as he replied.

"Yes, sir, er–ma'am!" he said, confusedly. "Are you Sheriff's sister, ma'am?"

"Yes," she answered. "Why do you ask? Has anything happened to him in this awful country?" she asked in alarm.

"No, ma'am, not yet," responded Bill in confusion. "He just didn't expect you 'til the next train, ma'am, that's all. He was going to meet you then."

"Now, isn't that just like a man?" she asked her companions. "I distinctly remember that I wrote him I would come on the twenty-fourth. How stupid of him!"

"Yes, ma'am, you did," interposed Bill, eagerly. "But this is only the twenty-first, ma'am."

She refused to notice the correction and waved her hand toward the coach.

"Get in, dears," she said. "I do so hope it isn't dirty and uncomfortable, and we have so far to go in it, too. Thirty miles–think of it!"

Bill thought of it, but refrained from offering correction. If Shields had said it was thirty miles when he knew it was eighty that was Shields' affair, and he didn't care to have any unpleasantness. He had offered correction about the date, and that was enough for him. Clambering down heavily he opened the side door of the vehicle and then helped the station agent put the trunks and valises and hat boxes on the hanging shelf behind the coach and saw that they were lashed securely into place. Then he threw the mail bag upon his seat, climbed after it and started on his journey with a whoop and rush, for this trip was to be a record-breaker. Shields had said it was thirty miles, and it behove the driver to make it seem as short as possible.

The unexpected arrival of the women had driven everything else from his mind, even The Orphan, and after he had covered a mile he had a strong desire to smoke. Giving his whip a jerk he threw it along the top of the coach and slipped the handle under his arm. Then he felt for his pouch, and as his fingers closed upon it he suddenly stiffened and gasped. He had forgotten The Orphan's half pound! Swearing earnestly and badly frightened at the close call he had from incurring the anger of a man like the outlaw, he pulled on the reins with a suddenness which caused the sextet to lay back their ears and indulge in a few heartfelt kicks. But the darting whip kept peace and he swung around and returned to town.

As he drove past the station Mary Shields, the sheriff's elder sister, poked her head out of the door and called to him.

"Driver!" she exclaimed. "Driver!"

Bill craned his neck and looked down.

"Yes, ma'am," he replied anxiously.

"Are we there already?" she asked.

"Why, no, ma'am, it's ei–thirty miles yet," he responded as he sprang to the ground.

"Then where are we, for goodness' sake?"

"Back in Sagetown, ma'am," he hurriedly replied. "I shore forgot something," he added in explanation of the return as he ran toward the saloon.

She turned to her companions with a gesture of despair:

"Isn't it awful," she asked, "what a terrible thing drinking is? A most detestable habit! Here we are back to where we started from and just because our driver must have a drink of nasty liquor! Why, we would have been there by this time. I will most assuredly speak to James about this!"

"Well, I suppose we may go on now!" she exclaimed as Bill bolted into sight again, holding a package firmly in his two hands. "I suppose he feels quite capable of driving now."

Bill, blissfully ignorant of the remarks he had called forth, tossed the tobacco upon the mail bag and climbed to his seat again. The long whip hissed and cracked as he bellowed to the team, and once more they started for Ford's Station.

The passengers had all they could do to keep their seats because of the gymnastics of the erratic stage. Bill, who had always found delight in seeing how near he could come to missing things and who was elated at the joy of getting over the worst parts of the trail with speed, decided that this was a rare and most auspicious occasion to show just what he could do in the way of fancy driving. The return to town had spoiled his chances for a record, but he still could do some high-class work with the reins. The weight of the baggage on the tailboard bothered him until he discovered that it acted as a tail to his Concord kite, and when he learned that he joyously essayed feats which he had long dreamed of doing. The result was fully appreciated by the terrified passengers who, choking with the dust which forced its way in to them, could only hold fast to whatever came to their grasp and pray that they would survive.

As he passed a peculiarly formed clump of organ cacti, which he regarded as being his half-way mark, he happened to glance behind, and his face blanched in a sudden fear which gripped his heart in an icy grasp.

He leaped to his feet, wrapping the reins about his wrists, and the "blacksnake" coiled and writhed and hissed. Its reports sounded like those of a gun, and every time it straightened out a horse lost a bit of hair and skin. Both of the leaders had limp and torn ears, and a sudden terror surged through the team, causing their eyes to dilate and grow red. The driver's voice, strong and full, rang out in blood-curdling whoops, which ended in the wailing howl of a coyote, wonderfully well imitated. The combination of voice and whip was too much, and the six horses, maddened by the terrible sting of the lash and the frightful, haunting howl, became frenzied and bolted.

Braced firmly on the footboard, poised carefully and with just the right tension on the reins, the driver scanned the trail before him, avoiding as best he could the rocks and deep ruts, and watching alertly for a stumble. His sombrero had deserted him and his long brown hair snapped behind him in the wind. Bill was frightened, but not for himself alone. With all his bravado he was built of good timber, and his one thought was for the women under his care. He unconsciously prayed that they might not be brought face to face with the realization of what menaced them; that they would not learn why the coach lurched so terribly; that the trunk which obstructed the back window of the coach would not shift and give them a sight of the danger. Oh, that the running gear held! That the king-bolt, new, thank God, proved the words of the boasting blacksmith to be true! He soon came to the beginning of a three-hundred-yard stretch of perfect road and he hazarded a quick backward glance. Instantly his eyes were to the front again, but his brain retained the picture he had seen, retained it perfectly and in wonderful clearness. He saw that the Apaches were no longer a mile away, but that they had gained upon him a very little, so very little that only an eye accustomed to gauging changing distances could have noticed the difference. And he also saw that the group was no longer compact, but that it was already spreading out into the dreaded, deadly crescent, a crescent with the best horses at the horns, which would endeavor to sweep forward and past the coach, drawing closer together until the circle was complete, with the stage as the center.

Another yell burst from him, and again and again the whip writhed and hissed and cracked, and a new burst of speed was the reward. Well it was that the horses were the best and most enduring to be found on the range. He was dependent on his team, he and his passengers. He could not hope to take up his rifle until the last desperate stand. Oh, if he only had the sheriff, the cool, laughing, accurate sheriff with him to lie against the seat and shoot for his sisters! Already the bullets were dropping behind him, but he did not know of it. They dropped, as yet, many yards too short, and he could not hear the flat reports. The wind which roared and whistled past his ears spared him that.

A stumble! But up again and without injury, for a master hand held the reins, a hand as cunning as the eyes were calculating. Could Bill's scoffing friends see him now their scoffing would freeze on lips open in admiring astonishment. If he attained nothing more in his life he was justifying his creation. He was doing his best, and doing it wonderfully well. Long since had fear left him. He was now only a superb driver, an alert, quick-thinking master of his chosen trade. He thrilled with a peculiar elation, for was he not playing his hand against death? A lone hand and with no hope of a lucky draw. All he could hope for was that he be not unlucky and lose the game because of the weakness of a wheel, or the traces, or that new king-bolt; that the splendid, ugly, terrorized units of his sextet would last until he had gained the cañon, where the stage would nearly block the narrow opening, and where he could exchange reins for rifle!

Within the coach three women were miserably huddled in a mass on the floor. Two would be more proper, because the third, a slim girl of nineteen, was temporarily out of her misery, having fainted, which was a boon denied to her companions. Thrown from side to side as if they were straws in weight, they first crashed into one wall and then into the other, buffeted from the edge of the front seat to that of the rear one. Bruised and bleeding and terrified, they dumbly prayed for deliverance from the madman up above them.

The driver's eye caught sight of the turn, which lay ten miles northeast of the cañon–then he had passed it.

"Only ten miles more, bronchs!" he shouted, imploringly, beseechingly. "Hold it, boys! Hold it, pets! Only ten miles more!" he repeated until the left-hand leader lurched forward and lost its footing. Another bit of masterly manipulation of the reins saved it from going down, and again the coyote yell rang out in all of its acute, quavering, hair-raising mournfulness. The blacksnake again and again mercilessly leaped and struck, and another wonderful burst of speed rewarded him.

His heart suddenly went out to his horses, as he realized what speed they were making and had been holding for so long a time, and he swore to treat them better than they had ever known if they pulled him safely to the mouth of the cañon.

A second backward glance, forced from him because of the awful uncertainty at his back, because if it was the last thing he ever did he must look behind him as a child looks back into the awful darkness of the room, caused his face to be convulsed with smiles, sudden and sincere. He shouted madly in his joy at what he saw, dancing up and down regardless of his perilous footing, bending his knees with a recklessness almost criminal, as he uncoiled the hissing blacksnake high up in the air. Again and again the whistling, hissing length of braided rawhide curled and straightened and cracked, faster and faster until the reports almost merged. He tossed his head and laughed wildly, hysterically, and danced as only a man can dance when eased of a terrible nervous tension; the rasping of the icy, grasping fingers of Death along his back suddenly ceased, and there came to him assurance of life and vengeance. Turning again he hurled the writhing length of his whip at the yelling Apaches, snapping the rifle-like reports at their faces, cursing them in shouted words; hot, joyous, cynical, taunting words fresh from the soul of him, throbbing with his hatred; venomous, contemptuous, scathing, too heartfelt to be over-profane.

"Come on, d—n you! Your slide to h–l is greased now! Come on, you wolves! You cheap, blind vultures! Come on! Come on!!" he yelled, well nigh out of his senses from the reaction. "Yes, yell! Yell, d—n you!" he shouted as they replied to his taunts. "Yell! Shoot your tin guns while you can, for you'll soon be so full of lead you'll stop forever! Come on! Come on!"

They came. All their energies were bent toward the grotesque figure that reviled them. They could not catch his words, but their eyes flashed at what they could see. Dust arose in huge, low clouds behind them, and they gained rapidly for a time, but only for a time, for their mounts had covered many miles in the last few days and were jaded and without their usual strength because of insufficient food. But they gained enough to drop their shots on the coach, although accurate shooting at the pace they were keeping was beyond their skill.

Puffs of dust spurted from the plain in front of the team and arose beside it, and a jagged splinter of seasoned ash whizzed past the driver's ear. A long, gray furrow suddenly appeared in the end of the seat and holes began to show in the woodwork of the stage. One bullet, closer than the others, almost tore the reins from the driver's hands as it hit the loose end of leather which flapped in the air. Its jerk caused him to turn again and renew his verbal cautery, tears in his eyes from the fervor of his madness.

"Hi-yi! Whoop-e-e!" he shouted at his straining, steaming sextet. "Keep it up, bronchs! Hold her for ten minutes more, boys! We'll win! We'll win! We'll laugh them into h–l yet! We'll dance on their painted faces! Keep her steady! You're all right, every d—d one of you! Hold her steady! Whoop-e-e!"

A new factor had drawn cards, and the new factor could play his cards better than any two men under that washed-out, faded blue sky.

CHAPTER VI
THE ORPHAN OBEYS AN IMPULSE

When Sneed promised to try to restrain his men he spoke in good faith, and when he discovered that half of them were missing his anger began to rise. But he was helpless now because they were beyond his reach, so he could only hope that they would not meet the sheriff, not only because of the displeasure of the peace officer, but also because good cowboys were hard to obtain, and he knew what such a meeting might easily develop into.

The foreman knew that Ford's Station bore him and his ranch no love and that if the sheriff should meet with armed resistance and, possibly, mishap at the hands of any members of the Cross Bar-8, that trouble would be the tune for him and his men to dance to. Angrily striding to and fro in front of the bunk house he gave a profane and pointed lecture to several of his men who stood near, abashed at their foreman's anger. He suddenly stopped and looked toward the rocky stretch of land and hurled epithets at what he feared might be taking place in its defiles and among its rocks and bowlders.

"Fools!" he shouted, shaking his fist at the Backbone. "Fools, to hunt a man like that on his own ground, and in the way you'll do it! You can't keep together for long, and as sure as you separate, some of you will be missing to-night!"

Had he been able, he would have seen six cowboys, who were keeping close together as they worked their way southward, exploring every arroyo and examining every thicket and bowlder. Their Colts were in their hands and their nerves were tensed to the snapping point.

They finally came to the stage road and, after a brief consultation, plunged into it and scrambled up the opposite bank, where they left one of their number on guard while they continued on their search. The guard found concealment behind a huge bowlder which stood on the edge of the cañon above the entrance. He lighted a cigarette, and the thin wisps of pale blue smoke slowly made their way above him, twisting and turning, halting for an instant, and then speeding upward as straight as a rod. It was strong tobacco and very aromatic, and when the wind caught it up in filmy clouds and carried it away it could be detected for many feet.

Five minutes had passed since the searchers had become lost to sight to the south when something moved on the other side of the cañon and then became instantly quiet as the smoke streamed up. The guard was cleverly hidden from sight, but he felt that he must smoke, for time passed slowly for him. Again something moved, this time behind a thin clump of mesquite. Gradually it took on the outlines of a man, and he was intently watching the tell-tale vapor, the odor of which had warned him in time.

Retreating, he was soon lost to sight, and a few minutes later he peered through a thin thicket which stood on the edge of the cañon wall. As he did so the guard stuck his head out from the shelter of his bowlder and glanced along the trail. Again seeking his cover he finished his cigarette and lighted another.

"He won't look again for a few minutes, the fool," muttered the other as he dropped into the road and darted across it. After a bit of cautious climbing he gained the top of the cañon wall and again became lost to sight.

Still the smoke ascended fitfully from behind the bowlder, and the prowler gradually drew near it, at last gaining the side opposite the smoker. He crouched and slowly crawled around it, his left hand holding a Colt; his right, a lariat. As the guard again turned to examine the lower end of the cañon his eyes looked into a steady gun, and while his wits were rallying to his aid the rope leaped at him and neatly dropped over his shoulders, pinning his arms to his side. It twitched and a loop formed in it, running swiftly and almost horizontally. It whipped over his head and tightened about his throat, while another loop sped after it and assisted in throttling the puncher. Then the lariat twitched and whirled and loops ran along it and fastened over the guard's wrists, rapidly getting shorter; and when it ceased, its wielder was brought to the side of his trussed victim. The bound man was turning purple in the face and neck and his captor, hastily crowding the guard's own neck-kerchief into the open, gasping mouth, released the throat clutch of the rawhide and then securely fixed the gag into place.

Roughly dragging his captive to a mass of débris he tore it apart and dragged and pushed the man into it, after which he pushed the rubbish back into place and then ran to the bowlder, where he covered all tracks. Picking up the puncher's revolver he took the cylinder from it and hurled it far out on the plain, throwing the frame across the defile into a tangled mass of mesquite. Looking carefully about him, to be sure he had not overlooked anything, he disappeared in the direction from which he had come.

He again appeared in the cañon, and ran swiftly along it until he came to the tracks made by the guard's horse, which he followed into an arroyo and where he found the animal hobbled. Loosening the hobbles he threw them over the horse's neck and sprang into the saddle. He picked his way carefully until he had reached the level plain, when he cantered northward, keeping close to the rock wall of the Backbone to avoid being seen by the searchers. When he had put a dozen miles behind him he turned abruptly to the east, soon becoming lost to sight behind the scattered chaparrals.

The Orphan, surmounting a rise, looked to the southwest and saw something which almost caused his hair to rise, and raising hair was not the rule with him, which latter is mentioned to give proper emphasis to the seriousness of what he looked upon. He leaped to the ground and saw that the cinches were securely fastened, after which he vaulted back into the saddle, and, instead of offering prayer for success, sent up profanity at the possibility of failure.

Two miles to the southwest of him he saw six horses flattened almost to earth in keeping the speed they had attained and were holding. Back of them lurched and rocked and heaved the sun-bleached coach, dull gray and dusty, its tall driver standing up to his work, hatless and with his arm rapidly rising and falling as he sent the cruel whip cruelly home. Behind the stage whipped the baggage flap, a huge leathern apron for the protection of luggage, standing out horizontally because of the rush of wind caused by the speed of the coach. It flapped defiantly at what so tenaciously pursued it. A thousand yards to the rear, riding in crescent formation, the horns now far apart and well ahead of the center, were five arm- and weapon-waving bronzed enthusiasts whose war paint could just be discerned by The Orphan's good eyes and field glasses.

As yet, the reason for the lifting hair has not been disclosed, because The Orphan was proud in his belief that he had few nerves and a dormant sympathy, and this scene alone would not have aroused much sympathy in his heart for the driver, and neither would it have changed the malevolent expression which disfigured his face, an expression caused by the remembrance of six cowboys who had searched for him as if he was a cowardly, cattle-killing coyote. But the exuberant baggage-flap revealed two trunks, three valises and a pile of white cardboard boxes; and as if this was not enough for a man adept at sign reading, the door of the coach suddenly became unfastened and alternately swung open and shut as the lurching of the coach affected it. And through the intermittent opening he could see a mass of gray and brown and blue.

The Orphan had spent ten years of his life battling against the hardest kinds of odds, and his brain had foresworn long methods of thinking and had adopted short cuts to conclusions. His mental processes were sharp, quick and acted instantly on his nerves, often completing an action before he became clearly conscious of its need. He forgot the pleasant sheriff and the unpleasant, blundering cowboys who, very probably, were now engaged in wondering where their companion had gone; and he forgot his determination to return and free that puncher. He asked himself no questions as to why or how, but simply sunk his spurs half an inch into a horse that had peculiar and fixed ideas about their use, and that now bucked, pitched and galloped forward because its rider had suddenly decided to save those gray and brown and blue dresses.

The Apaches had passed the point immediately south of him and were now more to the west, going at right angles to the course he took. They were so intent upon gaining yard upon yard that they did not look to the side–their thoughts were centered on the tall, lanky man who stood up against the sky and cursed them, and whose hat they had passed miles back. As he turned and stole the look at them which had so pleased him, they only waved guns and wasted cartridges more recklessly, yelling savagely.

Down from the north charged a brown, a dirty brown horse, and it was comparatively fresh. It gained steadily, silently, and its gains were measured in yards to each minute it ran, since it was coming at a sharp angle. Astride of it and lying along its neck was a man whose spurs and quirt urged it to its uttermost effort. Soon the man straightened up in his saddle, the horse braced its legs and slid to a stand as a rifle arose to the rider's shoulder, and at the shot the animal leaped forward at its top speed. A puff of smoke flashed past the marksman's head to mingle with the dust cloud in his wake, and the nearest brave, who was the last in the crescent, dropped sprawlingly to the ground and rolled rapidly several times. His horse, freed of its burden, ran off at an angle and was soon left behind. The excitement of the chase and the noise of the hoofbeats of their own horses and of the reports of their own rifles effectually lost the report of the shot and soon another, and nearest, Apache also plunged to the plain. This time the freed horse shot ahead and ranged alongside the wearer of the head-dress, who turned in his saddle and looked back. His eyesight was good, but not good enough to see the .50 caliber slug which passed through his abdomen and tore the ear of another warrior's horse.

The rider of the horse owning the mutilated ear looked quickly backward, screamed a warning and war-cry all in one and began to shoot rapidly. His surprised companion followed suit as the coach came to a stand, and another rifle, long silent, took a hand in the dispute with a vim as if to make up for lost time. The first warrior fell, shot through by both rifles, and the other, emptying his magazine at the new factor, who was very busily engaged in extracting a jammed cartridge, wheeled his pony about and fled toward the south, panic-stricken by the accuracy of the newcomer and terrorized by the awful execution. But the Apache's last shot nearly cleaned the sheriff's slate, grazing The Orphan's temple and stunning him: a fraction of an inch more to the right would have cheated the Cross Bar-8 of any chance of revenge.

Bill, still holding the rifle, leaped to the sand and ran to where his rescuer lay huddled in the dust of the plain.

"I've got yore smoking," he exclaimed breathlessly, at last getting rid of his mental burden. Then he stopped short, swore, and bent over the figure, and grasping the body firmly by neck and thigh, slung it over his shoulders and staggered toward the coach, his progress slow and laborious because of the deep sand and dust. As he neared his objective he glanced up and saw that his passengers had left the stage and were grouped together on the plain like lambs lost in a lion country.

They were hysterical, and all talked at once, sobbing and wringing their hands. But when they noticed the driver stumbling toward them with the body across his shoulders their tongues became suddenly mute with a new fear. Up to then they had thought only of their own woes and bruises, but here, perhaps, was Death; here was the man who had risked his life that they might live, and he might have lost as they gained.

They besieged Bill with tearful questions and gave him no chance to reply. He staggered past them and placed his burden in the scant shadow of the coach, while they cried aloud at sight of the blood-stained face, frozen in their tracks with fear and horror. Bill, ignoring them, hastily climbed with a wonderful celerity for him, to the high seat and dropped to the ground with a canteen which he had torn from its fastenings. Pouring its contents over the upturned face he half emptied a pocket flask of whisky into The Orphan's mouth and then fell to chafing and rubbing with his calloused, dust-covered hands, well knowing the nature of the wound and that it had only stunned.

Soon the eyelids quivered, fluttered and then flew back and the cruel eyes stared unblinkingly into those of the man above him, who swore in sudden joy. Then, weak as he was and only by the aid of an indomitable will, the wounded man bounded to his feet and stood swaying slightly as one hand reached out to the stage for support, the other instinctively leaping to his Colt. He swayed still more as he slowly turned his head and searched the plain for foes, the Colt half drawn from its holster.

As soon as he had gained his feet and while he was looking about him in a dazed way the women began to talk again, excitedly, hysterically. They gathered around this unshaven, blood-stained man and tried to thank him for their lives, their voices broken with sobs. He listened, vaguely conscious of what they were trying to say, until his brain cleared and made him capable of thought. Then he ceased to sway and spread his feet far apart to stand erect. His hand went to his head for the sombrero which was not there, and he smiled as he recalled how he had lost it.

"Oh, how can we ever thank you!" cried the sheriff's eldest sister, choking back a nervous sob. "How can we ever thank you for what you have done! You saved our lives!" she cried, shuddering at the danger now past. "You saved our lives! You saved our lives!" she repeated excitedly, clasping and unclasping her hands in her agitation.

"How can we ever thank you, how can we!" cried the girl who had fainted when the chase had begun. "It was splendid, splendid!" she cried, swaying in her weakness. She was so white and bruised and frail that The Orphan felt pity for her and started to say something, but had no chance. The three women monopolized the conversation even to the exclusion of Bill, who suddenly felt that his talking ability was only commonplace after all.

Blood trickled slowly down the outlaw's face as he smiled at them and tried to calm them, and the younger sister, suddenly realizing the meaning of what she had vaguely seen, turned to Bill with an imperative gesture.

"Bring me some water, driver, immediately," she commanded impatiently, and Bill hurried around to the rear axle from which swung a small keg of three gallons' capacity. Quickly unsnapping the chain from it he returned and pried out the wooden plug, slowly turning the keg until water began to flow through the hole and trickle down to the sand. Miss Shields took a small handkerchief from her waist and unfolded it, to be stopped by Bill.

"Don't spoil that, miss!" he hastily exclaimed. "Take one of mine. They ain't worth much, and besides, they're a whole lot bigger."

"Thank you, but this is better," she replied, smiling as she regarded the dusty neck-kerchief which he eagerly held out to her. She wet the bit of clean linen and Bill followed her as she stepped to the side of the outlaw, holding the keg for her and thinking that the sheriff was not the only thoroughbred to bear the name of Shields. He turned the keg for her as she needed water, and she bathed the wound carefully, pushing back the long hair which persisted in getting in her way, all the time vehemently declining the eager offers of assistance from her companions. The Orphan had involuntarily raised his hand to stop her, feeling foolish at so much attention given to so trivial a wound and not at all accustomed to such things, especially from women with wonderful deep, black eyes.

"Please do not bother me," she commanded, pushing his hand aside. "You can at least let me do this little thing, when you have done so much, or I shall think you selfish."

He stood as a bad boy stands when unexpectedly rewarded for some good deed, uncomfortable because of the ridiculous seriousness given to his gash, and ashamed because he was glad of the attention. He tried not to look at her, but somehow his eyes would not stray from her face, her heavy mass of black hair and her wonderful eyes.

"You make me think that I'm really hurt," he feebly expostulated as he capitulated to her deft hands. "Now, if it was a real wound, why it might be all right. But, pshaw, all this fuss and feathers about a scratch!"

"Indeed!" she cried, dropping the stained handkerchief to the ground as she took another from her dress, plastering his hair back with her free hand. "I suppose you would rather have what you call a real wound! You should be thankful that it is no worse! Why, just the tiniest bit more, and you would have–" she shuddered as she thought of it and turned quickly away and tore a strip of linen from her skirt. Straightening up and facing him again she ripped off the trimming and carefully plucked the loose threads from it. Folding it into a neat bandage she placed the handkerchief over the wound after pushing back the rebellious hair and bound it into place with the strip, deftly patting it here and pushing it there until it suited her. Then, drawing it tight, she unfastened the gold breast-pin which she wore at her throat and pinned the bandage into place, stepping back to regard her work with satisfaction.

"There!" she cried laughing delightedly. "You look real well in a bandage! But I am sorry there is need for one," she said, sobering instantly. "But, then, it could have been much worse, very much worse, couldn't it?" she asked, smiling brightly.

Before The Orphan could reply, Bill saw a break in the conversation, or thought he did, and hastened to say something, for he felt unnatural.

"I got yore smokin', Orphant!" he cried, clambering up to his seat. "Leastawise, I had before them war-whoops–yep! Here she is, right side up and fine and dandy!"

Could he have seen the look which the outlaw flashed at him he would have quailed with sudden fear. Three gasps arose in chorus, and the women drew back from the outlaw, fearful and shocked and severe. But with the sheriff's younger sister it was only momentarily, for she quickly recovered herself and the look of fear left her eyes. So this, then, was the dreaded Orphan, the outlaw of whom her brother had written! This young, sinewy, good-looking man, who had swayed so unsteadily on his feet, was the man the stories of whose outrages had filled the pages of Eastern newspapers and magazines! Could he possibly be guilty of the murders ascribed to him? Was he capable of the inhumanity which had made his name a synonym of terror? As she wondered, torn by conflicting thoughts, he looked at her unflinchingly, and his thin lips wore a peculiar smile, cynical and yet humorous.

Bill leaped to the ground with the smoking tobacco and, blissfully unconscious of what he had done, continued unruffled.

"That was d—n fine–begging the ladies' pardon," he cried. "Yes sir, it was plumb sumptious, it shore was! And when I tell the sheriff how you saved his sisters, he'll be some tickled! You just bet he will! And I'll tell it right, too! Just leave the telling of it to me. Lord, when I looked back to see how far them war-whoops were from my back hair, and saw you tearing along like you was a shore enough express train, I just had to yell, I was so tickled. It was just like I held a pair of deuces in a big jack-pot and drew two more! My, but didn't I feel good! And, say–whenever you run out of smoking again, you just flag Bill Howland's chariot: you can have all he's got. That's straight, you bet! Bill Howland don't forget a turn like that, never."

The enthusiasm he looked for did not materialize and he glanced from one to another as he realized that something was up.

"Come, dears, let us go," said Mary Shields, lifting her skirts and abruptly turning her back on the outlaw. "We evidently have far to go, and we have wasted so much time. Come, Grace," she said to her friend, stepping toward the coach.

Bill stared and wondered how much time had been wasted, since never before had he reached that point in so short a time. He had made two miles to every one at his regular speed.

"Come, Helen!" came the command from the elder, and with a trace of surprise and impatience.

"Sister! Why, Mary, how can you be so mean!" retorted the girl with the black eyes, angry and indignant at the unkindness of the cut, her face flushing at its injustice. Her spirit was up in arms immediately and she deliberately walked to The Orphan and impulsively held out her hand, her sister's words deciding the doubts in her mind in the outlaw's favor.

"Forgive her!" she cried. "She doesn't mean to be rude! She is so very nervous, and this afternoon has been too much for her. It was a man's act, a brave man's act! And one which I will always cherish, for I will never forget this day, never, never!" she reiterated earnestly. "I don't care what they say about you, not a bit! I don't believe it, for you could not have done what you have if you are as they paint you. I will not wait for our driver to tell my brother about your splendid act–he, at least, shall know you as you are, and some day he will return it, too."

Then she looked from him to her hand: "Will you not shake hands with me? Show me that you are not angry. Are you fair to me to class me as an enemy, just because my brother is the sheriff?"

He looked at her in wonderment and his face softened as he took the hand.

"Thank you," he said simply. "You are kind, and fair. I do not think of you as an enemy."

"Helen! Are you coming?" came from the coach.

He smiled at the words and then laughed bitterly, recklessly, his shoulders unconsciously squaring. There was no malice in his face, only a quizzical, baffling cynicism.

"Oh, it's a shame!" she cried, her eyes growing moist. She made a gesture of helplessness and looked him full in the eyes. "Whatever you have done in the past, you will give them no cause to say such things in the future, will you? You will leave it all behind you and get work, and not be an outlaw any more, won't you? You will prove my faith in you, for I have faith in you, won't you? It will all be forgotten," she added, as if her words made it so. Then she leaned forward to readjust the bandage. "There, now it's all right–you must not touch it again like that."

"You are alone in your faith," he replied bitterly, not daring to look at her.

"Oh, I reckon not," muttered Bill, scowling at the stage as if he would like to unhitch and leave it there. Then seeing The Orphan glance at the horse which was grazing contentedly, he went out to capture the animal. "D—d old hen, that's what she is!" he muttered fiercely. "I don't care if she is the sheriff's sister, that's just what she is! Just a regular ingrowing disposition!"

"You are kind, as kind as you are beautiful," The Orphan responded simply. "But you don't know."

She flushed at his words and then decided that he spoke in simple sincerity.

"I know that you are going to do differently," she replied as she extended her hand again. "Good-by."

He bowed his head as he took it and flushed: "Good-by."

She slowly turned and walked toward the coach, where she was received by a chilling silence.

Bill brought the horse to where The Orphan stood lost in thought, unbuckled his cartridge belt and wrapped it around the pommel of the saddle, the heavy Colt still in the holster. Then he clambered up for his rifle and tied it to the saddle skirt by the thongs of leather which dangled therefrom. Looking about him he espied the keg on the sand and, driving home the plug, slung it behind the cantle of the saddle where he fastend it by the straps which held the outlaw's "slicker." Jamming the package of tobacco into the pocket of the garment he stepped back and grinned sheepishly at his generous gifts. He turned abruptly and strode to the outlaw and shoved out his hand.

"There, pardner, shake!" he cried heartily. "Yore the best man in the whole d—d cow country, and I'll tell 'em so, too, by God!"

The outlaw came out of his reverie and looked him searchingly in the face as he gripped the outstretched hand with a grip which made the driver wince.

"Don't be a fool, Bill," he replied. "You'll get yourself disliked if you enthuse about me." Then he noticed the additions to his equipment and frowned: "You better take those things, I can't. The spirit is enough."

"Oh, you borrow them 'til you see me again," replied Bill. "You may need 'em," he added as he wheeled and walked to the coach. He climbed to his seat and wrapped the lines about his hands, cracking the whip as soon as he could, and the coach lurched on its way to Ford's Station, the driver grunting about fool old maids who didn't know enough to be glad they were alive.

The Orphan hesitated about the gifts and then decided to take them for the time. He mounted and rode past the coach door, keeping near to the flank of the last horse, where he listened to Bill's endless talk.

"How is it that you've got a Cross Bar-8 cayuse?" Bill asked at length, too idiotically happy to realize the significance of his question.

The Orphan's hand leaped suddenly and then stopped and dropped to the pommel, and he looked up at the driver.

"Oh, one of their punchers and I sort of swapped," he laughingly replied, thinking of the man under the débris. "Say, if I don't get as far as the cañon with you, just climb up above on the left hand side near the entrance and release a fool puncher that is covered up under a pile of rubbish, will you? I came near forgetting him, and I don't want him to die in that way."

As he spoke he saw a group of horsemen swing over a rise and he knew them instinctively.

"There's the gang now–tell them, I'm off for a ride," he said, dropping back to the coach door, where he raised his hand to his head and bowed.

CHAPTER VII
THE OUTFIT HUNTS FOR STRAYS

As the group of punchers and the stage neared each other Bill saw two horsemen ride out into view beside a chaparral half a mile to the northwest, and he recognized Shields and Charley, who were loping forward as if to overtake the cowboys, their approach noiseless because of the deep sand. As the cowboys came nearer Bill recognized them as being the five worst men of the Cross Bar-8 outfit, and his loyalty to his new friend was no stronger than his dislike for the newcomers. They swept up at a canter and stopped abruptly near the front wheel.

"Who was that?" asked Larry Thompson impatiently, with his gloved hand indicating the direction taken by The Orphan.

"Friend of mine," replied Bill, who was diplomatically pleasant. "Say," he began, enthusing for effect, "you should have turned up sooner–you missed a regular circus! We was chased by five Apaches, and my friend cleaned 'em up right, he shore did! You should a seen it. I wouldn't a missed it for—"

"Cheese it!" relentlessly continued Larry, interrupting the threatened verbal deluge. "Don't be all day about it, Windy," he cried; "who is he?"

"Why, a friend of mine, Tom Davis," lied Bill. "He just wiped out a bunch of Apaches, like I was telling you. They was a-chasing me some plentiful and things was getting real interesting when he chipped in and took a hand from behind. And he certainly cleaned 'em up brown, he shore did! Say, I'll bet you, even money, that he can lick the sheriff, or even The Orphant! He's a holy terror on wheels, that's what he is! Talk about lightning on the shoot–and he can hit twice in the same place, too, if he wants to, though there ain't no use of it when he gets there once. The way he can heave lead is enough to make—"

"Choke it, Bill, choke it!" testily ordered Curley Smith, whose reputation was unsavory. "Tell us why in h–l he hit th' trail so all-fired hard. Is yore friend some bashful?" he inquired ironically.

"Well," replied Bill, grinning exasperatingly, "it all depends on how you looks at it. Women say he is, men swear he ain't; you can take your choice. But they do say he ain't no ladies' man," he jabbed maliciously, well knowing that Curley prided himself on being a "lady-killer."

"Th' h–l he ain't!" retorted Curley, with a show of anger, preparing to argue, which would take time; and Bill was trying to give the outlaw a good start of them. "Th' h–l he ain't!" he repeated, leaning aggressively forward. "Yu keep yore opinions close to home, yu big-mouthed coyote!"

"Well, you asked me, didn't you?" replied Bill. "And I told you, didn't I? He's a good man all around, and say, you should oughter hear him sing! He's a singer from Singersville, he is. Got the finest voice this side of Chicago, that's what."

"That's real interesting, and just what we was askin' yu about," replied Larry with withering sarcasm. "An' bein' so, Windy, we'll shore give him all the music he wants to sing to before dark if we gets him. Yore lying ability is real highfalutin'. Now, suppose yu tell th' truth before we drag it outen yu–who is he?"

"You ought to know it by this time. Didn't I say his name is Tom Davis?" he replied, crossing his legs, his face wearing a bored look. "How many names do you think he's got, anyhow? Ain't one enough?"

"Look a-here!" cried Curley, pushing forward. "Was that th' d––d Orphant? Come on, now, talk straight!"

"Orphant!" ejaculated Bill in surprise. "Did you say Orphant? Orphant nothing!" he responded. "What in h–l do you think I'd be lying about him for? Do I look easy? He ain't no friend of mine! Besides, I wouldn't know him if I saw him, never having seen that frisky gent. Holy gee! is the Orphant loose in this country, out here along my route!" he cried, simulating alarm.

"Well, we'll take a chance anyhow," interposed Jack Kelly. "I can tell when a fool lies. If it is yore friend Tom Davis we won't hurt him none."

"Honest, you won't hurt him?" asked Bill, grinning broadly. "No, I reckon you won't, all right," he added, for the sheriff was close at hand now and was coming up at a walk, and Bill had an abiding faith in that official. He could be a trifle reckless how he talked now. He laughed sarcastically and hooked his thumbs in the armholes of his vest. "Nope, I reckon you won't hurt him, not a little bit. Not if he knows you're going to try it on him. And if it should be Mister Orphant, well, I hear that he's dead sore on being hunted–don't like it for a d—n. I also hear he drinks blood instead of water and whips five men before breakfast every morning to get up an appetite. Oh, no, and you won't hurt him neither, will you?"

"Yore real pert, now ain't yu?" shouted Curley angrily. "Yore a whole lot sassy an' smart, ain't yu? But if we find that he is that Orphant, we'll pay yu a visit so yu can explain just why yore so d—d friendly with him. He seems to have a whole lot of friends about this country, he does! Even the sheriff won't hurt him. Even th' brave sheriff loses his trail. Must be somethin' in it for somebody, eh?"

"You'd better tell that to somebody else, the sheriff, for instance. He'd like to think it over," responded Bill easily. "It's a good chance to see a little branding, a la Colt, as the French say. Tell it to him, why don't you?"

"I'm a-tellin' it to yu, now, an' I'll tell it to Shields when I sees him, yu overgrown baby, yu!" shouted Curley, his hand dropping to his Colt. "Everybody knows it! Everybody is a-talkin' about it! An' we'll have a new sheriff, too, before long! An' as for yu, if we wasn't in such a hurry, we'd give yu a lesson yu'd never forget! That d—d Orphant has got a pull, but we're goin' to give him a push, an' plumb into hell! Either a pull or our brave sheriff is some ascairt of him! He's a fine sheriff, he is, th' big baby!"

"Pleasant afternoon, Curley," came from behind the group, accompanied by a soft laugh. The voice was very pleasant and low. Curley stiffened and turned in his saddle like a flash. The sheriff was smiling, but there was a glint in his fighting eyes that gave grave warning. The sheriff smiled, but some men smile when most dangerous, and as an assurance of mastery and coolness.

"Looking for strays, or is it mavericks?" he casually asked, a question which left no doubt as to what the smile indicated, for it was a challenge. Maverick hunting was at that time akin to rustling, and it was occurring on the range despite the sheriff's best efforts to stop it.

Curley flushed and mumbled something about a missing herd. He had suddenly remembered the scene at the corral, and it had a most subduing effect on him. The sheriff regarded him closely and then noted the bullet holes in the coach. The door of the vehicle was closed, the curtains down, and no sound came from within it. The baggage flap had settled askew over the tell-tale trunks and hid them from sight on that side.

"Oh, it's a missing herd this time, is it?" he inquired coolly. "Well, I reckon you won't find it out here. They don't wander over this layout while the Limping Water is running."

"Well, we'll take a look down south aways; it won't do no harm now that we've got this far," replied Larry. "Come on, boys," he cried. "We've wasted too much time with th' engineer."

"Wait!" commanded the sheriff shortly. "Your foreman made me certain promises, and I reckon that you are out against orders. I wouldn't be surprised if Sneed wants you right now."

Larry laughed uneasily. "Oh, I reckon he ain't losin' no sleep about us. We won't hurt nobody" –whereat Bill grinned. "Come on, fellows."

"Well, I hope you get what you're looking for," replied the sheriff, whereat Bill snickered outright and winked at Charley, who sat alert and scowling behind the sheriff, rather hoping for a fight.

Larry flashed the driver a malicious look and, wheeling, cantered south, followed by his companions. They rode straight for the point at which The Orphan had disappeared, Bill waving his arms and crying: "Sic 'em." The chase was on in earnest.

The stage door suddenly flew open with a bang and interrupted the explanations which Bill was about to offer, and in a flash the sheriff was almost smothered by the attentions showered on him. Laughing and struggling and delighted by the surprise, the peace officer could not get a word edgewise in the rapid-fire exclamations and questions which were hurled at him from all sides.

But finally he could be heard as he extricated himself from the embraces of his sisters.

"Well, well!" he cried, smiles wreathing his face as he stepped back to get a good look at them. "You're a sight to make a sick man well! My, Helen, but how you've grown! It's been five years since I saw you–and you were only a schoolgirl in short dresses! And Mary hasn't grown a bit older, not a bit," addressing the elder of the two. Then he turned to the friend. "You must pardon me, Miss Ritchie," he said as he shook hands with her. "But I've been looking forward to this meeting for a long time. And I'm really surprised, too, because I didn't expect you all until the next stage trip. I had intended meeting you at the train and seeing you safely to Ford's Station, because the Apaches are out. I couldn't get word to you in time for you to postpone your visit, so I was going to take Charley and several more of the boys and escort you home."

Then he looked about for Charley, and found that person engaged in conversation with Bill as the two examined the bullet-marked stage.

"Come here, Charley!" he cried, beckoning his friend to his side. "Ladies, this is Charley Winter, and he is a real good boy for a puncher. Charley, Miss Ritchie, my sisters Mary and Helen. I reckon you ladies are purty well acquainted with Bill Howland by this time, but in case you ain't, I'll just say that he is the boss driver of the Southwest, noted locally for his oppressive taciturnity. I reckon you two boys don't need any introducing," he laughed.

Then, while the conversation throbbed at fever heat, Bill suddenly remembered and wheeled toward the sheriff.

"The Orphant!" he yelled in alarm, hoping to gain attention that way.

The sheriff and Charley wheeled, guns in hand, and leaped clear of the women, their quick eyes glancing from point to point in search of the danger.

"Where?" cried the sheriff over his shoulder at Bill.

"Down south, ahead of them fool punchers," Bill exclaimed. "He's only got a little start on 'em. And they know he's there, too. That's why they're looking for cows on a place cows never go."

Then he related in detail the occurrences of the past few hours, to the sheriff's great astonishment, and also to his delight at the way it had turned out. Shields thought of his own personal experiences with the outlaw, and this put him deeper in debt. His opinion as to there being much good in his enemy's makeup was strengthened, and he smiled at the fighting ability and fairness of the man who had declared a truce with him by the big bowlder on the Apache Trail.

"Oh, I hope they don't catch him!" Helen cried anxiously. "Can't you do something, James?" she implored. "He saved us, and he is wounded, too! Can't you stop them?"

The sheriff looked to the south in the direction taken by the cow-punchers, and a hard light grew in his eyes.

"No, not now," he replied decisively. "They've had too much time now. And it's safe to bet that they rode at full speed just as soon as they got out of my sight. They knew Bill would tell me. They're miles away by this time. But don't you worry, Sis–they won't get him.

Five curs never lived that could catch a timber wolf in his own country–and if they do catch him, they will wish they hadn't. And I almost hope they win the chase, for they'll lose their fool lives. It will be a lesson to the rest of the bullies of the Cross Bar-8–and small loss to the community at large, eh, Charley?"

"Yore shore right, Jim," replied Charley, smiling at Miss Ritchie. "Did you ever hear tell of the dog that retrieved a lighted dynamite cartridge?" he asked her. "No? Well, the dog left for parts unknown."

"That's good, Charley," Shields responded with a laugh. "The dog just wouldn't mind, and he was only a snarling, no-account cur at that, wasn't he?" Then he looked at the coach, and his heart softened to the hunted man. "I can see it all, now," he said slowly. "Those punchers must have forced him out of the Backbone, and he was getting away when he saw the plight you were in. By God!" he cried in appreciation of the act. "It wasn't no one man's work, five Apaches! One man stopping five of those devils–it was no work for a murderer, not much! It was clean-cut nerve, and if I ever see him I'll tell him so, too! I'll let him know that he's got some friends in this country. They can say what they please, but there's more manhood in him to the square inch than there is in all the people who cry him down; and who are in a great way responsible for his being an outlaw. I'm ready to swear that he never wantonly shot a man down; no, sir, he didn't. And I reckon he never had much show, from what I know of him."

"Helen was real kind to him," remarked the spinster. "She bathed his wound and bandaged it. Spoiled her very best skirt, too."

"You're a good girl, Sis," Shields said, looking fondly at the beautiful girl at his side. His arm went around her shoulder and he affectionately patted her cheek. "I'm proud of you, and we'll have to see if we can't get another 'very best skirt,' too." Then he laughed: "But I'll bet he blesses the warrior who fired that shot–he's not used to having pretty girls fuss about him."

Mary looked quickly at her sister. "Why, Helen! You've lost your gold pin! Where do you suppose it has gone? I'll look in the stage for it before we forget about it. Dear me, dear me," she cried as she entered the vehicle, "this has indeed been a terrible day!"

Bill grinned and turned toward his team. "I reckon she'll find it some day," he said in a low aside as he passed the sheriff. "I'll just bet she does. It'll be in at the finish of a whole lot of things, and people, too, you bet," he added enigmatically.

Shields looked quickly at the driver, his face brightened and he smiled knowingly at the words. "I reckon it will; fool punchers, for instance?"

Bill turned his head and one eye closed in an emphatic wink. "Keno," he replied.

Mary bustled out again, very much agitated. "I can't find it. Where do you suppose you lost it, dear? I've looked everywhere in the stage."

"Probably back where we stopped before," Helen replied quietly. "We were so agitated that we would never have noticed it if it slipped down."

"Well–" began Mary.

"No use going back for it, Miss Shields," promptly interrupted Bill from his high seat. "We just couldn't find it in all that trampled sand, not if we hunted all week for it with a comb."

"You're right, Bill," gravely responded the sheriff. "We never could."

As they entered the defile of the Backbone the sheriff suddenly remembered what Bill had told him and he stopped and dismounted.

"You keep right on, Bill," he said. "I'm going up to hunt that fool puncher. Lord, but it's a joke! This game is getting better every day–I'm getting so I sort of like to have The Orphan around. He's shore original, all right."

"He's better than a marked deck in a darkened room," laughed the driver. "He shore ought to be framed, or something like that."

"You better go with them, Charley," the sheriff said as his friend made a move at dismounting."There ain't no danger, but we won't take no chances this time; we've got a precious coachful."

"All right," replied Charley as he wheeled toward the disappearing stage. "So long, Sheriff."

The sheriff looked the wall over and then picked out a comparatively easy place and climbed to the top. As he drew himself over the edge he espied a pair of boots which showed from under a pile of débris, and he laughed heartily. At the laugh the feet began to kick vigorously, so affecting the sheriff that he had to stop a minute, for it was the most ludicrous sight he had ever looked upon.

Shields grabbed the boots and pulled, walking backward, and soon an enraged and trussed cow-puncher came into view. Slowly and carefully unrolling the rope from the unfortunate man, he coiled it methodically and slung it over his shoulder, and then assisted in loosening the gag.

The puncher was too stiff to rise and his liberator helped him to his feet and slapped and rubbed and chuckled and rubbed to start the blood in circulation. The gag had so affected the muscles of the puncher's jaw that his mouth would not close without assistance and effort, and his words were not at all clear for that reason. His first word was a curse.

"'Ell!" he cried as he stamped and swung his arms. "'Ell! I'm asleep all o'er! —! 'Ait till I get 'im! —! 'Ait till I get 'im!"

"Sort of continuing the little nap you was taking when he roped you, eh?" asked Shields, holding his sides.

"Nap nothing! Nap nothing!" yelled the other in profane denial. "I wasn't asleep, I tell yu! I was wide awake! He got th' drop on me, and then that cussed rope of his'n was everywhere! Th' air was plumb full of rope and guns! I didn't have no show! Not a bit of a show! Oh, just wait till I get him! Why, I heard my pardners talking as they hunted for me, and there I was not twenty feet away from them all the time, helpless! They're fine lookers, they are! Wait till I sees them, too! I'll tell 'em a few things, all right!"

"Well, I reckon you may see one or two of them, if they're lucky–and you can't beat a fool for luck," replied the sheriff. "They want to be angels; they're on his trail now."

"Hope they get him!" yelled the puncher, dancing with rage. "Hope they burn him at th' stake! Hope they scalp him, an' hash him, an' saw his arms off, an' cave his roof in! Hope they make him eat his fingers and toes! Hope—"

"You're some hopeful to-day," responded the sheriff. "If you like them, you better hope they don't get him. That's hoping real hope."

"Wait till I get him!" the puncher repeated, grabbing for his Colt, being too enraged to notice its absence. "I'll show him if he can tie a man up an' leave him to choke to death, an' starve an' roast! I'll show him if he can run this country like he owns it, shooting and abusing everybody he wants to!"

"All right, Sonny," Shields laughed. "I'll shore wait till you gets him, if I live long enough. But for your sake I shore hope you never finds him. He wouldn't get any more reputation if he killed you, and your friends would miss you."

"Don't yu let that worry yu!" retorted the enraged man. "I can take care of myself in a mix-up, all right! An' I'm going to chase after my friends an' take a hand in th' game, too, by God! He ain't going to leave me high an' dry an' live to boast about it! But I suppose you reckon yu'll stop me, hey?"

Shields raised both hands high in the air in denial. "I wouldn't think of such a thing, not for the world," he cried, laughter shaking his big frame. "You can go any place you please, only I'd take a gun if I was going after him," he added, eyeing the empty holster. "You know, you might need it," he was very grave in his use of the subjunctive.

The puncher slapped his hand to his thigh and then jumped high into the air: "—! —!" he shouted. "Stole my gun! Stole my gun!" Then he paused suddenly and his face cleared. "But I've got something better'n a Colt on my cayuse!" he cried as he leaped toward the edge of the cañon. "An' I'll give him all it holds, too!" he threatened as he bumped and slid to the bottom. The sheriff took more care and time in descending and had just reached the trail when he heard a heart-rending yell, followed by a sizzling stream of throbbing profanity.

"Where's my cayuse?" yelled the puncher as he rounded the corner of the cañon wall on a peculiar lope and hop. "Where's my cayuse, yu law-coyote?" he shouted, temporarily out of his senses from rage. "Where's my cayuse!" dancing up to the sheriff and shaking both fists under the laughter-convulsed face.

When the sheriff could speak, he leaned against the cañon wall for support and broke the news.

"Why, Bill Howland said as how The Orphan was riding a Cross Bar-8 cayuse–dirty brown, with a white stocking on his near front foot. It had a big scar on its neck, too."

"Th' d—d hoss thief!" began the puncher, but Shields kept right on talking.

"There was a dandy Cheyenne saddle," he said, counting on his fingers, "a good gun, a pair of hobbles and a big coil of rawhide rope on the cayuse. Was they yours?"

"Was they mine! Was they mine!" his companion screamed. "My new saddle gone, my gun gone and my fine rope gone! Oh, h–l! How'll I hunt him now? How'll I get home? How'll I get back to th' ranch?" Words failed him, and he could only wave his arms and yell.

"Well, it wouldn't hardly be worth while chasing him on foot without a gun, that's shore," the sheriff said, grave once more. "But you can get home all right; that's easy."

"How can I?" asked the puncher, eyeing the sheriff's horse and waiting for the invitation to ride double on it.

"Why, walk," was the reply. "It's only about twenty miles as the crow flies–say twenty-five on the trail."

"Walk! Walk!" cried his companion, savagely kicking at a lizard which looked out from a crevice in the rock wall. "I never walked five miles all at once in my life!"

"Well, it'll be a new experience, and you can't begin any younger," replied Shields as he swung into his saddle. "It'll do you good, too–increase your appetite."

"I'm so hungry now I'm half starved," replied the other. "But I'll pay up for all this, you see if I don't! I'll get square with that d—d outlaw!"

"You don't know enough to be glad you were found," retorted the sheriff. "And if he hadn't told Bill where to look for you, you wouldn't have been, neither. You got off easy, Bucknell, and don't you forget it, neither. Men have been killed for less than what you tried to do."

The puncher wilted, for twenty-five miles in high-heeled boots, over rocks and sand, and with an empty stomach, was terrible to contemplate, and he turned to the sheriff beseechingly.

"Give me a lift, Sheriff," he implored. "Take me up behind you–I can't walk all the way!"

Shields looked at the sun, which was nearing the western horizon, and thought for a minute. Then he shrugged his shoulders.

"Well, I hadn't ought to help you a step, not a single, solitary step, and you know it. You tried your best to run against me. You tried to hold me up there by the corral, and then after I had warned you not to go out for The Orphan you went right ahead. Now you're asking me to help you out of your trouble, to make good for your fool stupidity. But I'll take you as far as the end of the cañon–no, I'll take you on to the ford, and then you can do the rest on foot. That'll leave you ten or a dozen miles. Get aboard."

CHAPTER VIII "A TIMBER WOLF IN HIS OWN COUNTRY"

When The Orphan said good-by to Bill he sat quietly in his saddle for a minute watching the departing stage and wondered how it was that he had the decency to avoid a fight with the cowboys in the presence of the women. Then Helen's words came to him and he smiled at the idea of peace when he would have to fight the outfit before sundown. The heat of the sun on his bare head recalled him from his mental wanderings and he wheeled abruptly and galloped along the trail to where he remembered that a tiny, blood-stained handkerchief lay in the dust and sand. Soon he espied it and, swinging over in the saddle, deftly picked it up and regained his upright position, his head reeling at the effort. Unfolding it he examined the neat "H" done in silk in one corner and smiled as he put it in his chaps pocket where he kept his extra ammunition.

"Peace and war in one pocket," he muttered, grinning at his cartridges' new and unusual companion.

Then he espied a Winchester near a fallen brave, and he procured it as he had the handkerchief. Describing an arc he picked up another, discarding it after he had emptied the magazine, for ammunition was what he wanted. Two Winchesters were all right, but three were too many. As he threw it from him he glanced through a slight opening in the chaparral and saw the outfit approach the stage. Then he galloped to where his sombrero lay, picked it up and turned to the south for the Cimarron Trail. When thoroughly screened by the chaparral he pushed on with the swinging lope which his horse could maintain for hours, and which ate up distance in an astonishing manner. He had lost time in going for his sombrero and the handkerchief, and every minute before nightfall was precious. His thoughts now bent to the problem of how either to elude or ambush his pursuers, and the Winchesters bespoke his forethought, for up to six hundred yards they were not a pleasant proposition to face. If he eluded the cowboys in the darkness he was morally certain that they would take up his trail at dawn, and what distance he had gained would be at the expense of the freshness of his horse. While he would average ten miles an hour through the night, their mounts, freshened by a night's rest, might cut down his gain before the nightfall of the next day.

One of the Winchesters worked loose from its lashings and started to slide toward the ground. He quickly grasped it and made it secure, smiling at the number of rifles he had had and lost during the past three weeks.

"Funny how this country has been shedding Winchesters lately," he mused. "There was the five I got by the big bowlder, which I lost playing tag with that d—d Cross Bar-8 gang, and here's two more, and I just left three what I didn't want. Well, they're real handy for stopping a rush, and I reckons that's what I'm up against this time. If I can find a likely spot for a scrap before dark I may stop that gang in bang-up style, d—n them."

Half an hour later he caught sight of a moving body of horsemen to the southeast of him and his glasses enabled him to make them out.

"'Paches!" he exclaimed, and then he smiled grimly and continued on his way toward them, taking care to keep himself screened from their sight by rises and chaparrals. His first thought had been of danger, but now he laughed at the cards fate had put in his hand, for he would use the Indians to great advantage later on.

He counted them and made their number to be twenty-two, which accounted for the five warriors who had pursued the stage coach. The odds were fine and he laughed joyously, recklessly: "All is fair in love and war," he muttered savagely.

Before the Indians had come upon the scene he had been alone to face five angry and vengeful men, and whom he had every reason to believe were at least fair fighters. Had the positions been reversed they would not have hesitated to make use of any stratagem to save themselves–and here were two contingents, both of which would take his life at the first opportunity. He felt no distaste at the game he was about to play; on the other hand, it pleased him immensely to know that he was superior in intellect to his enemies. They both wanted blood, and they should have it. If they found too much, well and good–that was their lookout. And no less pleasing was the knowledge that he had sent them north and that now he could make use of them. He wondered what they had been doing for the last three weeks and why they were still in that part of the country, but he did not care, for they were where he wanted them to be.

"Twenty-two mad Apaches on the warpath against five cow-wrastlers!" he exulted. "More than four to one, and just aching to get square on somebody! That Cross Bar-8 gang will have something to weep about purty d—n soon! And I shore hope they don't get tired and quit chasing me."

He stopped and waited when he had gained a screened position from where he could look back over his trail, and he had not long to wait, for soon he saw five cowboys galloping hard in his direction. Another look to the southeast showed him that the war party was now riding slowly toward him, not knowing of his presence, and they would arrive at his cover at about the same time the cowboys would come up. Neither the Indians nor the cowboys knew of the proximity of the other, while The Orphan could see them both. He glanced at the thicket to the west of him and saw that it was thin, being a connecting link between the two larger chaparrals.

"I don't know how you are on the jump, bronch," he said to his mount, "but I reckon you can get through that, all right."

The cowboys disappeared from his sight behind the northern chaparral, and as they did so he sunk his spurs into his horse and rode straight at the prickly screen and, going partly over and partly through it, galloped westward as the war party and the ranch contingent met. The shots and yells were as music to his ears, and he bowed in mockery and waved his hand at the turmoil as he made his escape. The timber wolf had won.

CHAPTER IX
THE CROSS BAR-8 LOSES SLEEP

Sneed was angry, which could be seen by the way he talked, ate, moved and swore. He had many cattle to care for and they were strewn over six hundred square miles of territory. The work was hard enough when he had his full dozen punchers, but now it forced groans from the tired bodies of his men, who fell asleep while removing their saddles at night, and who worked in a way almost mechanical. The extra work was not conducive to sweetness of temper, and he was continually quelling fights among the members of the outfit. Where only argument formerly would have arisen over differences of opinion, guns now leaped forth; and the differences were multiplied greatly, and getting worse every day. Things which ordinarily would have provoked no notice, or a laugh at most, now caused hot words and surliness. And the reason for the extra work was the continued absence of five cow punchers.

Sneed, tired of cursing the missing men and of offering himself explanations as to why they had not returned, fell, instead, to planning an appropriate reception for them on their return to the ranch. He needed no rehearsing, for while he did not know in just what manner he would reveal his ideas concerning them, he knew what his ideas were and he had always been good at extemporizing when under pressure, and he was under pressure now if he had ever been.

The extra work was hard enough in itself to cause his anger to rise and to create sensitiveness and surliness on the part of his men, but it was only one factor of his discontent. Busy all day at driving the scattered cattle away from the Backbone and closer to the ranch proper where they would be less likely to fall prey to Apache raiders; working all day from the first sign of dawn to the prohibitive blackness of the night, they could have stood up under the strain, for these were men of iron, inured to hardships and constant riding. But hardy as they were there was one thing which they must have, and that was sleep. If they could have only four hours of unbroken sleep when they threw themselves, fully dressed with the exception of their boots, in their bunks, they could have endured the labor for weeks. But this was denied them, and constantly on their minds were thoughts of fire, slaughtered cattle and death.

For a week night had been a terror on the Cross Bar-8. No sooner had the exhausted outfit fallen asleep than bits of window glass would fly about them, cutting and stinging. There was not a whole window pane in the house and the door was so full of lead that it sagged on its half-shattered hinges. Cooking utensils were fast deserving premiums, for hardly an unperforated tin could be found on the premises. And their cook, a Mexican, who most devoutly believed in a personal devil and a brimstone hell, and who feared that he was living in uncomfortable proximity to both, stood the strain for just two nights and then, panic-stricken, had fled from the accursed place and left them to get their own meals as best they could. The protection of the saints was all very well and good under ordinary circumstances, but when they failed to stop the bullets which passed through his cook shack and which more than once had grazed him, it was time for him to find some place far removed from the Cross Bar-8, and where the devil was less strong. When the saints allowed a devil-sped bullet to completely shatter a crucifix it was time to migrate, which he did, but in broad daylight when the outfit had departed and when the devil was not in evidence.

The interiors of both the ranch house and the bunk house were wrecked. The clock, the pride of the foreman, stood with half its wheels buried in the wall behind it by a .50 caliber slug, its hands pointing to half-past one. Lead filled the interior walls, where opposite windows, and the holes and splinters were a disgrace. Sombreros, equipment and the few pictures the walls boasted were like tops of pepper shakers. No sooner was a light shown than it became the target for a shot, and more than one wound gave proof as to the accuracy of the perpetrator. So tired that they fell asleep at supper, the men were constantly awakened by the noise of devastation and the whining hum of the bullets. Pursuit was a failure, and was also hazardous, as proven by Bert Hodge's arm, broken by a .50 caliber slug from somewhere.

The two houses, wrecked as they were, were fortunate when compared to the condition of the other appurtenances of the ranch. Horses were found dead at all points, and always with a bullet hole in the center of the forehead. The carcasses of cows dotted the plain, and fire had half-destroyed the three corrals. The three new cook wagons, unsheltered, were denuded of bolts and nuts, and their tarpaulins were hopelessly ruined. A wheel was missing from each of them and their poles had been cut through in the middle, the severed ends being found on the roof of the ranch house three minutes after their crashing descent had awakened the foreman, who heard the hum and thud of a bullet as he opened the door. The best grass had been burned off and the outfit had fought fire on several nights when it should have slept. And the small water hole near the cook shack, which furnished water for the bunk house, had been cleared of a dead calf on two mornings. Scouting was of no avail, for the few remaining horses (which now spent the night in the bunk house) were as exhausted as their riders. Keeping guard was a farce, for it had been tried twice, and the guards had fallen asleep; and, awakened by their foreman at dawn, found that their rifles, sombreros and even their spurs were missing. With all his hatred for The Orphan, Sneed was fair-minded enough to give his enemy credit for being the better man. When the harassing outrages had first begun and the foreman and his men were comparatively fresh, he had given the matter his whole attention; and he was no fool. But he had gained nothing but a sense of defeat, which fact did not improve his peace of mind or cause him to lose a whit of his anger. Do what he could, plan as he might, he was beaten, and beaten at every turn. He had to deal with a man whose cunning and ingenuity were far above the average; a man who, combining a rare courage and a wonderful accuracy in shooting with devilish strategy, towered far above the ordinary rustler and outlaw. Sneed knew that he was absolutely at the mercy of his persistent enemy and wondered why it was that he did not steal up in the night and kill the outfit as it slept, which was entirely feasible. Finally, when the strain had grown too much for even his iron nerves the sheriff was implored to take command on the ranch and give it his personal protection. The relations between the sheriff and the ranch were not as cordial as they might have been, and the asking of this favor was gall and wormwood to the foreman and his outfit.

When Shields arrived to take charge of the trouble, accompanied by Charley and two others, he sought the foreman, for Charley had news of a grave nature for the Cross Bar-8.

The foreman ran out of the bunk house and met them near the corral, where the disagreement had taken place.

"By the living God, Sheriff!" he cried, white with anger. "This thing has got to stop if we have to call out the cavalry! We can't get a decent breakfast–not a whole plate or pan in the house! Our cayuses and cows are being slaughtered by the score! And as for the rest of our possessions, they are so full of holes that they whistle when the wind blows!"

"So I heard," replied the sheriff. "I'll do my best."

"We've been doing our best, but what good is it?" cried the foreman. "We are so plumb sleepy we go to sleep moving about! We dassent show our faces after dark without being made a target of! Our new wagons are wrecks, the corrals destroyed and the best grass made us fight for our lives while it burned! That cursed outlaw has got to be killed, d—n him!"

"We'll do our best, Sneed," responded Shields. "I reckon we can stop it; at least we can give you a good night's rest."

"Where are my five punchers?" Sneed asked; his words bellowed until his voice broke. "And Bucknell! D—n near dead before you found him above the cañon, tied up like a package of flour!"

"Well, Charley can tell you about your men," Shields responded, viewing the devastation on all sides of him.

"Well, what about them?" cried the foreman turning to the sheriff's deputy, anger flashing anew in his eyes.

"Well," Charley slowly began, "I was taking a short cut this morning, and when I got to a place about a dozen miles southeast of the mouth of Bill's cañon, I saw five bodies on the desert. They were your cow-punchers, and they was so full of arrows that they looked like big brooms. Apaches, I reckon," he added sententiously.

Sneed tore his hair and swore when he was not choking.

"And after I told them to let up on that blasted outlaw's trail!" he yelled. "Where will it end, between war-whoops and murders? What sort of a God-forsaken layout is this, anyhow? A man can't stick his nose out of his own house after dark without having it skinned by a slug! He's a h–l of a hefty orphant, he is! Poor thing, ain't got no paw or maw to look after his dear little hide! He needs a regiment of cavalry for a papa, that's what he needs, and a good strong lariat for a mamma! Orphant! He's a h–l of a sumptious orphant!"

"Have you trailed him?" asked the sheriff, having to smile in spite of himself at the execution on all sides of him, and at the foreman's words.

"Trailed him!" yelled Sneed, raising on his toes in his vehemence. "Trailed him! Good God, yes! But what good is it, what can we do when our cayuses are so dod-gasted tired that they can't catch a tumble bug? Trailed him! Yes, we trailed him, all right! We trailed him until we fell asleep in the saddles on our sleeping cayuses! And while we were gone, d—d if he didn't blow in and smash up our furniture! We trailed him, all right; just like a lot of cross-eyed, locoed drunken ants! We had to wake each other up, and he could-a killed the whole crowd of us with a club! And my punchers who were so cock-sure they'd get him! How in h–l did they go and mess up with Apaches? They wasn't no fool kids!"

"The last time we saw them they were leaving the stage to go south after him," Charley said. "They hadn't got more than ten miles south when they must have met the Apaches. I have a suspicion that The Orphan had a hand in that meeting, but how he did it I don't know. But I know that the spot was lovely for a head-on collision. Punchers riding south would turn the corner of the chaparral and run into the war party before they knowed it. And I didn't see The Orphant's body laying around all full of arrows, neither."

Sneed's rage was pathetic. He almost frothed, and tears stood in his blood-shot eyes. His neck and his face were red as fire and the veins of his neck and forehead stood out like whip-cords, while his face worked convulsively. He was incapable of coherent speech, his words being unintelligible growls, a series of snarls, and he could only pace back and forth, waving his arms and cursing wildly.

Shields glanced about the ranch and gave a few orders, his men executing them without delay. One man was to keep guard in the bunk house while Sneed and his woe-begone men slept. The sheriff and Charley rode away toward the north to begin the search for the outlaw; and there was to be no quarter asked or given if his deputies had anything to do with it.

The remaining deputy busied himself about the ranch in executing a plan the sheriff had thought out, and his actions were peculiar. First selecting a position from which a man could command an extensive view of the premises, he began to pace off distances in all directions. The place was about eight hundred yards west of the ranch house and bunk house, and formed one angle of a triangle with them; and from it it was possible to look in through the windows of both of them. Any one passing within good rifle range of either house would show up against the lights in the windows; and if a man had been covered over with sand on that particular outlying angle, he could pick off the intruder without being seen. The Orphan was due to meet with a surprise if he paid his regular visit the coming night.

The deputy, after completing his work to his satisfaction found three more positions where they respectively commanded the corrals, the wagons and the rear of the bunk house. Then he paced more distances and was careful that bulky objects interposed in the direct lines between the positions, this latter precaution being to make it impossible for the deputies to shoot each other. This done, he went into the house and consulted with his companion in arms, laughing immoderately about the joke they would play on the marauder.

While Shields and Charley vainly searched the plain and while the deputy paced and thought and paced, and while Sneed and his exhausted cow-punchers slept as if in death, safely under guard, two men were riding along the Ford's Station Sagetown Trail well to the east of the Backbone, chatting amicably and smoking the same brand of tobacco. One of them sat high up in the air on the seat of a stage coach, from where he overlooked his six-horse team. His face was wreathed in grins and his expression was one of beatific contentment. The other cantered alongside on a dirty brown horse which had a white stocking on the near front foot, keeping close watch of the surrounding plain, his mind active and alert.

Bill Howland laughed suddenly and slapped his thigh with enthusiasm: "Say, Orphant," he cried, "you are shore raising h–l with that Cross Bar-8 gang! You has got them so tangled up and miserable that they don't know where they are! If their brains was money they'd have to chalk up their drinks. They're about as dangerous as ossified prairie dogs. They remind me of the feller who kicked a rattlesnake to see if it was alive, and found out that it was. No, sir, they shore won't die of brain fever. Why, they ain't had any sleep for a week, have to work double hard, eat what they can cook in sieve tins, and can't say their soul's their own after dark. They could get rest if they quit working one day and all but one get plenty of sleep. Then the other feller could get his at night. But they don't know enough. Oh, it's rich: the whole blamed town is laughing at 'em fit to bust. It's the funniest thing ever happened in these parts since I've been out here."

Then he suddenly paused: "Say, Sneed sent a puncher to town this morning. It was that brass-headed, flat-faced Bucknell, what you tied up by the cañon. He begged the sheriff to swear in a dozen bad men and come out and protect his foreman and the rest of the outfit. And the pin-headed wart went and blabbed the whole thing right in front of the Taggert's saloon crowd, and he shore had to blow, all right. He shore did, and that gang's always thirsty."

The horseman flecked the ashes from his cigarette and smiled: "Well?" he asked, looking up.

"So Shields took Charley Winter and the two Larkin boys and went out to the ranch right after the puncher went back. So you want to go easy to-night or you'll touch off some unexpected fireworks and such. Shields and his men will stay out there for several days and nights. That'll give the crazy hens a chance to rest up a bit nights. But you be blamed careful about them pinwheels and skyrockets or you'll get burned some. Now, don't you even remember that I told you about it. I wouldn't-a said nothing at all, seeing as it ain't none of my business, only you went and got me out of a tight place, and Bill Howland don't forget a favor, no siree! You gave me a square deal and a ace full on kings with them animated paint shops, and I'll give you a lift every time I can. It wouldn't be a bad scheme to watch for me once in a while–I might have some news for you."

Bill's offer, plain as it was that he wished to help, not only because he was in debt to the outlaw, but also because he wished to have safe trips, touched the horseman deeply. Never in his life had The Orphan been offered a helping hand from a stranger; all he could hope for was to get the drop first. He rode on silently, buried in thought, and then, suddenly flipping his cigarette at a cactus, raised his head and looked full at the man above him.

"You play square with me, Bill, and I'll take care of you," he replied. "The less you say, the less apt you are to put your foot in it. I'll hold my mouth about your information, for if Shields knew what you've just said he'd play a tune for you to dance to. The Cross Bar-8 would shoot you before a day passed. Any time you have news for me, tie your kerchief to that cactus," pointing to an exceptionally tall plant close at hand. "Do it on your outward trip. If I see it in time I'll meet you somewhere on the Sagetown end of the trail on your return. I'm going back now, so by-by."

"So long, and good luck," replied Bill heartily. "I'll do the handkerchief game, all right. Be some cautious about the way you buzz around that stacked deck of a Cross Bar-8 for the next few days."

The Orphan wheeled and cantered back, making a detour to the south, for he had a plan to develop and did not wish to be interrupted by meeting any more hunting parties. Bill lashed his team and rolled on his way to Sagetown, a happy smile illuminating his countenance.

"They can't beat us, bronchs," he cried to his team. "Me and The Orphant can lick the whole blasted territory, you bet we can!"

CHAPTER X
THE ORPHAN PAYS TWO CALLS

Shortly after nightfall a rider cantered along the stage route, fording the Limping Water and rode toward the town, whose few lights were bunched together as if for protection against the spirits of the night. He soon passed the scattered corrals on the outskirts of Ford's Station and, slowing to a walk, went carelessly past the row of saloons and the general store and approached a neat, small house some two hundred yards west of the stage office. He appeared careless as to being seen; in fact a casual observer would have thought him to be some cowboy who was familiar with the town and who feared the recognition of no man. But while he had no fear, he was alert; under his affected nonchalance nerves were set for instant action. He was in the heart of the enemy's country, in the crude stronghold of the Law, and if anything hostile to him occurred it would happen quickly. And he was familiar with the town, because he had on more than one occasion ridden through and explored it, but never before at such an early hour.

Arriving at his destination he dismounted and, leaving his horse unrestrained by rope or strap, walked boldly up to the door of the sheriff's house and knocked. Soon he heard footsteps within and the door opened wide, revealing him standing hat in hand and smiling.

"Good evening, ma'am," he said uneasily.

The sheriff's wife stepped aside and the light fell full on his face. For an instant she was at a loss, and then the fresh scar on his forehead and her husband's good description came to her aid. She gasped and stepped back involuntarily, astonished at his daring. Her act allowed her companions to see him and the effect was marked. Miss Ritchie sat upright in expectation, her face beaming, for this was as romantic and unexpected as she could wish. Mary gasped and dropped her hands to her side, not knowing what to do or say, while Helen slowly laid her work aside and leaned forward slightly, regarding him intently, a curious expression on her face.

"I only called to ask how the ladies were," he continued slowly, turning his hat in his hands, apparently not noticing Mrs. Shields' surprise. "I was afraid they might have–that their recent experience might have bothered them some."

Evidently it was to be only a social call, and Mrs. Shields owed something to this fair-minded and chivalrous man. She smiled kindly, remembering that the caller was rather well thought of by her husband–he was not a man for women to fear, whatever else he might be.

"It is very kind of you," she replied. "Won't you come in?" she asked from the habit of politeness, hardly expecting that he would do so.

"Thank you, I will be glad to for a minute," he responded, slowly stepping into the room, where he suddenly felt awkward and not at all comfortable.

Helen picked up her work to fasten a thread, and he found himself marveling at the cleverness of her fingers. Again laying the work aside, she arose to meet him, a mischievous twinkle in her dark eyes. It was so unusual to have been saved by an outlaw whom her brother had tried to capture, and still more unusual to have him dare to call on her in her brother's own house, especially after her sister's direct cut at the coach.

"Won't you be seated?" she asked, indicating her own chair by the light and taking his hat. When the hat left him he suffered a loss, for he had nothing to twist and grip. He replied by dropping into the chair, not even seeing that it was out of range of the door as a compliment to his hostess. There was no sign of a weapon on him, his holster being empty; but his blue flannel shirt was unbuttoned, the opening hidden by his neck-kerchief. He had, however, only put his Colt there to have it out of sight, and not because he feared trouble. Habitual caution was responsible for the shirt being open, for he was not even sure that he would fight if trouble should come upon him, unless the women gave him a clear field.

Helen drew a chair from the wall and seated herself in the semi-circle which faced him.

"I am very glad that your wound has healed so nicely," she said with a smile. "We are very sorry that you were hurt in our defense."

"Oh, it wasn't anything," he quickly replied, smiling deprecatingly. "You fixed it up so nice that it didn't bother me at all–didn't hurt a bit."

"I am glad it was no worse," she replied, looking around the circle. "Grace, Mary, you surely remember Mr.–Mr.—"

"Please call me by the name you know me by–The Orphan," smiling broadly. "I've almost forgotten that I ever had any other name."

"Mr. Orphan–how funny it sounds," she laughed. "It's most original. Margaret, this is the gentleman to whom we certainly owe our lives. Oh! I know you don't like to be reminded of it," she went on, answering his deprecatory gesture, "no doubt you are accustomed to that sort of thing out here, but in the East such an experience does not often occur."

"I am glad indeed to know and thank you," said Mrs. Shields, impulsively extending her hand. "Your bravery has put me still deeper in your debt. My husband–" her feelings overcame her as she realized that this was the man who had spared to her that husband, her laughing, burly, broad-shouldered, big-hearted king of men. Was it possible that this handsome, confident stripling was his peer?

Helen relieved the tension: "Mr. Orphan, this is Miss Ritchie, the same Miss Ritchie who was so badly frightened when she first met you. Perhaps you'll remember it. And this—"

"I wasn't! I wasn't one bit frightened!" declared Miss Ritchie hotly, to The Orphan's great enjoyment.

"Now, Grace, don't fib–you can't deny it. And this is my sister who was mean enough to keep her senses when I didn't. We thought highly of you then, but even more so now. You see, my brother has been talking about you, he takes a keen interest in you, Mr. Orphan–I declare I can't help laughing at that name, it sounds so funny; but you will forgive me, won't you? I knew you would. Well, James has been saying nice things about you, and so you see we know you better now. He likes you real well, as well as you will let him, and I'm awful sorry that he is not at home," she dared, her eyes flashing with delight. "I am sure he would like to meet you very much; in fact he has said as much. Oh, he speaks of you quite often."

The caller flushed, but he was determined to let them think him perfectly at ease.

"I am glad that he remembers me," he responded gravely. "I have only met him once, but I thought he was rather glad to see me. We had a very enjoyable time together and I found him very pleasant." He was forced to smile as he recalled the six Apaches in the sheriff's rear.

"Helen was just saying what awful risks her brother ran," Miss Ritchie remarked, intently studying the rugged face before her. "But then, he's a man. If I was a man, I wouldn't be afraid of them!"

"My, how brave you are, Grace," laughed Mrs. Shields. "I heard quite to the contrary about the stage ride."

"Goodness, Margaret!" retorted Miss Ritchie, up in arms at the remark. "You would have been afraid in that old coach if you had been banged about in it as I was. The noise was terrible, and that awful driver!"

The caller smiled at her spirit and then replied to her, serious at once.

"Well, he does take chances," he said. "But for that matter every man out in this country has to run risks. Now, I've taken some myself," he added, smiling quizzically. "But, you know, we get used to them after a while–we get used to everything but hunger and thirst–and life. I've even gotten used to being lonesome, and I find that it really isn't so bad after all. And then, you know, lonesomeness does have its advantages at times, for it certainly promotes peace, and the cartridges that it saves are worth considerable. But it took me several years before I could accept it in that light with any degree of ease."

Helen laughed merrily, for she most of all appreciated this outcast's humor, and she liked him better the more he talked.

"Yes, in time I suppose one does become accustomed to danger," she replied, "although I'll be frank enough to admit that I don't believe I could," glancing at her friend. "You risked much by coming here to-night–just suppose that you had called last night!"

"The danger was only from a chance recognition in the street," he replied, smiling, "and it would have been equally dangerous for the man who recognized me, and perhaps more so, since I was on the lookout–that balances. I would be the last man anyone would expect to be in Ford's Station at this time, and once free of the town, I could elude the pursuers in the dark. And as for the sheriff, I knew that he was not at home to-night, and, had he been so, I doubt if it would have stayed me, for he is fair and square, and an unarmed man is safe with him in his own house. He understands what a truce means, and we had one before."

Mrs. Shields smiled at him in such warmth that he thanked his stars that he had played fair out by the bowlder.

"He told us of that!" Helen exclaimed, laughingly. "It was splendid of you, both of you. And, do you know, I liked you much better for it. And I wanted to meet you again and talk with you; I'm dreadfully curious."

"Helen!" reproved her sister, and, turning from the girl to him, she tried to explain away her sister's boldness. "You must excuse Helen, Mr.–Mr. Orphan, because she is not a day older than she was five years ago."

"Why, Mary!" cried Helen, reproachfully, "how can you say that? Just the other day you said that I was quite grown up and dignified. I am sure that Mr.–oh, goodness, there's that name again!" she bewailed. "Why don't you get another name–that one sounds so funny!"

The Orphan laughed: "I am not responsible for the name, I had no hand in it. But, let's see what we can do," he said, counting on his fingers. "There's Smith, Brown, Jones–Jones sounds well, why not say it?" he asked gravely. "I am sure that's easier to say and remember."

"Yes, that is better!" she cried. "Let's see," she said, experimenting. "Mr. Jones, Mr. Jones–oh, pshaw, I like the other much better. I trust that I'll get accustomed to it in time, and I certainly should, because I hear it enough; only then it hasn't that formal Mister before it. And it is the Mister that causes all the trouble. Now, I'll try it again: I'm sure that The Orphan (I said that real nicely, didn't I?) I'm sure that The Orphan doesn't think me lacking in dignity, does he?" she asked, regarding him merrily, and with a dare in her eyes.

"Well, now really," he began, and then, seeing the look of warning in her face, he laughed softly. "Why, really, I think that you must be much more dignified than you were five years ago."

"That's such a neat evasion that I hardly know whether to be angry or not," she retorted, and then turned to Miss Ritchie, who was smiling.

"Grace," she cried, "for goodness sake, say something! You don't want me to do all the talking, do you?" and before her friend could say a word she began a new attack, her eyes sparkling at the fun she was having.

"What have you done since I told you to behave yourself?" she asked, assuming a judicial seriousness which was extremely comical.

He laughed heartily, for she was so droll, her eyes flashing so with vivacity, and so rarely beautiful that he breathed deep in unconscious effort to absorb some of the atmosphere she had created. And he was not alone in his mirth, for Helen's audacity had caused smiles to come to Miss Ritchie and Mrs. Shields, who were content to take no part in the conversation, and even Mary forgot to be serious.

"Well, I haven't had time to do much," he replied in humble apology, "although I have been occupied in a desultory way on the Cross Bar-8 for a week, and before that I was quite busily engaged in traveling for my health. You see, this climate occasionally affects me, and I am forced to go south or west for a change of air. I was just starting out on my last trip when I first met you, and I have reason to believe that my promptness in leaving you saved me much annoyance. But I have cooked quite a few meals in the interim–and I've learned how mutton should be broiled, too. I'll have to confess, however, that I have been out late nights. But then, I'll have a better record to report next time, honest I will."

Helen leveled an accusing finger at him: "You spoiled all the cooking utensils on that ranch, and you scared that poor cook so bad that he fled in terror of his life and left those poor, tired men to get all their own meals. Now, that was not right, do you see? The poor cook, he was almost frightened to death. I am almost ashamed of you; you will have to promise that you will not do anything like that again."

"I promise, cross my heart," he replied eagerly, thinking of the five dead punchers she had been kind enough to overlook. "I solemnly promise never to scare that cook again," then seeing that she was about to object, he added, "nor any other cook."

"And you'll promise not to spoil any more tins, or terrorize that poor outfit, or burn any more corrals, and everything like that?" she asked quickly, for she detected a trace of seriousness in his face and wished to drive home her advantage. If she could get a serious promise from him she would rest content, for she knew he would keep his word.

He thought for an instant and then turned a smiling face to her. Seeing veiled entreaty in her eyes, he suddenly felt a quiet gladness steal over him. Perhaps she really cared about his welfare, after all, though he dared not hope for that. He grew serious, and when he spoke she knew that he had given his word.

"I promise not to take the initiative in any warfare, nor to harass the Cross Bar-8 unless they force me to in self-defense," he replied.

She hid her elation, for she had gained the point her brother had failed to win, and did not wish to risk anything by showing her feelings. As if to reward him for yielding to her, she led the conversation from the personal grounds it had assumed and cleverly got him to talk about the country and everything pertaining to it.

He was thoroughly at ease now, and for an hour held them interested by his knowledge of the trails and the natural phenomena. He told them of cattle herding, its dangers and sports; and his description of a stampede was masterly. He recounted the struggles of the first settlers with the Indians, and even quite extensively covered the field of practical prospecting, lightening his story with naïve bits of humor and witty personal opinions which had them laughing heartily. It was not long before they forgot that they were entertaining, or, rather, being entertained by an outlaw; and as for himself, it was the most pleasant evening he had ever known. There was such an air of friendliness and they were so natural and human that he was stimulated to his best efforts; the barriers had been broken down.

"Oh, James says that you are a wonderful shot!" cried Helen, interrupting his description of a shooting match at a cowboy carnival he had once attended in a northern town. "He says that no man ever lived who could hope to beat you with either rifle or revolver, six-shooter, as he calls it. Won't you let me see you shoot, some day?"

He laughed deprecatingly: "You ask the sheriff to shoot for you," he responded. "He can beat me, I'm sure."

"No, he can't!" she cried impulsively, "because he said he couldn't. That was why he couldn't get you–" she stopped, horrified at what she had said. Then, determined to make the best of it, and knowing that excuses or apologies would make it worse, she hurriedly continued: "He says that you are so fair and square that he just will not take any advantage of you. He likes square people, and he isn't afraid to say it, either."

The Orphan sat silently for half a minute, thinking hard, while Mrs. Shields looked anxiously at him. Here was peace and happiness. The sheriff could come and go as he pleased, and every good citizen was his friend. He had a home–a pleasant contrast to the man who spent his nights under the stars, not sure of his life from day to day, hounded from point to point, having no friend, no one who cared for him; he was just an outlaw, and damned by his fellow men. Then he remembered what Helen had said before leaving him at the coach. She had faith in him, for she had told him so–and she would not lie. Her kindness and faith in him, an outcast, had been with him in his thoughts ever since, and he had felt the loneliness of his life heavily from that day. He felt a strange gnawing at his heart and he slowly raised his eyes to her, eagerly drinking in her radiant beauty, a beauty wonderful to him, for never before had he seen a beautiful woman. To him women had always been repellent–and no wonder. He scorned those usually found in the cow towns. At their best they were only ornaments, and to The Orphan's mind ornaments were trash. But now he suddenly awoke to the fact that she was more, that she was all that was worth fighting for, that she was the missing half of his consciousness. And she herself had given him heart for the fight, slight as it was, for he was like a drowning man clutching at straws. But still his cynicism swayed him and made him fear that it would be a hopeless battle. Again he thought of her brother and suddenly envied him, and the liking he had felt for the sheriff became strong and clear. Shields was a white man, just and square.

He slowly raised his eyes to Mrs. Shields and smiled, which caused her look of anxiety to clear.

"The Sheriff is the whitest man in this whole country," he said quietly, a trace of his mood being in his voice, "and only for that did I play square with him. In confidence, just to let you know that I am not as bad as people say, I will tell you that I have had him under my sights more than once, and that I will never try to harm him while he remains the man he is. I do not exaggerate when I say that I am naturally a good judge of men, and I knew what he was in less than a minute after I met him.

"At this minute he is watching for me, he and Charley Winter and the Larkin brothers. They are lying quietly out on the plain, waiting for me to show up between them and the lights of the windows. This is not guesswork, for I know it. And if it was only the sheriff, and I did show up over his sights, he would call out and give me a chance to surrender or fight, and not shoot me down like a dog; the others wouldn't. And because of my faith in his squareness, and because I above all others can fully appreciate it at its highest value, I am going to ask you to remember this, Mrs. Shields: If he ever needs a man to stand at his back, and I can be found, he has only to let me know. He is compromising himself with certain people because he has been fair to me, so please remember what I said. He is the sheriff, and he only does his duty, for which I cannot blame him. Bill Howland may be able to find me if trouble should come upon you and yours.

"Others have hunted for me as if I was a cattle-killing wolf. They have tracked me and hounded me in gangs, determined to shoot me down at the first opportunity, and unawares, if possible. They have laid traps for me, tried to ambush me, and even stooped so low as to poison the water of a remote water hole with wolf poison–strychnine. They knew that I occasionally filled my canteen from it. Those who fight me foully I repay in kind–but never with poison! It is my wits and gunplay against theirs and against their cowardice and dirty tricks. When I fight, it is not because I want to, except in the case of Indians, but because I must. But your husband is a white man, madam, a thoroughbred. He stands so far above the rest of the men in this country that I have only respect and liking for him. Can you imagine the sheriff using poison to kill a man?

"Once when I had finally found a good berth punching cows, once when I had started out aright, I was discovered. They didn't get me, though they tried to hard enough. And they call me a murderer because I declined to remain inactive while they prepared for my funeral! Ever since I was a lad of fifteen I have fought for my life at every turn, and continually. I have no friends, not a living soul cares whether I live or die. There is no one whom I can trust, and no one who trusts me. I have to be ever on the lookout, and suspicious. Every man is my enemy, and all I have is my life, worthless as it is. But pride will not let me lose it without making a fight.

"I hope the time will come when you can see me shoot, Miss Shields, that the time will come when I can turn my back to my fellow men without fearing a shot. Only once have I done that–it was with your brother, and I enjoyed it immensely. And no one will welcome that day more devoutly than the outlawed Orphan–the many times murderer–but by necessity: for I never killed a man unless he was trying to kill me, and I never will. I know what is said, but what I say is the truth. I can only ask you to believe me, although I realize that I am asking much."

He arose and walked over to his sombrero, taking it up and turning toward the door.

"To-night is the first time in ten years that I have been in a stranger's house unarmed, and at ease. You have made the evening so pleasant for me, so delightfully strange, and you all have been so good to talk to me and treat me white that I find it impossible to thank you as I wish I could. Words are hopelessly inadequate, and more or less empty, but you will not lose by it," he said as he opened the door. "Good night, ladies."

The door closed softly, quickly, and the women heard the cantering hoofbeats of his horse as they grew fainter and finally died out on the plain.

His departure was seemingly unnoticed. They sat in silence for a minute or more, each lost in her own thoughts, each deeply affected by his words, staring before them and picturing each as her temperament guided, the hunted man's dangers and loneliness. Mrs. Shields sat as he had left her, her chin resting in her hand, seeing only two men in a chaparral, one of whom was the man she loved. She could hear the shooting and the war cries, she could see them meet, and clasp hands at the parting; and her heart filled with kindly pity for the outcast, a pity the others could not know. Helen, her face full in the light, her arms outstretched on the table before her and her eyes moist, wondered at the savage unkindness of men, the almost unbelievable harshness of man for man. Her head dropped to her arms, and her sister Mary, also under the spell, wondered at the expression she had seen on Helen's face. Miss Ritchie, who had scarcely given more than a passing thought to the sadness in his words, was picturing his fights, drinking in the dash and courage which had so exalted him in her mind. With all his loneliness, his danger, she almost envied him his devil-may-care, humorous recklessness and good fortune, his superb self-confidence and prowess. Here was a man who fought his own battles, who stood alone against the best the world sent against him, giving blow for blow, and always triumphing.

Mrs. Shields stirred, glanced at Helen's bowed head and sighed:

"Now I understand why James likes him so. Poor boy, I believe that if he had a chance he would be a different and better man. James is right; he always is."

"I think he is just splendid!" cried Miss Ritchie with a start, emerging from her dreams of deeds of daring. "Simply splendid! Don't you Helen?" she asked impulsively.

Helen arose and walked to the door of her room, turning her face toward the wall as she passed them: "Yes, dear," she replied. "Good night."

"Oh, why are men so cruel!" she cried softly as she paused before her mirror. "Why must they fight and kill one another! It's awful!"

The door had softly opened and closed and Miss Ritchie's arms were around her neck, hugging tightly.

"It is awful, dear," she said. "But they can't kill him! They can't hurt him, so don't you care. Come on to bed–I have so much to talk about! Don't put your hair up to-night, Helen–let's go right to bed!"

Helen impulsively kissed her and pushed her away, her face flushed.

"You dear, silly goose, do you think I am worrying about him? Why, I had forgotten him. I'm thinking about James."

"Yes, of course you are," laughed Miss Ritchie. "I was only teasing you, dear. But it is too bad that nobody cares anything about him, isn't it, Helen?"

Tears trembled in Helen's eyes and she turned quickly toward the bed. "Well, it's his own fault–oh, don't talk to me, Grace! Poor James, all alone out there on that awful plain! I'm just as blue as I can be, so there!"

"Have a good, long cry, dear," suggested Miss Ritchie. "It does one so much good," she added as she stepped before the mirror. "But I think he is just as splendid as he can be–I wish I was a man like him!"

And while they played at pretending, the man who was uppermost in their thoughts was playing a joke on the sheriff at the Cross Bar-8 which would open that person's eyes wide in the morning.

On the ranch the darkness was intense and no sounds save the natural noises of the night could be heard. The sky was overcast with clouds and occasionally a drop of rain fell. The haunting wail of a distant coyote quavered down the wind and the cattle in the corral were restless and uneasy. A mounted man suddenly topped a rise at a walk and then stopped to stare at the dim lights in the windows of the houses nearly a mile away. He laughed softly at the foolishness of the inmates trying to plot for his death by doing something they had not dared to do for a week. Who would be so foolish as to ride up to those lighted windows unless he was a tenderfoot?

Leaping lightly to the grass, he hobbled his horse and then took a bundle from his saddle, which he strapped on his back and then went quietly forward on foot, peering intently into the darkness before him. Soon he dropped to his hands and knees and crawled cautiously and without a sound. After covering several hundred yards in this manner he dropped to his stomach and wriggled forward, his eyes strained for dangers. A quarter of an hour elapsed, and then he heard a sneeze, muffled and indistinct, but still a sneeze. Avoiding the place from whence it came, he made a wide detour and finally stopped, chuckling silently. Untying the bundle he removed it from his back and placed it upon a pile of sand, which he heaped up for the purpose, and, printing his name in the sand at its base, retreated as he had come and without mishap. After searching for a quarter of an hour for his horse he finally found it, removed the hobbles and vaulted to the saddle. Wheeling, he rode off at a walk, soon changing to a canter, in the direction of the Limping Water. When he had gained it he chanced the danger of quicksands and rode north along the middle of the stream. If he was to be followed, the probability was that his pursuers would ride south to find where he had left the water; and they must be delayed as long as possible.

An hour later daylight swiftly developed and a peculiarly shaped pile of sand quaked and split asunder as a man arose from it. He shook himself and spent some time in digging the sand from his pockets and boots and in cleaning his rifle of it. Then he walked wearily toward the bunk-house, whose occupants were still lost in the sleep of the exhausted. It was very tedious to stay awake all night peering at the lights in the distant windows; and it was very hard to keep one's eyes from closing when lying in that position, and without any sleep for twenty-four hours. The sheriff determined to crawl into a bunk as soon as he possibly could and be prepared for his next vigil.

As he glanced over the plain he espied something which caused him to stare and rub his tired eyes, and which immediately banished sleep from his mind. Running to it, he suddenly stopped and swore: "Hell!" he shouted.

His wife's blue flower pot sat snugly on the apex of a pile of sand and from it arose a geranium, which was tied to a supporting stick by a white ribbon. He had whittled that stick himself, and he knew the flower pot. Roughly traced in the sand at its base was one word– "Orphan."

"Margaret's geranium in its blue pot, by God!" cried the sheriff, his mouth open in amazement. "Well, I'll be d—d!" he exclaimed, running toward the corral for his horse. "If that son-of-a-gun ain't been out here under my very nose while I watched for him!"

CHAPTER XI
A VOICE FROM THE GALLERY

Matters were fast coming to a head as far as the sheriff and the Cross Bar-8 were concerned. The loss of the five men who had won the friendship of their fellows, the reign of terror caused by the outlaw, the loss of their cook, the devastation and the extra work had only deepened the hatred which the members of the outfit held for The Orphan; and it went farther than The Orphan.

Sneed was not long in learning what took place at the stage and of the driver's loyalty to the outlaw, because Bill would talk; and the working of his mind was the same as that of his men, for it followed the line of least resistance. Questions of the nature of arraignments, and which were answerable by the outfit in only one way, constantly presented themselves in the minds of the men. They asked themselves why it was that a man of the sheriff's proven courage, marksmanship and cleverness should fail to get the man who so terrorized the ranch. Why was the sheriff so apparently reluctant to take up the chase in earnest and push it to a finish? Why was he so firm against the assistance of the ranchmen? Why did he keep to his determination to allow no lynch law when the evil was so great and the danger so pressing? And he was prepared to go to great lengths to see that his orders were not disobeyed, as proven by the scene at the corral. Why could he not have overlooked one lynching party when property was being destroyed and lives in danger? And why had the outrages suddenly ceased when Shields took charge of the defense of the ranch?–there had been no molestation, not a shot had been fired, not a cow killed. And how was it that a flower pot, which Shields had admitted as belonging to his wife, had been placed at a point hardly two hundred yards in front of the peace officer as he lay on guard? It was true that it was out of line of him and the lights, but that could be explained by events. From whom did The Orphan learn of the trap set for him, and all of its details, even to the placing of the men, enabling him to avoid the eager deputies and choose the position occupied by the sheriff when he had so recklessly flaunted his contempt from a pile of sand?

The cowboys were naturally enough warped and prejudiced because of their blind rage and hatred, and the questions which ran so riotously through their minds found their answers waiting for them; in fact, the answers induced the questions, and each recurrence gave them added weight until they ceased to be questions and became, in reality, statements of facts. Bill had talked too much when he had told in careful detail of the attentions shown The Orphan by the sheriff's sister; and to minds eager for confirmation of their suspicions this was the crowning proof of the double dealing of the sheriff. And to make matters worse, Tex Williard, who was as unscrupulous a man as ever wore the garb of honesty, had tried to force his attentions on Helen when she rode for exercise. His ideas of women had been developed among those who frequented frontier bar-rooms, and he was enraged at his rebuff, which had been sharp and final. She actually preferred a murdering outlaw to a hardworking cowboy! His profane oratory as to the collusion, or at least passive sympathy between the sheriff and the outlaw found eager ears and receptive minds awaiting the torch of initiative, and it was not long before low-voiced consultations began to plan a drastic course of action. Credit must be given to Sneed, because he knew only of the natural discontent and nothing of what was in the wind. Had he known what was brewing he would have stamped it out with no uncertain force, for he was wise enough to realize the folly of increasing the antagonism which already was held by Ford's Station for his ranch.

At first the conspirators had hopes of undermining Shields among the citizens of the town, not knowing the feeling there as well as their foreman knew it, but they were wise enough to go about it cautiously; and the returns justified their caution, for they found the inhabitants of Ford's Station unassailably loyal to the peace officer. To accuse him, either directly or by suggestion, of double dealing would be to array the two score inhabitants of the town on his side in hot and belligerent partisanship, and this they wished to avoid by all means, for they had no stomach for such a war as might easily follow. They then hit upon what appeared to them to be an excellent plan, inasmuch as it was indirect and would give the results desired; and the medium was to be the driver.

The talkative one had shown more than passing friendliness for The Orphan, and they had his boasting words for it and he could not deny it, for Bill was very proud of the part he had played on that memorable day, and he took delight in recounting the conversation he had held with the outfit at the coach–and he had a way of adding to the tartness of his repartee in its repetition. Tex Williard reasoned from experience that it would not appear at all strange and unusual for Bill to be called to account for his friendliness and assistance to the outlaw and for his contemptuous words concerning the cowboys if it was done by some member or members of the ranch as a personal affair and without the appearance of being sanctioned by the foreman. And through the driver he hoped to strike at Shields, for the sheriff would not remain passive in such an event; and once he was drawn into a brawl, hot tempers or accident would be the plea if he should be killed. The apologies and remorse of the sorrowful participants could be profound. And thus was cold-blooded murder planned by the very men who reviled The Orphan because they claimed he was a murderer, and who cried aloud for his death on that charge.

Tex was the ringleader and in his own way he was not without cunning, and neither was he lacking in daring. He selected his assistants for the game with cool, calculating judgment. The three he finally decided upon were reckless and not lacking in intelligence and physical courage for such work. After having made his selection he sounded them carefully and finally made his plans known, going into minute rehearsal of every phase and detail of the game with thoughtful care and studied sequence. When he believed them to be well drilled he fixed upon the time and place and caused word to get to Bill that he might expect trouble for his assistance to The Orphan, and for having had a hand in sending the five cowboys to their deaths. The news immediately reached the ears of the sheriff, who determined to see that Bill received no injury at the hands of the Cross Bar-8. He quietly made up his mind to be near the stage route on the days when Bill drove through the defile of the Backbone, and to be within call if he should be needed. If he should think it necessary, he would even go so far as to become a regular passenger in the coach until the trouble died down. To the masterly driving and cool-headed courage of Bill no less than to the daring and accuracy of The Orphan was the sheriff indebted for the lives of his sisters; and the protection of Bill clove close to the line of duty, and not one whit less to the line of law and order.

Bill laughed and boasted and made a joke of the thought of any danger from the malcontents of the Cross Bar-8, and flatly refused to allow the sheriff to ride with him. He talked volubly until the agent profanely sent him on his journey, and he tore through the streets of the town in the same old way. He forded the Limping Water in safety and crossed the ten mile stretch of open plain without a sign of trouble. As he left the water of the stream the sheriff started after him from town, intending to be not far behind him when he entered the rough country.

When Bill plunged into the defile through the Backbone he began to grow a little apprehensive, and he intently watched each stretch of the road as each successive turn unfolded it to his sight. His foot was on the brakes and he was braced to stop the rush of his team at the first glimpse of an obstruction, or to tear past the danger if he could. One coyote yell and one snap of the whip would send the team wild, for they remembered well.

All was nice until he neared the place where The Orphan had held him up for a smoke, and it was there the trouble occurred. As he swung around the sharp turn he saw four cowboys bunched squarely in the center of the trail and at such a distance from him that to attempt to dash past them would be to lay himself open to several shots. They had him covered, and as he grasped the situation Tex Williard rode forward and held up his hand.

"Stop!" Tex shouted. "Get down!"

"What in thunder do you want?" Bill asked, setting the brakes and stopping his team, wonder showing on his face.

"Yu!" came the laconic reply. "Get down!"

"What's eating you?" Bill asked in no uncertain inflection. Had Tex been less imperative and kept the insulting tone out of his words Bill might have had time to become afraid, but the sting made him leap over fear to anger; and genuine anger takes small heed of fear.

Tex motioned to one of his men, who instantly leaped to the ground and ran to the turn, where he knelt behind a rock, his rifle covering the back trail. Then Tex returned to the driver.

"Curiosity is eating me, yu half-breed!" he cried. "Get down! d––n yu, get down!! Don't wait all day, neither, do yu hear? What th' h–l do yu think I'm a-talkin' for!"

"Well, I'll be blamed!" ejaculated Bill, wrapping the reins about the back of his seat. "Anybody would think you was the boss of the earth to hear you! You ain't no road agent, you're only a fool amature with more gall than brains! But I'll tell you right here and now that if you are playing road agent, I wouldn't be in your fool boots for a cool million. And if you are joking you are showing d—d bad taste, and don't you forget it. You're holding up a sack of U. S. mail, and if you don't know what that means—"

"Shut yore face! Yu talk when I ask yu to!" shouted Tex as the driver dropped to the ground. "But since yore so unholy strong on th' palaver, suppose yu just explains why yu are so all-fired friendly to Th' Orphant? Suppose yu lisp why yu take such a peculiar interest in his health and happiness. Come now, out with it–this ain't no Quaker meeting."

"Warble, birdie, warble!" jeered one of the cowboys. "Sing, yu — —!"

"We're shore waitin', darlin'," jeered another. "Tune up an' get started, Windy."

"Well, since you talks like that," cried Bill, stung to reckless fury at the cutting contempt of the words, "you can go to h–l and find out from your fool friends!" he shouted, beside himself with rage. "Who are you to stick me up and ask questions? It's none of your infernal business who I like, you hog-nosed tanks! Why didn't you bring some decent men with you, you flat-faced skunks? Why didn't you bring Sneed! White men would a told you just what you are if you asked them to help you in your dirty work, wouldn't they? Even a tin-horn gambler, a crooked cheat, would give me more show for my money than you have, you bowlegged coyotes! Ain't you man enough to turn the trick alone, Williard? Can't you play a lone hand in ambush, you bob-tailed flush of a bad man! You're only a lake-mouthed, red-headed wart of a two-by-four puncher, that's what—"

Tex had been stunned by surprise at such an outburst from a man whom he had always regarded as woefully lacking in courage. Then his face flamed with an insane rage at the taunting insults hurled venomously at him and he sprang to action as though he had been struck. It would have been bad enough to hear such words from an equal, but from Bill!

"Yu cur!" he yelled as he leaped forward into the tearing sting of the driver's whip, which had been hanging from the wrist.

"You're the fourth dog I cut to-day," Bill said, jerking it back for another try.

Tex shivered with pain as the lash cut through his ear, as it would have cut through paper, and screamed his words as he avoided the second blow. "I'll show yu if I am man enough! I'll kill yu for that, d—n yu!"

As Tex threw his arms wide open to clinch, Bill leaped aside and drove his heavy fist into the cowman's face as he passed, knocking him sidewise against the wall of the defile; and then struggled like a madman in the toils of two ropes. He was a Berserker now, a maniac without a hope of life, and he screamed with rage as he tore frantically at the rough hair ropes, wishing only to destroy, to kill with his bare hands. The blow had not been well placed, being too high for the vital point, but it had smashed the puncher's nose flat to his face and one eye was fast losing its resemblance to the other. Tex staggered to his feet and returned to the attack, striking savagely at the face of the bound man. Bill avoided the blow by jerking his head aside and snarled like a beast as he drove the heel of his heavy boot into his enemy's stomach. Then everything grew black before his eyes and a roaring sound filled his ears. The rope slackened and the men who had thrown him head-first on a rock leaped from their horses and ran to him.

When his senses returned he found himself bound hand and foot and under a spur of rock which projected from the bank of the cut. His face was cut and bruised and his scalp laid open, but through the blood which dripped from his eyebrows he vaguely saw Tex, bent double and rocking back and forth on the ground, intoned moans coming from him with a sound like that made by a rasp on the edge of a box.

As Bill's brain cleared he became conscious of excruciating pains in his head, as if hammers were crashing against his skull. Glancing upward he saw that a rope ran from his neck to the rock, over it and then to the pommel of a saddle, and his face twitched as its meaning sifted through his mind. Then he thought of the time The Orphan had held him up in the defile–how unlike these men the outlaw was! If he would only come now–what joy there would be in the flashing of his gun; what ecstasy in the confusion, panic, rout that he would cause. He was dazed and the throbbing, heavy, monotonous pain dulled him still more. He seemed to be apart from his surroundings, to be an onlooker and not an actor in the game. He wondered if that whip was his: yes, it must be . . . certainly it was. He ought to know his own whip . . . of course it was his. He regarded Tex curiously . . . there had been Indians, or was it some other time? What was Tex doing there on the ground? He struggled to think clearly, and then he knew. But the deadening pain was merciful to him, it made him apathetic. Was he going to die? Perhaps, but what of it? He didn't care, for then that pain wouldn't beat through him. Tex looked funny. . . . He closed his eyes wearily and seemed to be far away. He was far away, and, oh, so tired!

Tex finally managed to gain his feet and straighten up and revealed his face, bloody and swollen and black from the blow. His words came with a hesitation which suggested pain, and they were mumbled between split and swollen lips.

"Now, d—n yu!" he cried, brokenly, staggering to the helpless man before him. "Now mebby yu'll talk! Why did yu help Th' Orphant? If yu lie yu'll swing!"

Bill swayed and his eyes opened, and after an interval he slowly and wearily made reply, for his senses had returned again.

"He saved my life," he said, "and I'll help–anybody for that."

"Oh, he did, did he?" jeered Tex. "An' why? That ain't his way, helpin' strangers at his own risk. Why?"

"There was women–in the coach."

"Oh, there was, hey?" ironically remarked Tex. "Mebby he wanted 'em all to himself, eh?"

"He's a white man, not a cur."

"He's a cub of th' devil, that's what he is!" Tex cried. "He ain't no orphant, not by a d—d sight–th' devil's his father, an' all hell is his mother. Now, I want an answer to this one, and I want it quick: no lie goes. Why don't th' sheriff get busy an' camp on his trail? What interest has th' sheriff an' Th' Orphant in each other? Come on, out with it!"

"I don't know," replied Bill, wishing that the sheriff was at hand to make an appropriate answer. "Ask him, why don't you?" he asked, stretching his neck to ease the hairy, bristling clutch of the lariat.

"Oh, yu don't, an' yore still cheeky, eh?" cried the inquisitor. "An' yu want yore d—d neck stretched, do yu?"

He motioned to the man on the horse at the end of the rope and Bill straightened up and daylight showed under his heels. As he struggled there was an interruption from the man who covered the back trail: "'Nds up!" he cried. "Don't move!"

Tex signalled for Bill to be let down and ran backward to the opposite side of the defile until he could see around the turn; and he discovered the sheriff, who sat quietly under the gun of the cowboy.

"Stop! Don't yu even wiggle!" cried the guard. "I'll blow yore head off at the first move!" he added in warning; and for once in his eventful life Shields knew that he was absolutely helpless, for the time, at least. His hands were clasped over his sombrero, for it would be tiresome to hold them out, and he felt that he might have need of fresh, quick muscles before long.

"All right, all right, bub," he responded in perfect good nature, apparently. "Don't get nervous and let that gun go off, for it's shore your turn now," he added, smiling his war smile. "Any particular thing you want, or are you just practicing a short cut to eternity?"

"I want yu to stay just like yu are!" snapped the man with the drop. "And yu keep yore mouth shut, too!"

"Since it's your last wish, why, it goes," replied the sheriff, ignoring the command for silence. "Got any message for your folks? Any keep-sakes you'd like to have sent back East? Give me the address of your folks and I'll send them your last words, too."

"That's enough, Sheriff," said Tex, moving cautiously forward behind his leveled Colt. "I'll do all th' talkin' that's necessary; yu just listen for a while."

"Well, well," replied the sheriff, grinning and simulating surprise. "If here ain't Tex Williard, too! What's your pet psalm, sonny? Good God, what a face!"

"What's that got to do with this?" asked Tex, intently watching for war.

"Oh, nothing, nothing at all," replied the sheriff. "But, Lord, that cayuse of yours can shore kick! Was you tickling it? They do go off like that some times. Any of your nose coming out the back of your head yet? But to reply to your touching inquiry, I'll say that the psalm might work in handy after while, that's all. If you'll only tell me, I'll see that it is sung over your grave. But, honest, how did you get that face?"

"That'll just about do for yu!" cried the cowboy, angrily. "An' sit still, yu!" he added.

"Say, bub," confidentially said Shields, "my stomach itches like blazes. Can't I scratch it, just once?"

"No! Think I'm a fool!" yelled Tex, his finger tightening on the trigger. "Yu sit still, d—n yu!"

"Well, I only wanted to see just how much of a fool you really are," grinned the sheriff exasperatingly. "Judging from your present position I must say that I thought you didn't have any sense at all, but now I reckon you've got a few brains after all. But suppose you scratch it for me, hey? Just rub it easy like with your left paw."

Tex swore luridly, too tense to realize what a fool the sheriff was making of him. He could think of only one thing at a time, and he was thinking very hard about the sheriff's hands.

"Tut, tut, don't take it so hard," jeered the sheriff, smiling pleasantly. "Now that I know that you are some rational, suppose you tell me the joke? What's the secret? Who skinned his shin? What in thunder is all this artillery saluting me for?"

"Since yu want to know, I'll tell yu, all right," replied Tex. "Why are yu an' Th' Orphant so d—d thick? Don't be all day about it?"

"You d—d excuse!" responded the sheriff. "You mere accident! As the poet said, it's none of your business! Catch that?"

"Yes, I caught it," retorted Tex. "I reckon we needs a new sheriff, an' d—d soon, too," he added venomously.

"Well, people don't always get what they need," replied Shields easily. "If they did, you would get yours right now, and good and hard, too," he explained, making ready to put up the hardest fight of his life. Three men had him covered, and he knew they would all shoot if he made a move, for they had placed themselves in a desperate situation and could not back out now. He knew that never before had he been in so tight a hole, but he trusted to luck and his own quickness to crawl out with a whole skin. If he was killed, he would have company across the Great Divide; of that he was certain.

"I reckon I'll take yore guns for a while, just to be doin' somethin'," Tex said as he advanced a step. "Mebby that itch will go away then."

"I reckon you'll be a d—n sight wiser if you don't force matters, for they are purty well forced now," Shields replied. "No man gets my guns' butts first without getting all mussed up inside. You'll certainly be doing something if you try it."

"Well, then," compromised Tex, "answer my question!"

"And no man gets an answer to a question like that in words," the sheriff continued, as if there had been no interruption. "But I'll give you and your white-faced bums a chance for your lives–and I don't wonder The Orphan shot up Jimmy, neither. Put up your wobbling guns and get out of this country as fast as God will let you! If you ever come back I'll fill you plumb full of lead! It's your move, Lovely Face, and the quicker you do it the better it'll be for your health."

"Oh, I don't know about that," replied Tex with a leer and swagger. "To a man up a tree it looks like yu are up agin a buzz saw this time."

"To a man on the ground it looks like your tin buzz saw has hit the hardest knot it ever struck, and you'll feel the jar purty soon, too," Shields countered, his hazel eyes beginning to grow red. "You put up that gun and scoot before I blow your d—d head off!"

"I'll give yu 'til I counts three to answer my question," Tex said, ignoring the advice. "One!"

"The less you count the longer you'll live," said Shields, gripping his horse with his knees in readiness to jump it sideways.

"Two!"

"Afternoon, gents," said a pleasant voice up above them, and all jumped and looked up. As they did so Shields jerked his guns loose and laughed softly: "That itch has plumb gone away," he said. "It's a new deal," he exulted, his face wreathed in grins.

CHAPTER XII
A NEW DEAL ALL AROUND

On the edge of the bank, thirty feet above them, a man squatted on his heels, his forearms resting easily on his knees. In each hand was a long-barreled Colt, held in a manner oppressively businesslike. One of the guns was leveled at the stomach of the man who guarded Bill, and who still held the rope; the other covered the man who had baited the sheriff. Shields took care of the remaining two. One of the newcomer's eyes was half closed, squinting to keep out the smoke which curled up from the cigarette which protruded jauntily from a corner of his mouth. If anything was needed to strengthen the air of pertness of the man above it was supplied by his sombrero, which sat rakishly over one ear. A quizzical grin flickered across his face and the cigarette bobbed recklessly when he laughed.

"Was you counting?" he asked of Tex in anxious inquiry. "And for God's sake, who stepped on your face?"

Tex made no reply, for his astonishment at the interruption had given way to the iron hand of fear which gripped him almost to suffocation. In the space of one breath he had been hurled from the mastery to defeat; from a good fighting chance, with all the odds on his side, to what he believed to be certain death, for to move was to die. Had it been anyone but The Orphan who had turned the scale he would have hazarded a shot and trusted to luck, for his gun was in his hand; but The Orphan's gunplay was as swift as light and never missed at that distance, and The Orphan's reputation was a host in itself. He had threatened the sheriff with death, he had used Bill worse than he would have used a dog, and now his cup of bitterness was full to overflowing. Above him a pair of cruel gray eyes looked over a sight into his very soul and a malevolent grin played about the thin, straight lips of the man who had killed Jimmy, who had led his five friends to an awful death, and who had instilled terror night after night into the hearts of seven good men. His mind leaped back to a day ten years before, and what he saw caused his face to blanch. Ten years of immunity, but at last he was to pay for his crime. Before him stood the son of the man he had been foremost in hanging, before him stood the man he had cruelly wronged. His nerve left him and he stood a broken, trembling coward, a living lie to the occupation he had made his own, an insult to his dress and his companions. Had he by some miracle been given the drop he could not have pulled the trigger. He now had no hope for mercy where he had denied it. He had played a good hand, but he had made no allowance for the joker, and no blame to him.

No sooner had The Orphan spoken and the sheriff discovered that he had things safely in his hands, than Shields had leaped to the ground and quickly disarmed his opponents, tossing the captured weapons to the top of the bank near the outlaw. Then he folded his arms and waited, laughing silently all the while.

As soon as Shields had disposed of the last gun, The Orphan gave his whole attention to the man who was guarding Bill, and that person changed the course of his hand just in time.

"No, I wouldn't try to use that gun, neither, if I was you," The Orphan said, still smiling. "You can just toss it up on the bank over your head–that's right. Now drop that rope–I'm surprised that you didn't do it before. When you get Bill all untangled from those fixings come right around here, where I can see how nice you all look in a bunch. It'll take you one whole minute to get out of sight around that turn, so I wouldn't try any running."

The Orphan was ignorant of the condition of Bill's face, since he had only seen the driver's back as he had crawled to the edge of the bank, and now the bend in the opposite wall just hid Bill from his sight. So he gave no great attention to the driver, but turned to the sheriff and laughed.

"I knew that you would pull through, Sheriff," he said, "but I couldn't help having a surprise party; I'm a whole lot fond of surprise parties, you know. And it's shore been a howling success, all right."

"You have a very pleasant way of making yourself useful," Shields replied. "From the holes you've pulled me out of within the past six weeks you must have a poor impression of me. But seeing that you have reason to laugh at me, I accept your apology and bid you welcome. It's all yours." Then he glanced quickly up the trail and his face went red with anger. "Hell!" he cried in amazement.

The Orphan looked in the direction indicated and he leaped to his feet in sudden anger at what he saw. A man, followed by a cowboy, staggered and stumbled drunkenly along the trail toward them, his face a mass of cuts and bruises and blood. His hair was matted with blood and dirt, and a red ring showed around his neck. His hands opened and shut convulsively and he made straight as he could for Tex, who shrank back involuntarily.

"My God! It's Bill!" cried The Orphan, hardly able to believe his eyes.

"You're the cur I want!" Bill muttered brokenly to Tex, straightening up and becoming rapidly steadier under the stimulus of his rage. "You're the — I want, d—n you!" he repeated as he slowly advanced. "It's my turn now, you cur! Lynch me, would you? Lynch me, eh? Tried to hit me when I was tied, eh? Sicked your dogs on me, eh? Keep still, d—n you–you can't get away!" he cried as Tex moved backward.

"Stand to it like a man, or I'll blow your head off!" cried The Orphan from his perch. "Go on, Bill!"

"You said you wanted me, didn't you? Do you still want me?" he asked, not hearing The Orphan's words. "Are you still curious?" he asked, backing Tex into a corner.

"Hash him up, Bill!" cried the man above, and then, "Hey, wait a minute–I want to see this," he added as he slid down the bank. "Go ahead with the slaughter–push his head off!"

Bill's one hundred and eighty pounds of muscle and rage suddenly hurled itself forward behind a huge fist and Tex hit the bank and careened into the dust of the trail, unconscious before he had moved.

"I told you you wasn't man enough to play a lone hand!" yelled the driver as he leaped after his victim. But he was stopped by the sheriff, who sprang forward and deflected him from his course.

"That's enough–no killing!" Shields cried, regaining his balance and swiftly interposing himself between the driver and Tex.

Bill didn't hear him, for he had just caught sight of the man who had told him to warble, and he lost no time in getting to him. A few quick blows and the enraged driver left his second victim face down in the dirt and passed on to the man who had held the rope.

"Hurrah for Bill!" yelled The Orphan, hopping first on one foot and then on the other in his joy. "Set 'em up in the other alley! I didn't know you had it in you, Bill! Good boy!" he shouted as Bill clinched with the third cowboy. "Oh, that was a beauty! Right on the nose–oh, what a whopper to get on the jaw! Whoop her up! Fine, fine!" he laughed as Bill dropped his man. "'And subsequent proceedings interested him no more!' Next!" he cried as Bill wheeled on the last of the group. "Eat him up, Bill!–that's the way! Just above the belt for his–Good! All down!" he yelled madly as Bill, drawing his arm back from the stomach of the falling puncher, sent a swift uppercut hissing to the jaw. "You lifted him five feet, Bill," The Orphan exulted as Bill wheeled for more worlds to conquer.

"Where's the rest of the gang?" savagely yelled the driver, looking twice at The Orphan before he was sure of his identity. "Where's the rest of 'em?" he shouted again, running around the bend in hot search. "Come out and fight, you cowards!" they heard him cry, and straightway the outlaw and the guardian of the law clung to each other for support as they cried with joy.

As Bill hurried back to the field of carnage one of his victims was mechanically striving to gain his hands and knees, to go down in a quivering heap by a blow from the insane victor. As Bill drew back his foot to finish his work, Shields broke from his companion and leaped forward just in time to hurl Bill back several steps. "D—n you!" he cried, standing over the prostrate figure, "If you hit another man while he's down I'll trim you right! Cool down and get some sense before I punch it into you!"

The Orphan, leaning limply against the bank of the defile, was making foolish motions with his hands, which still held the Colts, and was babbling idiotically, tears of laughter streaming down his face and dripping from his chin. His eyes were closed and he was bent over, rocking to and fro against the wall.

"Oh, Lord!" he sobbed senselessly. "Oh, Lord, oh, Lord! Let me die in peace! Take him away, take him away! Let me die in peace!"

"I'm a fine sight to hit Sagetown, ain't I?" yelled Bill, keeping keen watch on the four prostrate punchers. "They'll think I was licked! They'll point to my face and head and swear that some papoose kicked the stuffing outen me! That's what they'll do! But I'll show them, all right! I'll just take my game with me and prove that I am the best man, that's what I'll do! I'll pile 'em in the coach and lug 'em with me!" grabbing, as he finished, one of the men by the foot and dragging him toward the stage. It took The Orphan and Shields several strenuous minutes to dissuade him from his purpose. Shields placed his fingers on the bones of Bill's hand in a peculiar grip, and the driver loosened his hold without loss of time.

"You go back to town and get fixed up," ordered the sheriff. "I'll take your team out of this and turn them around, and then come back for you. Charley can make the trip if you can't. I would do it myself, only I've got to tell Sneed that he's shy four more men."

"I'll turn 'em around myself–I ain't hurt," asserted Bill with decision. "And when I get patched up I'll make the trip, Pop Westley or no Pop Westley. And I'll lick the whole blamed town, too, if they get fresh about my face! I'm a fighter from Fightersville, I am! I'm a man-eating bad-man, I am! I can lick anything that ever walked on hind legs, I can!" and he glared as if anxious to prove his words.

After the cowboys regained consciousness and got so they could stand, the sheriff lined them up with their backs to the wall and gave them the guns which The Orphan had obtained for him. The outlaw held them covered while the sheriff told them what they were, and he wound up his lecture with instructions and a warning.

"Get out of this country and don't never come back!" he told them. "I don't care where you go, so long as you go right now. If you even show your faces in these parts again I'll shoot first and talk after."

"Same here!" endorsed The Orphan, frowning down his desire to laugh at the wrecks in front of him.

"I'll kill you next time!" shouted Bill, prancing uneasily.

"The cayuses are yours," continued the sheriff. "I'll settle with Sneed if he has the gall to ask about them. Now git!"

Tex stared first at the sheriff and then at The Orphan and Bill as if doubting his ears. He was ten years nearer the grave than he had been before The Orphan had interrupted his counting. In less than half an hour he had gone through hell, and now he suddenly burst into tears from the reaction and staggered to his horse, which he finally managed to mount, a nervous wreck. "Oh, God!" he moaned, "Oh, God!"

The others stared at him in amazement until he had turned the bend, and then his companions slowly followed him and were lost to sight.

"D—n near dead from fright!" ejaculated the sheriff. "I never saw anybody go to pieces so bad!"

"He shore lost his nerve all right, all right," responded The Orphan. Then he turned to where Bill stood looking after them: "Bill, you're all right–you can fight like h–l!"

Bill slowly turned and grinned through the blood: "Oh, that wasn't nothing–you should oughter see me when I get real mad!"

Two men rode side by side after a lurching coach on their way toward the Limping Water, both buried in thought at what the driver had told them. As they emerged from the defile and left the Backbone behind, the elder looked keenly, almost affectionately, at his companion and placed a kindly hand on the shoulder of the man who had turned the balance, breaking the long silence.

"Son, why don't you get a job punching cows, or something, and quit your d—d foolishness?" he bluntly asked.

The younger man thought for a space, and a woman's words directed his reply:

"I've thought of that, and I'd like to do it," he said earnestly. "But, pshaw, who will give me a try in this country?" he asked bitterly. Then he added softly: "And I won't leave these parts, not now."

"You won't have to leave the country," replied the sheriff. "Why not try Blake, of the Star C?" he asked. "Blake is a shore square man, and he's a good friend of mine, too."

"Yes, I reckon he is square," replied The Orphan. "But he won't take no stock in me, not a bit."

"Tell him that you're a friend of mine, and that I sent you to punch for him, and see," responded Shields, examining his cinch.

"Do you mean that, Sheriff?" the other cried in surprise.

"Hell, yes!" answered Shields gruffly. "I'll give you a note to him, and if you watch your business you'll be his right-hand man in a month. I ain't making any mistake."

"By God, I'll do it!" cried the outlaw. "You're all right, Sheriff!"

"Well, I don't know about that," replied Shields, grinning broadly. "Mebby I just can't see the use of us shooting each other up, and that is what it will come to if things go on as they are, you know. I'd a blamed sight rather have you behaving yourself with Blake than bothering me with your fool nonsense and raising the devil all the time. Why, it's got so that every place I go I sort of looks for flower pots!"

The Orphan laughed: "I shore had a fine time that night!"

When half way to the Limping Water the sheriff said good-by to Bill and wheeled, facing in the direction of the Cross Bar-8.

"Orphan, you wait for me at the ford," he said. "I'm going up to break the news to Sneed, and I'll get paper and pencil while I'm there, and write a note to Blake. I'll get back as quick as I can–so long."

"So long, and good luck," replied The Orphan, heartily shaking hands with his new friend.

Shields loped away and arrived at the ranch as Sneed was carrying water to the cook shack.

"Hullo, Sneed! Playing cook?" he said, pulling in to a stop.

"I'll play on the cook if I ever get my hands on him," replied Sneed, setting the pail down. "Well, what's new? Seen Tex and the other three? I'll play on them, too, when they gets home! Off playing hookey from work when we all of us aches from double shifts–oh, just wait till I sees 'em sneaking in to bed! Just wait!"

"You ought to give 'em all a good thrashing, they need it," replied the sheriff, and then he asked: "Got any paper, and a pencil?" He wanted his needs supplied before he broke the news, for then he might not get them.

"Shore as you live I have," answered the foreman, picking up the pail and starting toward the bunk-house. "Come in and wet the dust–it's hot out here."

"Let me have the paper first–I want to scrawl a note before I forget about it," the sheriff responded as he seated himself on a bunk and looked critically about him at the bullet-riddled walls and pictures.

Sneed handed him an ink bottle and placed a piece of wrapping paper and a corroded pen on the table.

"That paper ain't for love letters, the ink is mud, and the pen's a brush, but I reckon you can make tracks, all right," the host remarked as he pushed a bench up to the table for his guest. "And if them punchers don't make tracks for home purty lively, I' ll salt their hides and peg 'em on the wall to cure," he grumbled, rummaging for a bottle and cup. When he placed the tin cup on the table he grinned foolishly, for it was plugged with a cork. "D—d outlaw!" he grunted.

"There," remarked the sheriff, fanning the note in the air. "That's done, if it'll ever dry."

"Blow on it," suggested Sneed, and then smiled.

"Here, wait a minute," he said, stepping to the door, where he scooped up a handful of sand. "Throw this on it–it can't get no muddier, anyhow."

Shields carefully folded the missive and tucked it in his hip pocket, and then he looked up at the foreman.

"Sneed," he slowly began, "your punchers ain't never coming back.

"What!" yelled the foreman, leaping to his feet, and having visions of his men being cut up by outlaws and Indians.

"Nope," replied Shields with an air of finality. "Bill Howland gave them the most awful beating up that I ever saw men get, the whole four of them, too! When he got through with them I took a hand and ordered them to get out of the country, and I told them that if they ever came back I'd shoot on sight, and I will."

Sneed's rage was pathetic, and was not induced by the beating his men had received, nor by the sheriff's orders, but because it left him only three men to work a ranch which needed twelve. As he listened to the sheriff's story he paced back and forth in the small room and swore luridly, kicking at everything in sight, except the sheriff. Then he cooled down, spread his feet far apart and stared at Shields.

"Why didn't you kill 'em, the d—d fools?" he cried. "That's what they deserved!" Then he paused. "But what am I going to do?" he asked. "Where'll I get men, and what'll I do 'til I do get 'em?"

"I'll send Charley and half a dozen of the boys out from town to stay with you 'til you get some others," replied the sheriff, walking toward the door. "And you might tell the three that are left that I'll kill the next man who tries that kind of work in this country. I'm getting good and tired of it. So long."

Sneed didn't hear him, but sat with his head in his hands for several minutes after the sheriff had gone, swearing fluently.

"Orphan h–l!" he yelled as he picked up the water pail and stamped to the cook shack.

CHAPTER XIII THE STAR C GIVES WELCOME

The Limping Water, within a mile after it passed Ford's Station, turned abruptly and flowed almost due west for thirty miles, where it again proceeded southward. At the second bend stood the ranch houses and corrals of the Star C, in a country rich in grass and water. Its cows numbered far into the thousands and its horses were the best for miles around, while the whole ranch had an air of opulence and plenty. Its ranch house was a curiosity, for even now there were lace curtains in some of the windows, badly torn and soiled, but still lace curtains; and on the floors of several rooms were thick carpets, now covered with dust and riding paraphernalia. Oddly shaped and badly scratched chairs were piled high with accumulated trash, and the few gilt-framed paintings which graced the walls were hanging awry and were torn and scratched. At one time an Eastern woman had tried to live there, but that was when the owner of the ranch and his wife had been enthusiasts. New York regained and kept its own, and they now would rather receive quarterly reports by mail than daily reports in person. The foreman and his wolf hounds reigned supreme, not at all bothered by the stiff furniture and lace curtains, because he would rather be comfortable than stylish, and so lived in two rooms which he had fitted up to his ideas. Carpets and two-inch spurs cause profanity and ravelings, and as for pictures, they have a most annoying way of tilting when one hangs a six-shooter on one corner of the frame, and they are so inviting that one is constantly forgetting. So the unstable pictures, the dress-parade chairs, bothersome curtains and clutching carpets were left under the dust.

The Star C, being in a part of the country little traversed and crossed by no trails, was removed from the zone of The Orphan's activities and had no cause for animosity, save that induced by his reputation. Several of its punchers had seen him, and all were well versed in his exploits, for frequently Ford's Station shared its hospitality with one or more of them; and in Ford's Station at that time The Orphan was the chief topic of conversation and the bone of contention. But the foreman of the Star C would not know him if he should see him, unless by intuition.

Blake was a man much after the pattern of Shields in his ideas, and the two were warm friends and had roughed it together when

Ford's Station had only been an adobe hut. Their affection for each other was of the stern, silent kind, which seldom betrayed itself directly in words, and they could ride together for hours in an understanding silence and never weary of the companionship; and when need was, deeds spoke for them. The Cross Bar-8 would have had more than Ford's Station to fight if it had declared war on the sheriff, which the Cross Bar-8 knew. The three cleverest manipulators of weapons in that section, in the order of their merit, were The Orphan, Shields and Blake, which also the Cross Bar-8 knew.

The foreman of the Star C rode at a walk toward a distant point of his dominions and cogitated as to whether he could ride over to Ford's Station that night to see the sheriff. It was a matter of sixty miles for the round trip, but it might have been sixty blocks, so far as the distance troubled him. He had just decided to make the trip and to spend a pleasant hour with his friend, and drink some of the delicious coffee which Mrs. Shields always made for him and eat one of her prize pies, or some of her light ginger bread, when he descried a horseman coming toward him at a lope.

The newcomer was a stranger to Blake and appeared to be a young man, which was of no consequence. But the thing which attracted more than a casual glance from the foreman was a certain jaunty, reckless air about the man which spoke well for the condition of his nerves and liver.

The stranger approached to within a rod of Blake before he spoke, and then he slowed down and nodded, but with wide-eyed alertness.

"Howdy," he said. "Are you the foreman of the Star C?"

"Howdy. I am," replied the foreman.

"Then I reckon this is yours," said the stranger, holding out a bit of straw-colored paper.

The foreman took it and slowly read it. When he had finished reading he turned it over to see if there was anything on the back, and then stuck it in his pocket and looked up casually.

"Are you The Orphan?" he asked, with no more interest than he would have displayed if he had asked about the weather.

"Yes," replied The Orphan, nonchalantly rolling another cigarette.

"How is the sheriff?" Blake asked.

"Shore well enough, but a little mad about the Cross Bar-8," answered the other as he inhaled deeply and with much satisfaction.

"He said there was some good coffee waiting for you to-night if you wanted it," he added.

"Did he?" asked Blake, grinning his delight.

"Yes, and some–apricot pie," added The Orphan wistfully.

Blake laughed: "Well, I reckon I've got some business over in town to-night, so you keep on going 'til you get to the bunk house. Tell Lee Lung to rustle the grub lively–I'll be there right after you. Apricot pie!" he chuckled as he pushed on at a lope.

Jim Carter was washing for supper, being urged to show more speed by Bud Taylor, when the latter looked up and saw The Orphan dismount. His mouth opened a trifle, but he continued his urging without a break. He had seen The Orphan at Ace High the year before, when the outlaw had ridden in for a supply of cartridges, and he instantly recalled the face. But Bud was not only easy-going, but also very hungry at the time, and he didn't care if the devil himself called as long as the devil respected the etiquette of the range. Besides, if there was to be trouble it would rest more comfortably on a full stomach.

"Give me a quit-claim to that pan, yu coyote," he said pleasantly to Jim. "Yu ain't taking no bath!"

"Blub–no I ain't–blub blub–but you will be–blub–if yu don't lemme alone," came from the pan. "Hand me that towel!"

"Don't wallow in it, yu!" admonished Bud as he refilled the basin. "Leave some dry spots for me, this time."

Jim carefully hung the towel on a peg in the wall of the house and then noticed the stranger, who was removing his saddle.

"Howdy, stranger!" he said heartily. "Just in time to feed. Coax some of that water from Bud, but get holt of the towel first, for there won't be none left soon."

The Orphan laughed and dusted his chaps.

"Where'll I find Lee Lung?" he asked. "Blake wants him to rustle the grub lively."

"He's in the cook shack behind the house a-doing it and trying to sing," replied Jim. "He's always trying to sing; it goes something like this: Hop-lee, low-hop yum-see," he hummed in a monotonous wail as he combed his hair before a broken bit of mirror stuck in a crack. "Hi-dee, hee-hee, chop-chop—"

"Gimme that comb, yu heathen Chinee," cried Bud, "and don't make that noise."

"Anything else yu wants?" asked Jim, deliberately putting the comb away in the box.

"I want to be in Kansas City with a million dollars and a whopper of a thirst," replied Bud as he filled the basin for the stranger. "It's all yourn, stranger. Grub's waiting for yu inside when yore ready."

"Do yu know who that feller is?" Bud asked in a whisper as they made their way to the table, from which came much laughter. "That's The Orphant," he added.

"Th' h–l it is!" said Jim. "Him? Him Th' Orphant? Tell another! I'm more than six years old, even if yu ain't."

"That's straight, fellers!" said Bud to the assembled outfit in a low voice. "I ain't kidding yu none, honest. I saw him up to Ace High last year. That's him, all right. Wait 'til he comes in and see!"

"Well, I don't care if he's Jonah," responded Jim. "Only I reckons you're plumb loco, all the same. But I'm too hungry to care if Gabriel blows if I can fill up before these Oliver Twists eats it all up," he said, revealing his last reading matter.

"He shore enough wears his gun plumb low–and the holster is tied to his chaps, too," muttered Jim as he seated himself at the table. "So would I, too, if I was him. Pass them murphys, Humble," he ordered.

"You has got to bust that piebald pet what you've been keeping around the house to-morrow, Humble," exulted the man nearest to him. "And it'll shore be a circus watching you do it, too!"

The blankets which divided the bunk house into two rooms were pushed aside and The Orphan entered, carrying his saddle and bridle, which he placed beside the others on the floor. Then he unbuckled his belts and hung them, Colts and all, over the pommel, which was etiquette and which gave assurance that the guest was not hunting anyone. Then he seated himself at the table in a chair which Humble pushed back for him. His entry in no degree caused a lull in the conversation.

"Well, you hasn't got no kick coming, has you?" asked Humble. "Hey, Cookie!" he shouted into the dark gallery which led to the cook shack. "Rustle in some more fixings for another place, and bring in the slush!" Then he turned to his tormentor: "You has allus got something to say about my business, ain't you, hey?"

"Sic 'em, Humble!" said Silent Allen. "Go for him!"

From the gallery came sounds of calamity and then a mongrel dog shot out and collided with the table, glancing off it and under the curtain in his haste to gain the outside world. A second later the cook, his face fiendish, grasping a huge knife, followed the dog out on the plain. Those eating sprang to their feet and streamed after the cook, yelling encouragement to their favorite.

"Go it, Old Woman!" "'Ray for Cookie!" "Beat him out, Lightning!" and other expressions met Blake as he came up from the corral.

"Cook got 'em again?" he asked, elbowing his way into the house. "I told you to keep liquor away from him."

"'Tain't liquor this time; it's th' kioodle," replied Docile Thomas as he led the way back to the table. "Him an' th' dog don't mix extra well."

Blake swept aside the blanket and saw The Orphan standing by the window and laughing. Turning, he disappeared into the gallery and soon returned with a tin plate, a steel knife, a tin cup and the coffee pot.

"Sit down–good Lord, they would let a man starve," he said, roughly clearing a place at the table for the new arrival. "I don't know how you feel," he continued, "but I'm so all-fired hungry that I don't know whether it's my back or stomach that hurts. Take some beef and throw those potatoes down this way. Here, have some slush," filling The Orphan's cup with coffee. "This ain't like the coffee the sheriff drinks, but it is just a little bit better than nothing. You see, Cook's all right, only he can't cook, never could and never will. But he's a whole lot better than a sailor I once suffered under."

"What's the matter between you and Lightning, Lee?" asked Bud as the cook passed by the table on his way to the shack.

"Wouldn't he drink yore slush? I allus said some dogs was smart," laughed Jack Lawson.

Lee's smile was bland. "Scalpee th' dlog," he asserted as he disappeared. "No dlamn good!" wafted from the gallery.

"Say, Humble," said Silent Allen in an aggrieved tone, "the beef will wag its tail some night if you don't shoot that cur!"

"That's right!" endorsed Jack. "I'll shoot him for a dollar," he added hopefully. "The boys will all chip in to make up the purse and it won't cost you a cent, not even a cartridge."

"Anybody that don't like that setter can move," responded Humble with decision. "He's a O. K. dog, that's what he is," he added loyally.

"Well, he's a setter, all right," laughed Silent. "He ain't good for nothing else but to set around all day in the shade and chew hisself up."

"He ain't, ain't he?" cried Humble, delaying the morsel on his fork in mid-air. "You ought to see him a-chasing coyotes!"

"I did see him chasing coyotes, and that's why I want you to have him killed," replied Silent, grinning. "His feet are too big. Every time he shoves his hind feet between the front ones he throws hisself."

"What did he ever catch except fleas and the mange?" asked Blake, winking at The Orphan, who was extremely busy burying his hunger.

"What did he ever catch!" indignantly cried Humble, dropping his fork. "You saw him catch that gray wolf over near the timber, and you can't deny it, neither!"

"By George, he did!" exclaimed Blake seriously. "You're right this time, Humble, he did. But he let go awful sudden. Besides, that gray wolf you're talking about was a coyote, and he would have died of old age in another week if you hadn't shot him to save the dog. And, what's more, I never saw him chase anything since, not even rabbits."

"He caught my boot one night," remarked Charley Bailey, reflectively, "right plumb on his near eye. Oh, he's a catcher, all right."

"He's so good he ought to be stuffed, then he could sit without having to move around catching boots and things," said Jim. "Why don't you have him stuffed, Humble?"

"Oh, yore a whole lot smart, now ain't you?" blazed the persecuted puncher, glaring at his tormentors.

"He can't catch his tail, Silent," offered Bud. "I once saw him trying to do it for ten minutes–he looked like a pinwheel what we used to have when we were kids. Missed it every time, and all he got was a cheap drunk."

Humble said a few things which came out so fast that they jammed up, and he left the room to hunt for his dog.

"Any particular reason why you call him Lightning, or is it just irony?" asked The Orphan as he helped himself to the beef for the third time. "I never heard that name used before."

"Oh, it ain't irony at all!" hastily denied the foreman. "That's a real good name, fits him all right," he assured. Then he explained: "You see, lightning don't hit twice in the same place, and neither can the dog when he scratches himself. And, besides, he can dodge awful quick. You have to figure which way he'll jump when you want him to catch anything."

"But you don't have to remember his name at all, Stranger," interposed Silent, who was not at all silent. "Any handle will do, if you only yells. Every time anybody yells he makes a crow line for the plain and howls at every jump. He's got a regular, shore enough trail worn where he makes his get-away."

Silence descended over the table, and for a quarter of an hour only the click of eating utensils could be heard. At the end of that time Blake pushed back his chair and arose. He glanced around the table and then spoke very distinctly: "Well, Orphan, get acquainted with your outfit." A head or two raised at the name, but that seemed to be all the effect of his words. "The boys will put you onto the game in the morning, and Bud will show you where to begin in case I don't show up in time. Better take a fresh cayuse and let yours rest up some. Don't hurt Humble's ki-yi and he'll be plumb nice to you; and if Silent wants to know how you likes his singing and banjo playing, lie and say it's fine."

The laugh went around and all was serene with the good fellowship which is so often found in good outfits.

"Joe, I'll bring the mail out with me, so you needn't go after it," continued the foreman as he strode towards the door. "That's what I'm going over for," he laughed.

"Lord, I'd go, too, if pie and cake and good coffee was on the card," laughed Silent.

"We'll shore have to go over in a gang some night and raid that pantry," remarked Bud. "It would be a circus, all right."

"The sheriff would get some good target practice, that's shore," responded Blake. "But I've got something better than that, and since you brought the subject up I'll tell you now, so you'll be good.

"Mrs. Shields has promised to get up a fine feed for you fellows as soon as Jim's sisters are on hand to help her, and as they are here now I wouldn't be a whole lot surprised if I brought the invitation back with me. How's that for a change, eh?" he asked.

"Glory be!" cried Silent. "Hurry up and get home!"

"Say, she's all right, ain't she!" shouted Jack, executing a jig to show how glad he was.

"Pinch me, Humble, pinch me!" begged Bud. "I may be asleep and dreaming–here! What the devil do you think I am, you wart-headed coyote!" he yelled, dancing in pain and rubbing his leg frantically. "You blamed doodle bug, yu!"

"Well, I pinched you, didn't I?" indignantly cried Humble. "What's eating you? Didn't you ask me to, you chump?"

"Hurry up and get that mail, Tom," cried Jim. "It might spoil–and say, if she leads at you with that invite, clinch!"

Blake laughed and went off toward the corral. As he found the horse he wished to ride he heard a riot in the bunk-house and he laughed silently. A Virginia reel was in full swing and the noise was terrible. Riding past the window, he saw Silent working like a madman at his banjo; and assiduously playing a harmonica was The Orphan, all smiles and puffed-out cheeks.

"Well, The Orphan is all right now," the foreman muttered as he swung out on the trail to Ford's Station. "I reckon he's found himself."

In the bunk-house there was much hilarity, and laughter roared continually at the grotesque gymnastics of the reel and at the sharp wit which cut right and left, respecting no one save the new member of the outfit, and eventually he came in for his share, which he repaid with interest. Suddenly Jim, catching his spurs in a bear-skin rug which lay near a bunk, threw out his arms to save himself and then went sprawling to the floor. The uproar increased suddenly, and as it died down Jim could be heard complaining.

"— —!" he cried as he nursed his knee. "I've had that pelt for nigh onto three years and regularly I go and get tangled up with it. It shore beats all how I plumb forget its habit of wrapping itself around them rowels, what are too big, anyhow. And it ain't a big one at that, only about half as big as the one I got for a tenderfoot up in Montanny," he deprecated in disgust.

The outfit scented a story and became suddenly quiet.

"Dod-blasted postage stamp of a pelt," he grumbled as he threw it into his bunk.

"The other skin couldn't 'a' been much bigger than that one," said Bud, leading him on. "How big was it, anyhow, Jim?"

"It couldn't, hey? It came off a nine-foot grizzly, that's how big it was," retorted Jim, sitting down and filling his pipe. "Nine whole feet from stub of tail to snoot, plumb full of cussedness, too."

"How'd you get it–Sharps?" queried Charley.

"No, Colt," responded Jim. "Luckiest shot I ever made, all right. I shore had visions of wearing wings when I pulled the trigger. Just one of them lucky shots a man will make sometimes."

"Give us the story, Jim," suggested Silent, settling himself easily in his bunk. "Then we'll have another smoke and go right to bed. I'm some sleepy."

"Well," began Jim after his pipe was going well, "I was sort of second foreman for the Tadpole, up in Montanny, about six years ago. I had a good foreman, a good ranch and about a dozen white punchers to look after. And we had a real cook, no mistake about that, all right.

"The Old Man hibernated in New York during the winter and came out every spring right after the calf round-up was over to see how we was fixed and to eat some of the cook's flapjacks. That cook wasn't no yaller-skinned post for a hair clothes line, like this grinning monkey what we've got here. The Old Man was a fine old cuss–one of the boys, and a darn good one, too–and we was always plumb glad to see him. He minded his own business, didn't tell us how we ought to punch cows and didn't bother anybody what didn't want to be bothered, which we most of us did like.

"Well, one day Jed Thompson, who rustled our mail for us twice a month, handed me a letter for the foreman, who was down South and wouldn't be back for some time. His mother had died and he went back home for a spell. I saw that the letter was from the Old Man, and wondered what it would say. I sort of figured that it would tell us when to hitch up to the buckboard and go after him. Fearing that he might land before the foreman got back, I went and opened it up.

"It was from the Old Man, all right, but it was no go for him that spring. He was sick abed in New York, and said as how he was plumb sorry he couldn't get out to see his boys, and so was we sorry. But he said as how he was sending us a friend of his'n who wanted to go hunting, and would we see that he didn't shoot no cows. We said we would, and then I went on and found out when this hunter was due to land.

"When the unfortunate day rolled around I straddled the buckboard and lit out for Whisky Crossing, twenty miles to the east, it being the nearest burg on the stage line. And as I pulled in I saw Frank, who drove the stage, and he was grinning from ear to ear.

"I reckon that's your'n, " he said, pointing to a circus clown what had got loose and was sizing up the town.

"The drinks are on me when I sees you again, Frank, " I said, for somehow I felt that he was right.

"Then I sized up my present, and blamed if he wasn't all rigged out to kill Indians. While my mouth was closing he ambled up to me and stared at my gun, which must 'a' been purty big to him.

"'Are you Mr. Fisher's hired man? " he asked, giving me a real tolerating look.

"Frank followed his grin into the saloon, leaving the door open so he could hear everything. That made me plumb sore at Frank, him a-doing a thing like that, and I glared.

"I ain't nobody's hired man, and never was, " I said, sort of riled. "We ain't had no hired man since we lynched the last one, but I'm next door to the foreman. Won't I do, or do you insist on talking to a hired man? If you do, he's in the saloon."

"Oh, yes, you'll do!" he said, quick-like, and then he ups and climbs aboard and we pulled out for home, Frank waving his sombrero at me and laughing fit to kill.

"We hadn't no more than got started when the hunter ups and grabs at the lines, which he shore missed by a foot. I was driving them cayuses, not him, and I told him so, too.

"But ain't you going to take my luggage?" he asked.

"Luggage! What luggage?" I answers, surprised-like.

"Then he pointed behind him, and blamed if he didn't have two trunks, a gripsack and three gun cases. I didn't say a word, being too full of cuss words to let any of 'em loose, until Frank wobbled up and asked me if I'd forgot something. Then I shore said a few, after which I busted my back a-hoisting his freight cars aboard, and we started out again, Frank acting like a d—n fool.

"The cayuses raised their ears, wondering what we was taking the saloon for, and I reckoned we would make them twenty miles in about eight hours if nothing busted and we rustled real hard.

"Well, about every twenty minutes I had to get off and hoist some of his furniture aboard, it being jolted off, for the prairie wasn't paved a whole lot, and us going cross-country. Considering my back, and the fact that he kept calling me 'My man,' and Frank's grin, I wasn't in no frame of mind to lead a religion round-up when I got home and dumped Davy Crockett's war-duds overboard for Jed to rustle in. I was still sore at Jed for bringing that letter.

"Davy Crockett dusted for the house and ordered Sammy Johns to oil his guns and put them together, after which he went off a-poking his nose into everything in sight, and mostly everything that wasn't in sight. When he got back to the house from his tour of inspection he found his guns just like he'd left them, and that was in their cases. Then he ambled out to me and registered his howl.

"My man," he said, "My man, that hired man what I told to put my guns together ain't done it!"

"Oh, he didn't?" I said, hanging on to my cuss words, for I was some surprised and couldn't say a whole lot.

"No, he hasn't, and so I've come out to report him," he said, looking mad.

"My man!" said I, mad some myself, and looking him plumb in the eyes. "My man, if he had I'd shore think he was off his feed or loco. He ain't no hired man, but he is a all-fired good cow-puncher, and I'm a heap scared about him not filling you full of holes, you asking him to do a thing like that! He must be real sick."

"He didn't have no come-back to that, but just looked sort of funny, and then he trotted off to put his guns together hisself. I hustled around and saw that some work was done right and then went in to supper. After it was over my present got up and handed me a gun, and I near fell over. It was a purty little Winchester, and I don't blame him a whole lot for being tickled over it, for it shore was a beauty, but it oozed out a ball about the size of a pea, and the makers would 'a' been some scared if they had known it was running around loose in a grizzly-bear country.

"I reckon that'll stop him," he said, happy-like.

"Stop what?" I asked him.

"Why, game–bears, of course," he said, shocked at my appalling ignorance.

"Yes," said I, slow-like, "I reckon Ephraim may turn around and scratch hisself, if you hits him."

"Why, won't that stop a bear?"

"Yes, if it's a stuffed bear," I said.

"Why, that's a blamed good rifle!"

"It shore is; it's as fine a gun as I ever laid my eyes on," I replied, "for prairie dogs and such."

"Then I felt plumb sorry for him, he being so ignorant, and so when he hands me a peach of a shotgun to shoot coyotes with I laid it down and got my breach-loading Sharps, .50 caliber, which I handed to him.

"There,' I said, 'that's the only gun in the room what any self-respecting bear will give a d—n for."

"He looked at it, felt its heft, sized up the bunghole and then squinted along the sights.

"Why, this gun will kick like the very deuce!" he said.

"Kick!" said I. "Kick! She'll kick like a army mule if you holds her far enough from your shoulder. But I'd a whole lot ruther get kicked by a mule than hugged by a grizzly, and so'll you when you sees him a-heading your way."

"But what'll you use?' says he, 'I don't want to take your gun."

"Well, when he said that I reckoned that he had some good stuff in him after all, and somehow I felt better. There he was, away from his mother and sisters, among a bunch of gamboling cow-punchers, and right in the middle of a good bear country. I sort of wondered if he was to blame, and managed to lay all the fault on his city bringing-up.

"That's all right,' says I, 'I'll take an old muzzle-loading Bridesburg what's been laying around the house ever since I came here. It heaves enough lead at one crack to sink a man-of-war, being a .60 caliber."

"Well, bright and early the next morning we started out for bear, and I knowed just where to look, too. You see, there was a thicket of berry bushes about three miles from the ranch house and I had seen plenty of tracks there, and there was a grizzly among them, too, and as big as a house, judging from the signs. The boys had wanted to ride out in a gang and rope him, but I said as how I was saving him for a dude hunter to practice on, so they left him alone.

"We footed it through the brush, and finally Davy Crockett, who simply would go ahead of me, yelled out that he had found tracks.

"I rustled over, and sure enough he had, only they wasn't made by no bear, and I said so.

"'Then what are they?' he asked, sort of disappointed.

"'Cow tracks,' said I. 'When you see bear tracks you'll know it right away,' and we went on a-hunting.

"We had just got down in a little hollow, where the green flies were purty bad, when I saw tracks, and they was bear tracks this time, and whoppers. It had rained a little during the night and the ground was just soft enough to show them nice. I called Davy Crockett and he came up, and when he saw them tracks he was plumb tickled, and some scairt.

"Where is he?" he asked, looking around sort of anxious.

"At the front end of these tracks, making more," said I.

"'And what are we going to do now?" he asked, cocking the Sharps.

"We're going to trail him,' said I, 'and if we finds him and has any accidents, you wants to telegraph yourself up a tree, and be sure that it ain't a big tree, too.'

"Be sure it ain't a big tree!" he repeated, looking at me like he thought I wanted him to get killed.

"Exactly," said I, and then I explained: "The bigger the tree, the sooner you'll be a meal, for he climbs by hugging the trunk and pushing hisself up. A little tree'll slide through his legs, and he can't get a holt."

"I hope I don't forget that!" he exclaimed, looking dubious.

"The less you forgets when bear hunting," said I, 'the longer you'll remember.'

"We took up the trail and purty soon we saw the bear, and he was so big he didn't hardly know how to act. He was pawing berries into his mouth for breakfast, and he turned his head and slowly sized us up. He dropped on all fours and then got up again, and Davy Crockett, not listening to me telling him where to shoot, lets drive and busted an ear. Ephraim preferred all fours again and started coming straight at us, and Moses and all his bullrushers couldn't have stopped him. He was due to arrive near Davy Crockett in about four and a half seconds, and that person dropped his gun and hot-footed it for a whopping big tree. I yelled at him and told him to take a little one, but he was too blamed busy hunting bear to listen to a no-account hired man like me, so he kept on a-going for the big tree.

"I figured, and figured blamed quick, that the bear would tag him just about the time he tagged the tree, and so, hoping to create a diversion, I whanged away at the bear's tail, him running plumb away from me. I was real successful, for I created it all right. When he felt that carload of lead slide up under his skin he braced hisself, slid and wheeled, looking for the son-of-a-gun what done it, and he saw me pouring powder hell-bent down my gun. He must 'a' knowed that I was the real business end of the partnership, and that he'd have trouble a-plenty if he let me finish my job, for he came at me like a bullet.

"Climb a little tree! Climb a little tree!" yelled Davy Crockett from his perch in his two-foot-through oak.

"I wasn't in no joyous frame of mind when a nine-foot grizzly was due in the next mail, but I just had to laugh at his advice when I sized up his layout. As I jumped to one side the bear slid past, trying awful hard to stop, and he was doing real well, too. As he turned I slipped on some of that green grass, and thought as how the Old Man would have to get another puncher.

"I ain't never going to peter out with a tenderfoot looking on if I can help it!" I said to myself, and I jerked loose my six-shooter, shooting offhand and some hasty. It was just a last hope, the kick of a dying man's foot, but it fetched him, blamed if it didn't! He went down in a heap and clawed about for a spell, but I put five more in him, and then sat down. Did you ever notice how long it takes a grizzly to die? I loaded my gun in a hurry, the sweat pouring down my face, for that was one of the times it ain't no disgrace to be some scared, which I was.

"Is he dead?" called Davy Crockett from his tree, hopeful-like and some anxious.

"He is," I said, "or, leastawise, he was."

"Davy was a sight. He was all skinned up from his clinch with the tree, though how he used his face getting up is more than I can tell. And he was some white and unsteady. He had all the hunting he wanted, and he managed to say that he was glad he hadn't come out alone, and that he reckoned I was right about his guns after all. So we took a last look at the bear and lit out for the ranch, where I told the boys to go out and drag our game home."

Jim knocked the ashes from his pipe and began to fill it anew, acting as though the story was finished, but Bud knew him well, and he spoke up:

"Well, what then?" he asked.

"Oh, the hunter left for New York the very next day, and I skinned the bear and sent the pelt after him as a present. When I wrote out my quarterly report, the foreman not being back yet, I told the Old Man that if he had any more friends what wanted to go hunting to send them up to Frenchy McAllister on the Tin Cup. I was some sore at Frenchy for the way he had cleaned me out at poker."

He threw the skin to the floor and began to undress.

"Come on, now, lights out," he said. "I'm tired."

CHAPTER XIV
THE SHERIFF STATES SOME FACTS

The foreman of the Star C impatiently tossed his bridle reins over the post which stood near the sheriff's door and knocked heavily, brushing the dust of his ride from him. Quick, heavy steps approached within the house and the door suddenly flew open.

"Hullo, Tom!" Shields cried, shaking hands with his friend. "Come right in–I knew you would come if we coaxed you a little."

"You don't have to do much coaxing–I can't stay away, Jim," replied Blake with a laugh. "How do you do, Mrs. Shields?"

"Very well, Tom," she answered. "Miss Ritchie, Helen, Mary, this is Tom Blake; Tom, Miss Ritchie and James' sisters. They are to stay with us just as long as they can, and I'll see that it is a good, long time, too.

"How do you do?" he cried heartily, acknowledging the introduction. "I am glad to meet you, for I've heard a whole lot about you. I hope you'll like this country–greatest country under the sky! You stay out here a month and I'll bet you'll be just like lots of people, and not want to go back East again."

"It seems as though we have always known Mr. Blake, for James has written about you so much," replied Helen, and then she laughed: "But I am not so sure about liking this country, although very unusual things seem to take place in it. The journey was very trying, and it seemed to get worse as we neared our destination."

"Well, I'll have to confess that the stage-ride part of it is a drawback, and also that Apaches don't make good reception committees. They are a little too pressing at times."

"But, speaking seriously," responded Helen, "I have had a really delightful time. James has managed to get me a very tame horse after quite a long search, and I have taken many rides about the country."

"Wait 'til you see that horse, Tom," laughed the sheriff. "It's warranted not to raise any devilment, but it can't, for it has all it can do to stand up alone, and can't very well run away."

"I see that The Orphan delivered my message, contrary to the habits of men," remarked the sheriff's wife as she took the guest's hat and offered him a seat. "I spoke to James about it several days ago, and asked him to send you word when he could, for you have not been here for a long time. And the wonderful thing about it is that he remembered to tell The Orphan."

"Thank you," he replied, seating himself. "Yes, he delivered it all right, it was about the second thing he said. But I just couldn't get here any sooner, Mrs. Shields. And I was just wondering if I could get over to-night when he told me. When he said 'apricot pie' he looked sort of sad."

"Poor boy!" she exclaimed. "You must take him one–it was a shame to send such a message by him, poor, lonesome boy!"

"Well, he ain't so lonesome now," laughed Blake.

Helen had looked up quickly at the mention of The Orphan's name, and the sheriff replied to her look of inquiry.

"I sent him out to punch for Blake, Helen," he said quickly. "If he has the right spirit in him he'll get along with the Star C outfit; if he hasn't, why, he won't get on with anybody. But I reckon Tom will bring out all the good in him; he'll have a fair show, anyhow."

"And you never told us about it!" cried Helen reproachfully.

"Oh, I was saving it up," laughed the sheriff. "What do you think of him, Tom?" he asked, turning to the foreman.

"Why, he's a clean-looking boy," answered Blake. "I like his looks. He seems to be a fellow what can be depended on in a pinch, and after all I had heard about him he sort of took me by surprise. I thought he would be a tough-looking killer, and there he was only a overgrown, mischievous kid. But there is a look in his eyes that says there is a limit. But he surprised me, all right."

"You want to appreciate that, Miss Ritchie," remarked the sheriff, smiling broadly. "Anything that takes Tom Blake by surprise must have merit of some kind. And he is a good judge of men, too."

"I do so hope he gets on well," she replied earnestly. "He was a perfect gentleman when he was here, and his wit was sharp, too. And out there on that awful plain, when he stood swaying with weakness, he looked just splendid!"

"Pure grit, pure grit!" cried the sheriff in reply. "That's why I'm banking on him," he added, his eyes warming as he remembered. "Any fellow who could turn a trick like that, and who has so much clean-cut courage, must be worth looking after. He's got a bad reputation, but he's plumb white and square with me, and I'm going to be square with him. And when you know all that I know about him you'll take his reputation as a natural result of hard luck, spunk, and other people's devilment and foolishness. But he's going to have a show now, all right."

"What did your men say when they saw him? Do they know who he is?" asked Mrs. Shields anxiously.

Blake laughed: "Oh, yes, they know who he is. They ain't the talking kind in a case like that; they won't say a word to him about what he has done. Besides, he was under their roof, eating their food, and that's enough for them. Of course, they were a little surprised, but not half as much as I thought they would be. He is a man who gives a good first impression, and the boys are all fine fellows, big-hearted, square, clean-living and peaceful. Reputations don't count for much with them, for they know that reputations are gossip-made in most cases. I asked him to stay, and they haven't got no reason to object, and they won't waste no time looking for reasons, neither. If there is any trouble at all, it will be his own fault. Then again, they know that he is all sand and that his gunplay is real and sudden; not that they are afraid of him, or anybody else, for that matter, but he is the kind of a man they like–somebody who can stand up on his own legs and give better than he gets."

"I reckon he fills that bill, all right," laughed the sheriff. "He can stand up on his own legs, and when he does he makes good. And as for gunplay, good Lord, he's a shore wizard! I reckoned I could do things with a gun, but he can beat me. He ain't no Boston pet, and he ain't no city tough, not nohow. And I'd rather have him with me in a mix-up than against me. He's the coolest proposition loose in this part of the country at any game, and I know what I'm talking about, too."

"You promised to tell us everything about him, all you knew," reproached Helen. "And I am sure that it will be well worth hearing."

"Well, I was saving it up 'til I could tell it all at once and when you would all be together," he replied. "There wasn't any use of telling it twice," he explained as he brought out a box of cigars. "These are the same brand you sampled last time you were here," he assured his friend as he extended the box.

"By George, that's fine!" cried the foreman, picking out the blackest cigar he could see. "I could taste them cigars for a whole week, they was so good. There's nothing like a good Perfecto to make a fellow feel like he's too lucky to live."

"Oh," said Mrs. Shields. "Then you won't care for the coffee and pie and gingerbread," she sighed. "I'm very sorry."

Blake jumped: "Lord, Ma'am," he cried hastily, "I meant in the smoking line! Why, I've been losing sleep a-dreaming of your cooking. Every time the cook fills my cup with his insult to coffee I feel so lonesome that it hurts!"

"You want to look out, Tom!" laughingly warned the sheriff, "or you'll get yourself disliked! When I don't care for Margaret's cooking I ain't fool enough to say so, not a bit of it."

"You're a nice one to talk like that!" cried his wife. "You are just like a little boy on baking day–I can hardly keep you out of the kitchen. You bother me to death, and it is all I can do to cook enough for you!"

After the laugh had subsided and a steaming cup of coffee had been placed at the foreman's elbow, Helen impatiently urged her brother to begin his story.

He lighted his cigar with exasperating deliberateness and then laughed softly: "Gosh! I'm getting to be a second fiddle around here. From morning to night all I hear is The Orphan. The first thing that hits me when I come home is, 'Have you seen The Orphan?' or, 'Have you heard anything about him?' The worst offenders are Miss Ritchie and Helen. They pester me nigh to death about him. But here goes:

"I reckon I'd better begin with Old John Taylor," he slowly began. "I've been doing some quiet hunting lately, and in the course of it I ran across Old John down in Crockettsville. You remember him, don't you, Tom? Yes, I reckoned you wouldn't forget the man who got us out of that Apache scrape. Well, I had a good talk with him, and this is what I learned:

"About twenty years ago a family named Gordon moved into northwestern Texas and put up a shack in one of the valleys. There was three of them, father, mother, and a bright little five-year-old boy, and they brought about two hundred head of cattle, a few horses and a whole raft of books. Gordon bought up quite a bit of land from a ranch nearby at almost a song, and he never thought of asking for a deed–who would, down there in those days? There wasn't a rancher who owned more than a quarter section; you know the game, Tom–take up a hundred and sixty acres on a stream and then claim about a million, and fight like the very devil to hold it. We've all done it, I reckon, but there is plenty of land for everybody, and so there is no kick. Well, he was shore lucky, for his boundary on two sides was a fair-sized stream that never went dry, and you know how scarce that is–a whole lot better than a gold mine to a cattleman.

"They got along all right for a while, had a tenderfoot's luck with their cattle, which soon began to be more than a few specks on the plain, and he was very well satisfied with everything, except that there wasn't no school. Old man Gordon was daffy on education, which is a good thing to be daffy over, and he was some strong in that line himself, having been a school teacher back East. But he took his boy in hand and taught him all he knew, which must have been a whole lot, judging from things in general, and the kid was a smart, quick youngster. He was plumb crazy about two things–books and guns. He read and re-read all the books he could borrow, and got so he could handle a gun with any man on the range.

"About five years after he had located, the ranchman from whom he bought his range and water rights went and died. Some of the heirs, who were not what you would call square, began to get an itching for Gordon's land, which was improved by the first irrigation ditch in Texas. There was a garden and a purty good orchard, which was just beginning to bear fruit. It was pure, cussed hoggishness, for there was more land than anybody had any use for, but they must grab everything in sight, no matter what the cost. Trouble was the rule after that, and the old man was up against it all the time. But he managed to hold his own, even though he did lose a lot of cattle.

"His brand was a gridiron, which wasn't much different from the gridiron circle brand of the big ranch. It ain't much trouble to use a running iron through a wet blanket and change a brand like that when you know how, and the Gridiron Circle gang shore enough knew how. Their expertness with a running iron would have caused questions to be asked, and probably a lynching bee, in other parts of the country, but down there they were purty well alone. They let Gordon know that he had jumped the range, which was just what they had done, that he didn't own it, and that the sooner he left the country the better it would be for his health. But he had peculiar ideas about justice, and he shore was plumb full of grit and obstinacy. He knew he was right, that he had paid for the land, and that he had improved it. And he had a lot of faith in the law, not realizing that he hadn't anything to show the law. And he didn't know that law and justice don't always mean the same thing, not by a long shot.

"Well, one day he went out looking for a vein of coal, which he thought ought to be thereabouts, according to his books, and it ought to be close to the surface of a fissure. He reckoned that coal of any quality would be some better than chips and the little wood he owned, so he got busy. But he didn't find coal, but something that made him hotfoot it to his books. When the report came back from the assay office he knew that he had hit on a vein of native silver, which was some better than coal.

"It didn't take long for the news to get around, though God Himself only knows how it did, unless the storekeeper told that a package had gone through his hands addressed to the assay office, and things began to happen in chunks. He caught three Gridiron Circle punchers shooting his cows, and he was naturally mad about it and just shot up the bunch before they knew he was around. He killed one and spoiled the health of the other two for some time to come, which naturally spelled war with a big W. Then about this time his wife went and died, which was a purty big addition to his troubles. As he stood above her grave, all broken up, and about ready to give up the fight and go back East, he was shot at from cover. He didn't much care if he was killed or not, until he remembered that he had a boy to take care of. Then he got fighting mad all at once, all of his troubles coming up before him in a bunch, and he got his gun and went hunting, which was only right and proper under the circumstances."

The sheriff flecked the ashes of his cigar into a blue flower pot which was gay with white ribbons, and poured himself a cup of coffee.

"I hate to think that it is possible to find a whole ranch of hellions from the owner down," he continued, "but the nature of the owner picks a dirty foreman, and a dirty foreman needs dirty men, and there you are. That fits the case of the Gridiron Circle to a T. There was not one white man in the whole gang," and he sat in silence for a space.

"Well, the boy, who was about fifteen years old by this time, took his gun and went out to find his daddy, and he succeeded. He cut him down and buried him and then went home. That night the shack burned to the ground, the orchard was ruined and the boy disappeared. Some people said that the kid took what he wanted and burned the house rather than to have it profaned as a range house by the curs who murdered his dad; and some said the other thing, but from what I know of the kid, I reckon he did it himself.

"Right there and then things began to happen that hurt the ease and safety of the Gridiron Circle. Cows were found dead all over the range–juglars cut in every case. Three of their punchers were found dead in one week–a .5O-caliber Sharps had done it. A regular reign of terror began and kept the outfit on the nervous jump all the time. They searched and trailed and searched and swore, and if one of them went off by himself he was usually ready to be buried. Ten experienced, old-time cowmen were made fools of by a fifteen-year-old kid, who was never seen by anybody that lived long enough to tell about it. When he got hungry, he just killed another cow and had a porterhouse steak cooked between two others over a good fire. He ate the middle steak, which had all the juices of the two burned ones, and threw the others away. Three meals a day for six months, and one cow to a meal, was the order of things on the ranges of the Gridiron Circle. He had plenty of ammunition, because every dead puncher was minus his belt when found and his guns were broken or gone; and early in the game the boy had made a master stroke: he raided the storehouse of the ranch one night and lugged away about five hundred rounds of ammunition in his saddle bags, with a couple of spare Colts and a repeating Winchester of the latest pattern, and he spoiled all the rest of the guns he could lay his hands on. Humorous kid, wasn't he, shooting up the ranch with its own guns and cartridges?

"Finally, however, after the news had spread, which it did real quick, a regular lynching party was arranged, and the U-B, which lay about sixty miles to the east, sent over half a dozen men to take a hand. Then the Gridiron Circle had a rest, but while the gang was hunting for him and laying all sorts of elaborate traps to catch him, the boy was over on the U-B, showing it how foolish it had been to take up another man's quarrel. By this time the whole country knew about it, and even some Eastern papers began to give it much attention. One of the punchers of the Gridiron Circle, when he found a friend dead and saw the tracks of the kid in the sand, swore and cried that it was 'that d—n Orphan' who had done it, and the name stuck. He had become an outlaw and was legitimate prey for any man who had the chance and grit to turn the trick. For ten years he has been wandering all over the range like a hunted gray wolf, fighting for his life at every turn against all kinds of odds, both human and natural. And I reckon that explains why he is accused of doing so much killing. He has been hunted and forced to shoot to save his own life, and a gray wolf is a fighter when cornered. I know that I wouldn't give up the ghost if I could help it, and neither would anybody else."

"Oh, it is a shame, an awful shame!" cried Helen, tears of sympathy in her eyes. "How could they do it? I don't blame him, not a bit! He did right, terrible as it was! And only a boy when they began, too! Oh, it is awful, almost unbelievable!"

"Yes, it is, Sis," replied Shields earnestly. "It ain't his fault, not by any manner or means–he was warped." And then he added slowly: "But Tom and I will straighten him out, and if some folks hereabouts don't like it, they can shore lump it, or fight."

"Tell me how you met him, Jim," requested Blake in the interval of silence. "I've heard some of it, second-handed, or third-handed, but I'd like to have it straight."

"Well," the sheriff continued, "when he came to these parts I didn't know anything about him except what I had heard, which was only bad. He had a nasty way of handling his gun, a hair-trigger and a nervous finger on his gun, and he had a distressing way of using one cow to a meal, so I got busy. I didn't expect much trouble in getting him. I knew that he was only a youngster and I counted on my fifty years, and most of them of experience, getting him. Being young, I reckoned he would be foolhardy and hasty and uncertain in his wisdom; but, Lord! it was just like trying to catch a flea in the dark. He was here, there and everywhere. While I was down south hunting along his trail he would be up north objecting to the sheep industry in ingenious ways and varying his bill of fare with choice cuts of lamb and mutton. And by the time I got down south he would be–God only knows where, I didn't. I could only guess, and I guessed wrong until the last one. And then it was the toss of a coin that decided it.

"After a while he began to get more daring, and when I say more daring I mean an open game with no limit. He began to prove my ideas about his age making him reckless, though he was cautious enough, to be sure. One day, not long ago, he had a run-in with two sheepmen out by the U bend of the creek, who had driven their herds up on Cross Bar-8 land and over the dead-line established by the ranch. They must have taken him for some Cross Bar-8 puncher and thought he was going to kick up a fuss about the trespass, or else they recognized him. Anyway, when I got on the scene they were ready to be planted, which I did for them. Then I went after him on a plain trail north–and almost too plain to suit me, because it looked like it had been made plain as an invitation. He had picked out the softest ground and left plenty of good tracks. But I was some mad and didn't care much what I run into. I thought he had driven the whole blasted herd of baa-baas over that high bank and into the creek, for the number of dead sheep was shore scandalous.

"I followed that cussed trail north, east, south, west and then all over the whole United States, it seemed to me. And it was always growing older, because I had to waste time in dodging chaparrals and things like that that might hold him and his gun. I went picking my way on a roundabout course past thickets of honey mesquite and cactus gardens, over alkali flats and everything else, and the more I fooled about the madder I got. I ain't no real, genuine fool, and I've had some experience at trailing, but I had to confess that I was just a plain, ordinary monkey-on-a-stick when stacked up against a kid that was only about half my age, because suddenly the plainness of the trail disappeared and I was left out on the middle of a burning desert to guess the answer as best I could. I knew what he had done, all right, but that didn't help me a whole lot. Did you ever trail anybody that used padded-leather footpads on his cayuse's feet, and that went on a walk, picking out the hardest ground? No? Well, I have, and it's no cinch.

"I got tired of chasing myself back to the same place four times out of five, and I reckons that it wouldn't be very long before he had made his circle and got me in front of him. It ain't no church fair to be hunting a mad devil like him under the best conditions, and it's a whole lot less like one when he gets behind you doing the same thing. I didn't know whether he had swung to the north or south, so I tossed up a coin and cried heads for north–and it was tails. I cut loose at a lope and had been riding for some time when I saw something through an opening in the chaparrals to the east of me, and it moved. I swung my glasses on it, and I'm blamed if it wasn't an Apache war party bound north. They were about a mile to the east of me, and if they kept on going straight ahead they would run across my trail in about three hours, for it gradually worked their way. I ducked right then and there and struck west for a time, turning south again until I hit the Cimarron Trail, which I followed east. Well, as I went around one side of the chaparral six mad Apaches went around the other, and they hit my trail too soon to suit me. I heard a hair-raising yell and lit out in the direction of Chattanooga as hard as I could go, with a hungry chorus a mile behind me.

"I had just passed that freak bowlder on the Apache Trail when the man I was looking for turned up, and with the drop, of course. We reckoned that two was needed to stop the war-paints, which we did, him running the game and doing most of the playing. I felt like I was his honored guest whom he had invited to share in the festivities. He had plenty of chances to nail me if he wanted to, and he had chipped in on a game that he didn't have to take cards in; and to help me out. He could have let them get me and they would have thought that I had done all the injury and that there wasn't another man on the desert. But he didn't, and I began to think he wasn't as bad as he was painted."

Then he told of the trouble between The Orphan and Jimmy of the Cross Bar-8, and of the rage which blossomed out on the ranch.

"That shore settled it for the Cross Bar-8. They wanted lots of gore, and they got it, all right, when he played five of their punchers against the very war party he had sent north to meet me, while I was chasing him. That war party must have found something to their liking, wandering about the country all that time."

Blake interrupted him: "War party that he sent north to meet you?" he asked in surprise. "How could he do that?"

"That's just what I said," replied Shields, and then he explained about the arrow. "Any man who could stack a deck like that and use one danger to wipe out another ain't going to get caught by an outfit of lunkheads–by George! if he didn't work nearly the same trick on the Cross Bar-8 crowd! Oh, it's great, simply great!"

The foreman slapped his knee enthusiastically: "Fine! Fine!" he exulted. "That fellow has got brains, plenty of them! And he'll make use of them to the good of this country, too, before we get through with him."

Shields continued: "After he sic'd the chumps of the Cross Bar-8 on the Apaches he shore raised the devil on the ranch and I was asked to go out and run things, which I did, or rather thought I would do. Charley and I and the two Larkin boys laid out on the plain all night, covered up with sand, waiting for him to show up between us and the windows–and the first thing I saw in the morning was Helen's flower pot here–it used to be Margaret's–setting up on top of a pile of sand under my very nose where he had stuck it while I waited for him–and blamed if he hadn't signed his name in the sand at its base!" He suddenly turned to his sister: "Tell Tom about him calling on you while I was waiting for him out on the ranch, Helen."

Helen did so and the way she told it caused the women to look keenly at her.

Blake laughed heartily: "Now, don't that beat all!" he cried.

"It don't beat this," responded the sheriff, turning again to Helen. "Tell him about the stage coach, Sis."

"Well, I don't know much about the first part of it," she replied. "All I remember is a terrible ride –oh, it was awful!" she cried, shuddering as she remembered the tortures of the Concord. "But when we stopped and after I managed to get out of the coach I saw the driver carrying a man on his shoulders and coming toward us. He laid his burden down and revived him–and he was a young man, and covered with blood." Then she paused: "He was real nice and polite and didn't seem to think that he had done anything out of the ordinary. Then we went on and he left us."

The sheriff laughed and leveled an accusing finger at her:

"You have left out a whole lot, Sis," he said affectionately. "Helen acted just like the thoroughbred she is, Tom," he continued. "I guess Bill told you all about it, for he's aired it purty well. Why, she even lost her gold pin a-helping him!" and he grinned broadly.

Helen shot him a warning glance, but it was too late; Mary suddenly sat bolt upright, her expression one of shocked surprise.

"Helen Shields!" she cried, "and I never thought of it before! How could you do it! Why, that horrid man will show your pin and boast about it to everybody! The idea! I'm surprised at you!"

"Tut, tut," exclaimed Shields. "I reckon that pin is all right. He might find it handy some day to return it, it'll be a good excuse when he gets on his feet. And I'd hate to be the man to laugh at it, or try to take it from him. Now, come, Mary, think of it right; it was the first kind act he had known since he lost his daddy. And that pin is one of my main stand-bys in this game. I believe that he'll be square as long as he has it."

"Well, I don't care, James," warmly responded Mary. "It was not a modest thing to do when she had never seen him before, and he her brother's enemy and an outlaw!"

"How could I have fastened the bandage, sister dear?" asked Helen, her complexion slightly more colored than its natural shade. "It was so very little to do after all he had done for us!"

"Well, Tom and I have some business to talk over, so we'll leave you to fight the matter out among yourselves," the sheriff said, arising. "Come to my room, Tom, I want to talk over that ranch scheme with you. You bring the coffee pot and the cigars and I' ll juggle the pie and gingerbread," he laughed as he led the way.

"Oh, Tom!" hastily called Mrs. Shields after good-nights had been said, and just before the door closed; "I promised you a dinner for your boys when Helen and Mary came, and if you think you can spare them this coming Sunday I will have it then."

"Thank you, Mrs. Shields," earnestly responded Blake, turning on the threshold. "It is awful good of you to put yourself out that way, and you can bet that the boys will be your devoted slaves ever after. If you must go to that trouble, why, Sunday or any day you may name will do for us. Gosh, but won't they be tickled!" he exulted as he pictured them feasting on goodies. "It'll be better than a circus, it shore will!"

"Why, it's no trouble at all, Tom," she replied, smiling at being able to bring cheer to a crowd of men, lonely, as she thought. "And you will arrange to have The Orphan with them, won't you?"

"I most certainly will," he heartily replied. "It'll do wonders for him." He glanced quickly at Helen, but she was busily engaged in threading a needle under the lamp shade.

"Good night, all," he said as he closed the door.

CHAPTER XV
AN UNDERSTANDING

Blake settled himself in the easy chair which his host pushed over to him and crossed his feet on the seat of another, and became the personification of contentment. One of the black Perfectos which a friend in the East kept Shields supplied with, was tenderly nursed by his lips, its fragrant smoke slowly issuing from his nose and mouth, yielding its delights to a man who knew a good cigar when he smoked it, and who knew how to smoke it. At his elbow stood a coffee pot, flanked on one side by a plate piled high with gingerbread; on the other by an apricot pie. His eyes half-closed and his arms were folded, and a great peace stole over him. He had the philosopher's mind which so readily yields to the magic touch of a perfect cigar. In that short space of time he was recompensed for a life of hardships, perils and but few pleasures.

They sat each lost in his own thoughts, in a silence broken only by the very low and indistinct hum of women's voices and the loud ticking of the clock, which soon struck ten. The foreman sighed, stirred to knock the ashes from his cigar, and then slowly reached his hand toward the pie. Shields came to himself and very gravely relighted his cigar, watching the blue smoke stream up over the lamp. He looked at his contented friend for a few seconds and then broke the silence.

"Tom," he said, "what I'm going to tell you now is all meat. I couldn't say anything about it while the women were around, for they shore worry a lot and there wasn't no good in scaring them.

"The Cross Bar-8 outfit got saddled with the idea that they wanted a new sheriff, and four of them didn't care a whole lot how they made the necessary vacancy. I got word that they were going to pay Bill Howland for the part he played, and on the face of it there wasn't nothing more than that. It was natural enough that they were sore on him, and that they would try to square matters. Well, of course, I couldn't let him get wiped out and I took cards in the game. But, Lord, it wasn't what I reckoned it was at all. He was in for his licking, all right, but he was the little fish–and I was the big one.

"They got Bill in the defile of the Backbone and were going to lynch him–they beat him up shameful. He wouldn't tell them that I was hand-in-glove with The Orphan, which they wanted to hear, so they tried to scare him to lie, but it was no go.

"Well, I followed Bill and, to make it short, that is just what they had figured on. They posted an outpost to get the drop on me when I showed up, and he got it. Tex Williard seemed to be the officer in charge, and he asked me questions and suggested things that made me fighting mad inside. But I was as cool as I could be apparently, for it ain't no good to lose your temper in a place like that. I suppose they wanted me to get out on the warpath so they could frame up some story about self-defense. It looked bad for me, with three of them having their guns on me, and Tex Williard had just given me an ultimatum and had counted two, when, d—d if The Orphan didn't take a hand from up on the wall of the defile. That let me get my guns out, and the rest was easy. We let Bill get square on the gang for the beating he had got, by whipping all of them to the queen's taste. When they got so they could stand up I told them a few things and ordered them out of the country, and they were blamed glad to get the chance to go, too.

"The Orphan didn't have to mix up in that, not at all, and it makes the third time he's put his head in danger to help me or mine, and he took big chances every time. How in h–l can I help liking him? Can I be blamed for treating him white and square when he's done so much for me? He is so chock full of grit and squareness that I'll throw up this job rather than to go out after him for his past deeds, and I mean it, too, Tom."

Blake reached for another piece of pie, held his hand over it in uncertainty and then, changing his mind, took gingerbread for a change.

"Well, I reckon you're right, Jim," he replied. "Anyhow, it don't make a whole lot of difference whether you are or not. You're the sheriff of this layout, and you're to do what you think best, and that's the idea of most of the people out here, too. If you want to experiment, that's your business, for you'll be the first to get bit if you're wrong. And it ain't necessary to tell you that your friends will back you up in anything you try. Personally, I am rather glad of what you're doing, for I like that man's looks, as I said before, and he'll be just the kind of a puncher I want. He's a man that'll fight like h–l for the man he ties up to and who treats him square. If he ain't, I'm getting childish in my judgment."

"I sent him to you," the sheriff continued, "because I wanted to get him in with a good outfit and under a man who would be fair with him. I knew that you would give him every chance in the world. And then Helen takes such an interest in him, being young and sympathetic and romantic, that I wanted to please her if I could, and I can. She'll be very much pleased now that I've given him a start in the right direction and there ain't nothing I can do for her that is not going to be done. She's a blamed fine girl, Tom, as nice a girl as ever lived."

"She shore is–there ain't no doubt about that!" cried the foreman, and then he frowned slightly. "But have you thought of what all this might develop into?" he asked, leaning forward in his earnestness. "It's shore funny how I should think of such a thing, for it ain't in my line at all, but the idea just sort of blew into my head."

"What do you mean?"

"Well, Helen, being young and sympathetic and romantic, as you said, and owing her own life and the lives of her sister and friend, not to mention yours, to him, might just go and fall in love with him, and I reckon that if she did, she would stick to him in spite of hell. He's a blamed good-looking, attractive fellow, full of energy and grit, somewhat of a mystery, and women are strong on mysteries, and he might nurse ideas about having some one to make gingerbread and apricot pie for him; and if he does, as shore as God made little apples, it'll be Helen that he'll want. He's never seen as pretty a girl, she's been kind and sympathetic with him, and I'm willing to bet my hat that he's lost a bit of sleep about her already. Good Lord, what can you expect? She pities him, and what do the books say about pity?"

The sheriff thought for a minute and then looked up with a peculiar light in his eyes.

"For a bachelor you're doing real well," he said, still thinking hard.

"Being a bachelor don't mean that I ain't never rubbed elbows with women," replied the foreman. "There are some people that are bachelors because they are too darned smart to get roped and branded because the moon happens to be real bright. But I'll confess to you that I ain't a bachelor because I didn't want to get roped. We won't say any more about that, however."

"Well," said Shields, slowly. "If he tries to get her before I know that he is straight and clean and good enough for her, I'll just have to stop him any way I can. First of all, I'm looking out for my sister, the h–l with anybody else. But on the other hand, if he makes good and wants her bad enough to rustle for two and she has her mind made up that she'd rather have him than stay single and is head over heels in love with him, I don't see that there's anything to worry about. I tell you that he is a good man, a real man, and if he changes like I want him to, she would be a d—d sight better off with him than with some dudish tenderfoot in love with money. He has had such a God-forsaken life that he will be able to appreciate a change like that–he would be square as a brick with her and attentive and loyal–and with him she wouldn't run much chance of being left a widow. Why, I'll bet he'll worship the ground she walks on–she could wind him all around her little finger and he'd never peep. And she would have the best protection that walks around these parts. But, pshaw, all this is too far ahead of the game. How about that herd of cattle you spoke of?"

"I can get you the whole herd dirt cheap," replied the foreman. "And they are as hungry and healthy a lot as you could wish."

"Well," responded the sheriff, "I've made up my mind to go ranching again. I can't stand this loafing, for it don't amount to much more than that now that The Orphan has graduated out of the outlaw class. I can run a ranch and have plenty of time to attend to the sheriff part of it, too. Ever since I sold the Three-S I have been like a fish out of water. When I got rid of it I put the money away in Kansas City, thinking that I might want to go back at it again. Then I got rid of that mine and bunked the money with the ranch money. The interest has been accumulating for a long time now and I have got something over thirty thousand lying idle. Now, I'm going to put it to work.

"I ran across Crawford last week, and he is dead anxious to sell out and go back East–he don't like the West. I've determined to take the A-Y off his hands, for it's a good ranch, has good buildings on it, two fine windmills over driven wells, good grass and shelters. Why, he has put up shelters in Long Valley that can't be duplicated under a thousand dollars. His terms are good–five thousand down and the balance in installments of two thousand a year at three per cent., and I can get over three per cent, while it is lying waiting to be paid to him. He is too blamed sick of his white elephant to haggle over terms. He was foolish to try to run it himself and to sink so much money in driven wells, windmills and buildings–it would astonish you to know how much money he spent in paint alone. What did he know about ranching, anyhow? He can't hardly tell a cow from a heifer. He said that he knew how to make money earn money in the East, but that he couldn't make a cent raising cows.

"If The Orphan attends to his new deal I'll put him in charge and the rest lies with him. I'll provide him with a good outfit, everything he needs and, if he makes good and the ranch pays, I'll fix it so he can own a half-interest in it at less than it cost me, and that will give him a good job to hold down for the rest of his life. It'll be something for him to tie to in case of squalls, but there ain't much danger of his becoming unsteady, because if he was at all inclined to that sort of thing he would be dead now.

"This ain't no fly-away notion, as you know. I've had an itching for a good ranch for several years, and for just about that length of time I've had my eyes on the A-Y. I was going to buy it when Crawford gobbled it up at that fancy price and I felt a little put out when he took up his option on it, but I'm glad he did, now. Why, Reeves sold out to Crawford for almost three times what I am going to pay for it, and it has been improved fifty per cent. since he has had it. But, of course, there was more cattle then than there is now. You get me that herd at a good figure and I'll be able to take care of them very soon now, just as soon as I close the deal. But, mind you, no Texas cattle goes–I don't want any Spanish fever in mine.

"I'm thinking some of putting Charley in charge temporarily, just as soon as Sneed gets some men, and when The Orphan takes it over things will be in purty fair shape. I won't move out there because my wife don't like ranching–she wants to be in town where she is near somebody, but I'll spend most of my time out there until everything gets in running order. Oh, yes–in consideration of the five thousand down at the time the papers are signed, Crawford has agreed to leave the ranch-house furnished practically as it is, and that will be nice for Helen and The Orphan if they ever should decide to join hands in double blessedness. You used to have a lot of fun about the high-faluting fixings in your ranch-house, but just wait 'til you see this one! An inside look around will open your eyes some, all right. It is a wonder, a real wonder! Running water from the windmills, a bath-room, sinks in the kitchen, a wood-burning boiler in the cellar, and all the comforts possible. If Crawford tries to move all that stuff back East it would cost him more than he could get for it, and he knows it, too. It's a bargain at twice the price, and I'm going to nail it. I can't think of anything else."

"Well," replied Blake, "I don't see how you could do anything better, that's sure. It all depends on the price, and if you're satisfied with that, there ain't no use of turning it down. I know you can make money out there with any kind of attention, for I ' m purty well acquainted with the A-Y. And I'll see about the cattle next week, but you better leave The Orphan stay with me a while longer. My boys are the best crowd that ever lived in a bunk-house, and if he minds his business they'll smooth down his corners until you won't hardly know him; and they'll teach him a little about the cow-puncher game if he's rusty.

"You remember the time we had that killing out there, don't you?" Blake asked. "Well, you also remember that we agreed to cut out all gunplay on the ranch in the future, and that I sent East for some boxing gloves, which were to be used in case anybody wanted to settle any trouble. They have been out there for two years now, and haven't been used except in fun. Give the boys a chance and they'll cure him of the itching trigger-finger, all right. They're only a lot of big-hearted, overgrown kids, and they can get along with the devil himself if he'll let them. But they are hell-fire and brimstone when aroused," then he laughed softly: "They heard about your trouble with Sneed and they shore was dead anxious to call on the Cross Bar-8 and make a few remarks about long life and happiness, but I made them wait 'til they should be sent for.

"They know all about The Orphan–that is, as much as I did before I called to-night. Joe Haines is a great listener and when he rustles our mail once a week he takes it all in, so of course they know all about it. They had a lot of fun about the way he made the Cross Bar-8 sit up and take notice, for they ain't wasting any love on Sneed's crowd. And it took Bill Howland over an hour to tell Joe about his experiences. So when The Orphan met the outfit they knew him to be the man who had saved the sheriff's sisters, which went a long way with them. Say, Jim," he exclaimed, "can I tell them what you said about him to-night? Let me tell them everything, for it'll go far with them, especially with Silent, who had some trouble with the U-B about five years ago. He was taking a herd of about three thousand head across their range and he swears yet at the treatment he got. Yes? All right, it'll make him solid with the outfit."

"Tell them anything you want about him," said the sheriff, "but don't say anything about the A-Y. I want to keep it quiet for a while."

Shields poured himself a cup of coffee and then glanced at the clock: "Too late for a game, Tom?" he asked, expectantly.

The foreman laughed: "It's seldom too late for that," he replied.

"Good enough!" cried his host. "What shall it be this time–pinochle or crib?"

The foreman slowly closed his eyes as he replied: "Either suits me–this feed has made me plumb easy to please. Why, I'd even play casino to-night!"

"Well, what do you say to crib?" asked the sheriff. "You licked me so bad at it the last time you were here that I hanker to get revenge."

"Well, I don't blame you for wanting to get it, but I'll tell you right now that you won't, for I can lick the man that invented crib to-night," laughed the foreman. "Bring out your cards."

Shields placed the cards on the table and arranged things where they would be handy while his friend shuffled the pack.

The foreman pushed the cards toward his host: "There you are–low deals as usual, I suppose."

"Oh, you might as well go ahead and deal," grumbled the sheriff good-naturedly. "I don't remember ever cutting low enough for you–by George! A five!"

Blake picked up the cards and started to deal, but the sheriff stopped him.

"Hey! You haven't cut yet!" Shields cried, putting his hand on the cards. "What are you doing, anyhow?"

Blake laughed with delight: "Well, anybody that can't cut lower than a five hadn't ought to play the game. What's the use of wasting time?"

"Well, you never mind about the time–you go ahead and beat me," cried the sheriff. "Of all the nerve!"

Blake picked up the cards again: "Do you want to cut again?" he asked.

"Not a bit of it! That five stands!"

"Well, how would a four do?" asked the foreman, lifting his hand. "It's a three!" he exulted. "All that time wasted," he said.

"You go to blazes," pleasantly replied the sheriff as he sorted his hand. "This ain't so bad for you, not at all bad; you could have done worse, but I doubt it." He discarded, cut, and Blake turned a six.

"Seven," called Shields as he played.

"Seventeen," replied Blake, playing a queen.

"No you don't, either," grinned the sheriff. "You can play that four later if you want to, but not now on twenty-seven. Call it twenty-five," he said, playing an eight.

Blake carefully scanned his hand and finally played the four, grumbling a little as his friend laughed.

"Thirty-one–first blood," remarked the sheriff, dropping the deuce. While he pegged his points Blake suddenly laughed.

"Say, Jim," he said, "before I forget it I want to tell you a joke on Humble. He thought it would be easy money if he taught Lee Lung how to play poker. He bothered Lee's life out of him for several days, and finally the Chinaman consented to learn the great American game."

Blake played a six and the sheriff scored two by pairing, whereupon his opponent made it threes for six, and took a point for the last card.

"As I was saying, Humble wanted the cook to learn poker. Lee's face was as blank as a cow's, and Humble had to explain everything several times before the cook seemed to understand what he was driving at. Anybody would have thought he had been brought up in a monastery and that he didn't know a card from an army mule."

Blake pegged his seven points and picked up his cards without breaking the story.

"But Lee had awful luck, and in half an hour he owned half of Humble's next month's pay. Now, every time he gets a chance he shows Humble the cards and asks for a game. 'Nicee game, ploker, nicee game,' he'll say. What Humble says is pertinent, profane and permeating. Then the boys guy him to a finish. He'll be wanting to teach Lee how to play fan-tan some day, so the boys say. Lee must have graduated in poker before Humble ever heard of the game."

Shields laughed heartily and swiftly ran over his cards.

"Fifteen two, four, six, a pair is eight, and a double run of three is fourteen. Real good," he said as he pegged. "Passed the crack that time. What have you got?"

The foreman put his cards down, found three sixes and then turned the crib face up. "Pair of tens and His Highness," he grumbled. "Only three in that crib!"

"That's what you get for cutting a three," laughed the sheriff.

The game continued until the striking of the clock startled the guest.

"Midnight!" he cried. "Thirty miles before I get to bed–no, no, I can't stay with you to-night –much obliged, all the same."

He clapped his sombrero on his head and started for the door: "Well, better luck next time, Jim–three twenty-four hands shore did make a difference. Right where they were needed, too. So long."

"Sorry you won't stay, Tom," called his friend from the door as the foreman mounted. "You might just as well, you know."

"I'm sorry, too, but I've got to be on hand to-morrow–anyway, it's bright moonlight–so long!" he cried as he cantered away.

"Hey, Tom!" cried the sheriff, leaping from the porch and running to the gate. "Tom!"

"Hullo, what is it?" asked the foreman, drawing rein and returning.

"Smoke this on your way, it'll seem shorter," said the sheriff, holding out a cigar.

"By George, I will!" laughed Blake. "That's fine, you're all right!"

"Be good," cried the sheriff, watching his friend ride down the street.

"Shore enough good–I have to be," floated back to his ears.

CHAPTER XVI
THE FLYING-MARE

The Sunday morning following Blake's visit to Ford's Station found the Star C in excitement. Notwithstanding the fact that on every pleasant night after the day's work had been done it was the custom for the outfit to indulge in a swim, and that Saturday night had been very pleasant, the Limping Water was being violently disturbed, and laughter and splashing greeted the sun as it looked over the rim of the bank. Cakes of soap glistened on the sand on the west bank and towels hung from convenient limbs of the bushes which fringed the creek.

Silent, who was noted among his companions for the length of time he could stay under water, challenged them to a submersion test. The rules were simple, inasmuch as they consisted in all plunging under at the same time, the winner being he who was the last man up. Silent had steadfastly refused to have his endurance timed, which his friends mistook for modesty, and no sooner had all "ducked under" than his head popped up–but this time he was not alone. Humble, whose utmost limit was not over half a minute, grew angry at his inability to make a good showing and craftily determined to take a handicap. The two stared at each other for a space and then burst into laughter, forgetting for the time being what they should do. Other heads bobbed up, and the secret was out. Only that Silent was the best swimmer in the crowd saved him from a ducking, and as it was he had to grab his clothes and run.

After being assured that he was forgiven for his trickery he rejoined his friends and his towel.

More fun was now the rule, for dressing required care. The sandy west bank sloped gradually to the water's edge, and it was necessary to stand on one foot on a small stone in the water while the other was dipped to remove the sand. Still on one foot the other must be dried, the stocking put on, then the trouser leg and lastly the boot, and woe to the man who lost his balance and splashed stocking and trouser leg as he wildly sought to save it! Humble splashed while his foot was only half-way through the trouser leg, and The Orphan fared even worse. Then a race of awkward runners was on toward the bunk house, where breakfast was annihilated.

"Hey, Tom, what time do we leave?" asked Bud for the fifth time.

"Nine o'clock, you chump," replied the foreman.

"Three whole hours yet," grumbled Jim as he again plastered his hair to his head.

"I'll lose my appetite shore," worried Humble. "We got up too blamed early, that's what we did."

"Why, here's Humble!" cried Silent in mock surprise. "Do you like apricot pie, and gingerbread and real coffee?"

"You go to the devil," grumbled Humble. "You wouldn't 'a' been asked at all, only she couldn't very well cut you out of it when she asked me along. I'm the one she really wants to feed; you fellers just happen to tag on behind, that's all."

"Going to take Lightning with you, Humble?" asked Docile, winking at the others.

"Why, I shore am," replied Humble in surprise. "Do you reckon I'd leave him and that d—-d Chink all alone together, you sheep?"

"I was afraid you wouldn't," pessimistically grumbled Docile, but here he smiled hopefully. "Suppose you take Lee Lung and leave the dog here?" he queried.

"Suppose you quit supposing with your feet!" sarcastically countered Humble. "I know you ain't got much brains, but you might exercise what little you have got once in a while. It won't hurt you none after you get used to it."

"How are you going to carry him, Humble–like a papoose?" queried Joe with a great show of interest.

Humble stared at him: "Huh!" he muttered, being too much astonished to say more.

"I asked you how you are going to carry your fighting wolfhound," Joe said without the quiver of an eyelash. "I thought mebby you was going to sling him on your back like a papoose."

"Carry him! Papoose!" ejaculated Humble in withering irony. "What do you reckon his legs are for? He ain't no statue, he ain't no ornament, he's a dog."

"Well, I knowed he ain't no ornament, but I wasn't shore about the rest of it," responded Joe. "I only wanted to know how he'd get to town. There ain't no crime in asking about that, is there? I know he can't follow the gait we'll hit up for thirty miles, so I just naturally asked, sabe?"

"Oh, you did, did you!" cried Humble, not at all humbly. "He can't follow us, can't he?" he yelled belligerently.

"He shore can't, cross my heart," asserted Silent in great earnestness. "If he runs to Ford's Station after us and gets there inside of two days I'll buy him a collar. That goes."

"Huh!" snorted Humble in disgust, "he won't wear your old collar after he wins it. He's got too much pride to wear anything you'll give him."

"He couldn't, you mean," jabbed Jim. "He's so plumb tender that it would strain his back to carry it. Why, he has to sit down and rest if more'n two flies get on the same spot at once."

"He can't wag his tail more'n three times in an hour," added Bud, "and when he scratches hisself he has to rest for the remainder of the day."

Humble turned to The Orphan in an appealing way: "Did you ever see so many d—d fools all at once?" he beseeched.

The Orphan placed his finger to his chin and thought for fully half a minute before replying: "I was just figuring," he explained in apology for his abstraction. Then his face brightened: "You can tie him up in a blanket–that's the best way. Yes, sir, tie him up in a blanket and sling him at the pommel. We'll take turns carrying him."

"Purple h–l!" yelled Humble. "You're another! The whole crowd are a lot of —!"

"Sing it, Humble," suggested Tad, laughing. "Sing it!"

"Whistle some of it, and send the rest by mail," assisted Jack Lawson.

"Seen th' dlog?" came a bland, monotonous voice from the doorway, where Lee Lung stood holding a chunk of beef in one hand, while his other hand was hidden behind his back. Over his left shoulder projected half a foot of club, which he thought concealed. "Seen th' dlog?" he repeated, smiling.

"Miss Mirandy and holy hell!" shouted Humble, leaping forward at sight of the club. There was a swish! and Humble rebounded from the door, at which he stared. From the rear of the house came more monotonous words: "Nice dlog-gie. Pletty Lightling. Here come. Gette glub," and Humble galloped around the corner of the house, swearing at every jump.

When the laughter had died down Blake smiled grimly: "Some day Lee will get that dog, and when he does he'll get him good and hard. Then we'll have to get another cook. I've told him fifty times if I've told him once not to let it go past a joke, but it's no use."

"He won't hurt the cur, he's only stringing Humble," said Bud. "Nobody would hurt a dog that minded his own business."

"If anybody hit a dog of mine for no cause, he wouldn't do it again unless he got me first," quietly remarked The Orphan.

Jim hastily pointed to the corner of the house where a club projected into sight: "There's Lee now!" he whispered hurriedly. "He's laying for him!"

There was a sudden spurt of flame and smoke and the club flew several yards, struck by three bullets. Humble hopped around the corner holding his hand, his words too profane for repetition.

Smoke filtered from The Orphan's holster and eyes opened wide in surprise at the wonderful quickness of his gunplay, for no one had seen it. All there was was smoke.

"Good God!" breathed Blake, staring at the marksman, who had stepped forward and was explaining to Humble. "It's a good thing Shields was square!" he muttered.

"Did you see that?" asked Bud of Jim in whispered awe. "And I thought I was some beans with a six-shooter!"

"No, but I heard it–was they one or six?" replied Jim.

"I didn't know it was you, Humble," explained The Orphan. "I thought it was the Chink laying for the dog."

"— —! Good for you!" cried Humble in sudden friendliness. "You're all right, Orphant, but will you be sure next time? That stung like blazes," he said as he held out his hand. "I can always tell a white man by the way he treats a dog. If all men were as good as dogs this world would be a blamed sight nicer place to live in, and don't you forget it."

"Still going to take Lightning with you, Humble?" asked Bud.

"No, I ain't going to take Lightning with me!" snapped Humble. "I'm going to leave him right here on the ranch," here his voice arose to a roar, "and if any sing-song, rope-haired, animated hash-wrastler gets gay while I'm gone, I'll send him to his heathen hell!"

"Come on, boys," said Blake, snapping his watch shut. "Time to get going."

"Glory be!" exulted Silent, executing a few fancy steps toward the corral, his companions close behind, with the exception of The Orphan, who had gone into the bunk house for a minute.

As they whooped their way toward the town Blake noticed that a gold pin glittered at the knot of the new recruit's neck-kerchief, and he chuckled when he recalled the warning he had given to the sheriff. He shrewdly guessed that the apricot pie and the rest of the feast were quite subordinated by The Orphan to the girl who had given him the pin.

Bud suddenly turned in his saddle and pointed to a jackrabbit which bounded away across the plain like an animated shadow.

"Now, if Humble's bloodhound was only here," he said, "we would rope that jack and make the cur fight it. It would be a fine fight, all right," he laughed.

"You go to the devil," grunted Humble, and he started ahead at full speed. "Come on!" he cried. "Come on, you snails!" and a race was on.

The citizens of Ford's Station saw a low-hanging cloud of dust which rolled rapidly up from the west and soon a hard-riding crowd of cowboys, in gala attire, galloped down the main street of the town. They slowed to a canter and rode abreast in a single line, the arms of each man over the shoulders of his nearest companions, and all sang at the top of their lungs. On the right end rode Blake, and on the left was The Orphan. Bill Howland ran out into the street and spotted his new friend immediately and swung his hat and cheered for the man who had helped him out of two bad holes. The Orphan broke from the line and shook hands with the driver, his face wreathed by a grin.

"You old son-of-a-gun!" cried Bill, delighted at the familiarity from so noted a person as the former outlaw. "How are you, hey?"

The line cried warm greeting as it swung around to shake his hand, and the driver's chest took on several inches of girth.

"Hullo, Bill!" cried Bud with a laugh. "Seen your old friend Tex lately?"

"Yes, I did," replied Bill. "I saw him out on Thirty-Mile Stretch, but he didn't do nothing but swear. He didn't want no more run-ins with me, all right, and, besides, my rifle was across my knees. He said as how he was going to come back some day and start things moving about this old town, and I told him to begin with the Star C when he did."

He looked across the street and waved his hand at a group of his friends who were looking on. "Come on over, fellows," he cried, and when they had done so he turned and introduced The Orphan to them.

"This ugly cuss here is Charley Winter; this slab-sided curiosity is Tommy Larkin, and here is his brother Al; Chet Dare, Duke Irwin, Frank Hicks, Hoke Jones, Gus Shaw and Roy Purvis. All good fellows, every one of them, and all friends of the sheriff. Here comes Jed Carr, the only man in the whole town who ain't afraid of me since I licked them punchers in the defile. Hullo, Jed! Shake hands with the man who played h–l with the Cross Bar-8 and the Apaches."

"Glad to meet you, Orphan," remarked Jed as he shook hands. "Punching for the Star C, eh? Good crowd, most of them, as they run, though Humble ain't very much."

"He ain't, ain't he?" grinned that puncher. "You're some sore about that day when I cleaned up all your cush at poker, ain't you? Ain't had time to get over it, have you? Want to borrow some?"

"You want to look out for Humble, Jed," bantered Bud. "He's taken a lesson at poker from our cook since he played you. Didn't you, Easy?" he asked Humble.

The roar of laughter which followed Bud's words forced Humble to stand treat: "Come on over and have something with the only man in the crowd that's got any money," he said.

When they had lined up against the bar jokes began to fly thick and fast and The Orphan felt a peculiar elation steal over him as he slowly puffed at his cigar. Suddenly the door flew open and Bill's glass dropped from his hand.

"Bucknell, by God! And as drunk as a fool!" he exclaimed.

The puncher whom The Orphan had tied up above the defile leaned against the door frame and his gun wavered from point to point unsteadily as he tried to peer into the dim interior of the room, his face leering as he sought, with a courage born of drink, for the man who had made a fool of him.

A bottle crashed against the wall at his side, and as he lurched forward, glancing at the broken glass, a figure leaped to meet him and with agile strength grasped his right wrist, wheeled and got his shoulder under Bucknell's armpit, took two short steps and straightened up with a jerk. The intruder left the floor and flew headforemost through the air, crashing against the rear wall, where he fell to the floor and lay quiet. The Orphan, having foresworn unnecessary gunplay, and always scorning to shoot a drunken man, had executed a clever, quick flying-mare.

As the sheriff stepped into the room Blake ran forward and lifted Bucknell to his feet, supporting him until he could stand alone. The puncher was greatly sobered by the shock and blinked confusedly about him. The Orphan was smoking nonchalantly at the bar and Bill had just given the sheriff the victim's gun.

"What's the matter?" asked Bucknell, rubbing his forehead, which was cut and bruised.

"Nothing's the matter, yet," answered Shields shortly. "But there would have been if you hadn't been too drunk to know what you was doing. I saw you and tried to get here first, but it's all right now. Take your gun and get out. Here," he exclaimed, "you promise me to behave yourself and you can go back to Sneed, for he needs you. Otherwise, it's out of the country after Tex for you. Is it a go?"

"What was that, and who done it?" asked Bucknell, clinging to the bar. "What was it?" he repeated.

"That was me trying to throw you through the wall," said the sheriff, wishing to give Bucknell no greater cause for animosity against The Orphan, and for the peace of the community; and also because he wished to help The Orphan to refrain from using his gun in the future. "And I'd 'a' done it, too, only my hand was sweaty. Will you do what I said?" he asked.

Bucknell straightened up and staggered past the sheriff to where The Orphan stood: "You done that, but it's all right, ain't it?" he asked. "You ain't sore, are you?" His eyes had a crafty look, but the dimness of the room concealed it, and The Orphan did not notice the look.

"It's all right, Bucknell, and I ain't sore," he replied. "I won't be sore if you do what the sheriff wants you to."

"All right, all right," replied Bucknell. "Have a drink on me, boys. It's all right now, ain't it? Have a drink on me."

"No more drinking to-day," quickly said the bartender at a look from Shields. "All the good stuff is used up and the rest ain't fit for dogs, let alone my friends. Wait 'til next time, when I'll have some new."

"That's too d—d bad," replied Bucknell, leering at the crowd. "Have a smoke, then. Come on, have a smoke with me."

"We shore will, Bucknell," responded Shields quickly.

As the cowboy started for the door the sheriff placed a hand on his shoulder: "You behave yourself, Bucknell," he said. "So long."

CHAPTER XVII
THE FEAST

Joyous whoops, loud and heartfelt, brought the women to the door of the sheriff's house in time to see their guests dismount. A perfect babel of words greeted their appearance as the cowboys burst into a running fire of jokes, salutations and comments. Even the ponies seemed to know that something important and unusual was taking place, for they cavorted and bit and squealed to prove that they were in accord with the spirit of their riders and that thirty miles in less than three hours had not subdued them. Bright colors prevailed, for the neck-kerchiefs in most cases were new and yet showed the original folding creases, while new, clean thongs of rawhide and glittering bits of metal flashed back the sunlight. Spurs glittered and the clean looking horses appeared to have had a dip in the Limping Water. Blake had hunted through the carpeted rooms of his ranch-house for decorations, and in the drawer of a table he had found a bunch of ribbons of many kinds and shades. These now fluttered from the pommels of the saddles and in one case a red ribbon was twined about the leg of a vicious pinto, and the pinto was not at all pleased by the decoration.

The sheriff led the way to the house closely followed by Blake, the others coming in the order of their nerve. The Orphan was last, not from lack of courage, but rather because of strategy. He thought that Helen would remain at the door to welcome each arrival and if he was in the van he would be passed on to make way for those behind him. Being the last man he hoped to be able to say more to her than a few words of greeting. As he mounted the steps she was drawn into the room for something and he stepped to one side on the porch, well knowing that she would miss him.

Bud poked his head out the door and started to say something, but The Orphan fiercely whispered for him to be silent and to disappear, which Bud did after grinning exasperatingly.

The man on the porch was growing impatient when he heard the light swish of skirts around the corner of the house. Sauntering carelessly to the corner he looked into the back-yard and saw Helen with a tray in her hands, nearing the back door. She espied him and stopped, flushing suddenly as he leaped lightly to the ground and walked rapidly toward her. Her cheeks became a deeper red when he stopped before her and took the tray, for his eyes were rebellious and would not be subdued, and the first thing she saw was the gold pin which stood out boldly against the dark blue neck-kerchief. She was rarely beautiful in her white dress, and the ribbon which she wore at her throat did not detract in its effect. Later her sister was to wonder if it was a coincidence that the ribbon and his neck-kerchief were so good a match in color.

She welcomed him graciously and he felt a sudden new and strangely exhilarating sensation steal over him as he took the hand she held out, the tray all the while bobbing recklessly in his other hand.

"Why aren't you in the house paying your respects to your hostess?" she chided half in jest and half in earnest.

"The delay will but add to my fervor when I do," he replied, "for I will have had a stimulus then. As long as the hostesses are four and insist on not being together, how can I pay my respects all at once?"

"But there is only one hostess," she laughingly corrected. "I am afraid you are not very good at making excuses. You probably never felt the need to make them before. You see, I, too, am only a guest."

"We two," he corrected daringly.

"I am very glad to see you," she said, leading away from plurals. "You are looking very well and much more contented. And then, this is ever so much nicer than our first meeting, isn't it? No horrid Apaches."

"I've gotten so that I rather like Apaches," he replied. "They are so useful at times. But you mustn't try to tempt me to subordinate that eventful day, not yet. It can't be done, although I've never tried to do it," he hastily assured her, making a gesture of helplessness. "Sometimes an unexpected incident will change the habits of a lifetime, making the days seem brighter, and yet, somehow, adding a touch of sadness. I have been a stranger to myself since then, restless, absentminded, moody and hungry for I know not what." He paused and then slowly continued, "I must beg to remain loyal to that day of all days when you bathed an outlaw's head and showed your love for fair play and kindness."

"Goodness!" she cried, for one instant meeting his eager eyes. "Why, I thought it was a terrible day! And you really think differently?"

"Very much so," he assured her as she withdrew her hand from his. "You see, it was such a new and delightful experience to save a stage coach and then find that it was a hospital with a wonderful doctor. I accused that Apache of being stingy with his lead, for he might just as well have given me a few more wounds to have dressed."

"Yes," she laughingly retorted, "it was almost as new an experience as starting on a long and supposedly peaceful journey and suddenly finding oneself in the middle of a desert surrounded by dead Indians and doctoring an Indian killer who was at war with one's brother. And that after a terrible shaking up lasting for over an hour.

Truly it is a day to be remembered. Now, don't you think you should hurry in and greet my sister-in-law?"

"Yes, certainly," he quickly responded. "But before I lose the opportunity I must ask you if you will care if I ride over and see you occasionally, because it is terribly lonely on that ranch."

"You know that we shall always be glad to see you whenever you can call," she replied, smiling up at him. "We are all very deep in your debt and brother and all of us think a great deal of you. Are you satisfied on the Star C, and do you like your work and your companions?"

"Thank you," he cried happily, "I will ride over and see you once in a while. But as for my work, it is delightful! The Star C is fine and my companions–well, they just simply can't be beat! they are the finest, whitest set of men that ever gathered under one roof."

"That's very nice, I am glad that you find things so congenial," she replied in sincerity. "James was sure that you would, for Mr. Blake is an old friend of his."

"I'm very anxious about this pin," he said, putting his hand on it. "May I keep it for a while longer?" he asked with a note of appeal in his voice.

"Why, yes," she replied, "if you wish to. But only as long as you do not displease me, and you will not do that, will you? James has such deep confidence in you that I know you will not disappoint him. You will justify him in his own mind and in the minds of his acquaintances and prove that he has not erred in judgment, won't you?"

"If I am the sum total of your brother's trouble, he will have a path of roses to wander through all the rest of his life," he responded earnestly. "And I'm really afraid that you will never again wear this pin as a possession of yours. Of course you can borrow it occasionally," and he smiled whimsically, "but as far as displeasing you is concerned, it is mine forever. It will really and truly be mine on that condition, won't it? My very own if I do not forfeit it?"

"If you wish it so," she replied quickly, her face radiant with smiles. "And you will work hard and you will never shoot a man, no matter what the provocation may be, unless it is absolutely necessary to do it for the saving of your own life or that of a friend or an innocent man. Promise me that!" she commanded imperatively, pleased at being able to dictate to him. "Men like you never break a promise," she added impulsively.

"I promise never to shoot a man, woman, child or–or anybody," he laughingly replied, "unless it is necessary to save life. And I'll work real hard and save my money. And on Sundays, rain or shine, I'll ride in and report to my new foreman." Then a bit of his old humor came to him: "For I just about need this pin–knots are so clumsy, you know."

She glanced at the knot which held the pin and laughed merrily, leading the way into the house.

As they entered Humble was extolling the virtues of his dog, to the broad grins of his companions, who constantly added amendments and made corrections sotto voce.

"Why, here they are!" cried the sheriff in such a tone as to suffuse Helen's face with blushes. The Orphan coolly shook hands with him.

"Yes, here we are, Sheriff, every one of us," he replied. "We couldn't be expected to stay away when Mrs. Shields put herself to so much trouble, and we're all happy and proud to be so honored. How do you do, Mrs. Shields," he continued as he took her hand. "It is awful kind of you to go to such trouble for a lot of lonely, hungry fellows like us."

"Goodness sakes!" she cried, delighted at his words and pleased at the way he had parried her husband's teasing thrust. "Why, it was no trouble at all–you are all my boys now, you know."

"Thank you, Mrs. Shields," he replied slowly. "We will do our very best to prove ourselves worthy of being called your boys."

The sheriff regarded The Orphan with a look of approbation and turned to his sister Helen.

"He ain't nobody's fool, eh, Sis?" he whispered. "I'm wondering how you ever made up your mind to share him with us!"

"Oh, please don't!" she begged in confusion. "Please don't tease me now!"

"All right, Sis," he replied in a whisper, pinching her ear. "I'll save it all up for some other time, some time when he ain't around to turn it off, eh? But I don't blame him a bit for exploring the yard first–you're the prettiest girl this side of sun-up," he said, beaming with love and pride. "How's that for a change, eh? Worth a kiss?"

She kissed him hurriedly and then left the room to attend to her duties in the kitchen, and he sauntered over to where The Orphan was talking with Mrs. Shields, his hand rubbing his lips and a mischievous twinkle in his kind eyes.

"Did you notice the new flower-bed right by the side of the house as you ran past it a while ago?" he asked, flashing a keen warning to his wife.

The Orphan searched his memory for the flower-bed and not finding it, turned and smiled, not willing to admit that his attention had been too fully taken up with a fairer flower than ever grew in earth.

"Why, yes, it is real pretty," he replied. "What about it?"

"Oh, nothing much," gravely replied the sheriff as he edged away. "Only we were thinking of putting a flower-bed there, although I haven't had time to get at it yet."

The Orphan flushed and glanced quickly at the outfit, who were too busy cracking jokes and laughing to pay any attention to the conversation across the room.

"James!" cried Mrs. Shields. "Aren't you ashamed of yourself!"

"When you tickle a mule," said the sheriff, grinning at his friend, "you want to look out for the kick. Come again sometime, Sonny."

"James!" his wife repeated, "how can you be so mean! Now, stop teasing and behave yourself!"

"For a long time I've been puzzled about what you resembled, but now I have your words for it," easily countered The Orphan. "Thank you for putting me straight."

The sheriff grinned sheepishly and scratched his head: "I'm an old fool," he grumbled, and forthwith departed to tell Helen of the fencing.

Mrs. Shields excused herself and followed her husband into the kitchen to look after the dinner, and The Orphan sauntered over to his outfit just as Jim looked out of a rear window. Jim turned quickly, his face wearing a grin from ear to ear.

"Hey, Bud!" he called eagerly. "Bud!"

"What?" asked Bud, turning at the hail.

"Come over here for a minute, I want to show you something," Jim replied, "but don't let Humble come."

Bud obeyed and looked: "Jimminee!" he exulted. "Don't that look sumptious, though? This is where we shine, all right." Then turned: "Hey, fellows, come over here and take a look."

As they crowded around the window Humble discovered that something was in the wind and he followed them. What they saw was a long table beneath two trees, and it was covered with a white cloth and dressed for a feast. Bud turned quickly from the crowd and forcibly led

Humble to a side window before that unfortunate had seen anything and told him to put his finger against the glass, which Humble finally did after an argument.

"Feel the pain?" Bud asked.

"Why, no," Humble replied, looking critically at his finger. "What's the matter with you, anyhow?"

"Nothing," replied Bud. "Think it over, Humble," he advised, turning away.

Humble again put his finger to the glass and then snorted:

"Locoed chump! Prosperity is making him nutty!" When he turned he saw his friends laughing silently at him and making grimaces, and a light suddenly broke in upon him.

"Yes, I did!" he cried. "That joke is so old I plumb forgot it years ago! Spring something that hasn't got whiskers and a halting step, will you?"

Jim laughed and suggested a dance, but was promptly squelched.

"You heathen!" snorted Blake in mock horror. "This is Sunday! If you want to dance wait till you get back to the ranch–suppose one of the women was here and heard you say that!"

"Gee, I forgot all about it being Sunday," replied Jim, quickly looking to see if any of the women were in the room. "We're regular barbarians, ain't we!" he exclaimed in self-condemnation and relief when he saw that no women were present. "We're regular land pirates, ain't we?"

"You'll be asking to play poker yet, or have a race," jabbed Humble with malice. "You ain't got no sense and never did have any."

"Huh!" retorted Jim belligerently, "I won't try to learn a Chinee cook how to play poker and get skinned out of my pay, anyhow! Got enough?" he asked, "or shall I tell of the time you drifted into Sagetown and asked—"

"Shut up, you fool!" whispered Humble ferociously. "Yu'll get skun if you say too much!"

"Skun' is real good," retorted Jim. "Got any more of them new words to spring on us?"

Helen had been passing to and fro past the window and Docile Thomas here put his marveling into words, for he had been casting covert glances at her, but now his restraint broke.

"Gee whiz!" he exclaimed in a whisper to Jack Lawson. "Ain't she a regular hummer, now! Lines like a thoroughbred, face like a dream and a smile what shore is a winner! See her hair–fine and dandy, eh? She's in the two-forty class, all right!" he enthused. "Why, when this country wakes up to what's in it the sheriff will have to put up a stockade around this house and mount guard. Everybody from Bill up will be stampeding this way to talk business with the sheriff. No wonder The Orphan has got a bee in his bonnet–lucky dog!"

"She can take care of my pay every month just as soon as she says the word," Jack replied. "But suppose you look away once in a while? Suppose you shift your sights! You, too, Humble," he said, suddenly turning on the latter.

"Me what?" asked Humble, without interest and without shifting his gaze. "What are you talking about?"

"Look at something else, see?"

"Shore I see," replied Humble. "That's why I'm looking. Do you think I look with my eyes shut! Gee, but ain't she a picture, though!"

"She shore is, but give it a rest, take a vacation, you chump!" retorted Jack. "You're staring at her like she had you hoodooed. Come out of your trance–wake up and make a fool of yourself some other way. Don't aim all the time at her. Mebby Lee Lung has killed your dog!"

"If he has we'll need a new cook," replied Humble with decision.

"Come on, boys! Don't start milling!" cried the sheriff, suddenly entering the room. "Dinner's all ready and waiting for us. And I shore hope you have all got your best appetites with you, because Margaret likes to see her food taken care of lively. If you don't clean it all up she'll think you don't like it," he said, winking at Blake, "and if she once gets that notion in her head it will be no more invitations for the Star C."

There was much excitement in the crowd, and the replies came fast.

"I ain't had anything good to eat for fifteen long, aching years!" cried Bud. "When I get through you'll need a new table.

"Same here, only for thirty years," replied Jim hastily. "I just couldn't sleep last night for thinking about the glorious surprise my abused stomach was due to have to-day. I'll bet my gun on my performance if the track is heavy, all right. I'm not poor on speed, and I'm a stayer from Stayersville."

"Well, I won't be among the also rans, you can bet on that," laughed Silent. "I don't weigh very much, but I'm geared high."

"I'll bet it's good!" cried Humble, "I'll bet it's real good!"

"D—n good, you mean!" corrected Jack. "Hey, fellows!" he cried, "did you hear what Humble said? He said that he'd bet it was real good!"

"Horray for Humble, the wit of the Star C," laughed Docile.

"Me for the apricot pie!" exulted Charley. "Here's where I get square on Blake for rubbing it in all these months about the fine pie he gets over here."

"There ain't no apricot pie," gravely lied the sheriff in surprise.

"What!" cried Charley in alarm. "There ain't none for me! Oh, well, you can't lose me in daylight, for I'll double up on everything else. I ain't going to get left, all right!"

"Don't wake me up," begged Joe Haines. "Let me dream on in peace and plenty. Grub, real, genuine grub, grub what is grub! Oh, joy!"

Mrs. Shields hurried into the room and then paused in surprise when she saw that the outfit had not moved toward the feast.

"Land sakes!" she cried. "Aren't you boys hungry, or is James up to some of his everlasting teasing again!"

"You talk to her, Bud," whispered Jim eagerly. "I'm so scary I shore can't."

"Yes, go ahead, Bud!" came instant and unanimous endorsement in whispers.

"Well, ma'am," began Bud, clearing his throat, glancing around uneasily to be sure that the crowd was giving him moral backing, and feeling uncomfortable, "we was just getting up a–a—"

"B, C, D," prompted Jim in a whisper.

"We was just getting up a resolution of thanks, Mrs. Shields," he continued, stabbing his elbow into the stomach of the offending Jim. "You shut up!" he fiercely whispered. "I'm carrying one hundred and forty pounds now without the saddle!" Then he continued: "We all of us are plumb tickled about this, so plumb tickled we don't hardly know what to say—"

"That's right," whispered Jim, folding his arms across his stomach. "You're proving it, all right."

Silent and Jack hauled Jim to the rear and Bud continued unruffled: "But we want to thank you, ma'am, from the bottoms, the very lowest bottoms of our hearts for your kindness to a orphant outfit what ain't had anything to eat since the war, and very little during it. Joe

Haines, here, ma'am, was just saying as how he was a-scared that it is all a dream—"

"I didn't neither!" fiercely contradicted Joe in a whisper, looking very self-conscious. He was whisked to the rear to join Jim and the speech went on.

"He is afraid it is a dream, ma'am, and I know we all of us have more or less doubts about it being really true. But, ma'am, we shore are anxious to find out all about it. We've rid thirty miles to see for ourselves, and I don't reckon you'll have any fears about our appetites being left at home when you sizes up the wreck left in the path of the storm after the stampede is over. The boys want to give you three cheers even if it is Sunday, ma'am, for your kindness to them, and I'm shore one of the boys!"

"Hip, hip, horray!" yelled the crowd, surging forward.

"Good boy, Bud!" they cried.

"I'm proud of you, Buddie!" exulted Charley, slapping him extra heartily on the back.

"I didn't know you had it in you, Bud!" cried Silent. "It was shore a dandy speech, all right."

"We'll send you to Congress for that, some day, Bud," cried Jack Lawson. "You're all right!"

"I once had a piece of pie, a piece of pie, a piece of pie,

I once had a piece of pie, when I was five years old," sang Charley as he pranced toward the door.

"Good! Go on, Charley, go on!" cried his companions joyously.

"Now I'll have another piece, another piece, another piece. Now I'll have another piece, that's two all told. Good bye, Lee Lung, good bye Lee Lung, Good bye, Lee Lung, we're going to forget you now!"

"Again on that Lee Lung, altogether–it hits me right!" cried Bud, and the matter pertaining to the farewells to Lee Lung was promptly and properly attended to in heartfelt sincerity.

The ladies laughed with delight, and Mrs. Shields whispered to her husband, who nodded and escorted The Orphan to a seat near the head of the table, where he was flanked by Helen and Blake.

"Grab your partners, boys," the sheriff cried, pointing to the chairs. There was a hasty piling of belts and guns on the ground, and after much confusion all were seated.

The sheriff arose: "Boys, Mrs. Shields wants me to tell you how pleased she is to have you all here. She has felt plumb sorry about you and she shore has shuddered at the thought of a Chinee cook—"

"Which same we all do–it's chronic," interposed Jim to laughter.

"She wants you to make yourselves at home," continued the sheriff, "learn the lay of the land around this range and never forget the trail leading here, because she insists that when any of you come to town you have simply got to pay us a visit and see if there is a piece of pie or cake to eat before you go back to that cook. And Tom says that he'll fire the first man who renigs—"

"I'm going to carry the mail hereafter!" cried Bud, scowling fiercely at Joe.

"Not if I can shoot first, you don't!" retorted the mail carrier. "I was just a-wondering if it wouldn't be better to come in twice a week for it instead of once. We might get more letters."

"We'll bid for your job next year," laughed Silent.

"Before I coax you to eat," continued the sheriff, "I—"

"Wrong word, Sheriff," interposed Humble. "Not coax, but force."

"I am going to ask you to reverse things a little, and drink a standing toast to the man who saved the stage, to the man who saved Miss Ritchie and my sisters and who made this dinner possible. This would be far from a happy day but for him. I want you to drink to the long life and happiness of The Orphan. All up!"

The clink of glasses was lost in the spontaneous cheer which burst from the lips of the former outlaw's new friends, and he sat confused and embarrassed with a sudden timidity, his face crimson.

"Speech!" cried Jim, the others joining in the cry. "Speech! Speech!"

Finally, after some urging, The Orphan slowly arose to his feet, a foolish smile playing about his lips.

"It wasn't anything," he said deprecatingly. "You all would have done it, every one of you. But I'm glad it was me. I'm glad I was on hand, although it wasn't anything to make all this fuss about," and he dropped suddenly into his seat, feeling hot and uncomfortable.

"Well, we have different ideas about its being nothing," replied the sheriff. "Now, boys, a toast to Bill Halloway," he requested. "Bill couldn't get here to-day, but we mustn't forget him. His splendid grit and driving made it possible for our friend to play his hand so well."

"Hurrah for Bill!" cried Silent, leaping to his feet with the others. When seated again he looked quickly at his glass and turned to Bud.

"Real sweet cider!" he exulted. "Good Lord, but how time gallops past! I'd almost forgotten what it was like! It's been over twenty years since I tasted any! Ain't it fine?"

"I was wondering what it was," remarked Humble, a trace of awe in his voice as he refilled his glass. "It's shore enough sweet cider, and blamed good, too!"

Charley was romping with the mail carrier and he had a sudden inspiration: "Speech from Joe! Speech for the pieces of pie and cake he's due to get!"

"Now, look here, boy," Joe gravely replied. "I'm the mail carrier. I don't have to go on jury duty, lead religion round-ups, go to war or make speeches. As the books say, I'm exempt. All I have to do is punch cows, rustle the mail and eat pie and cake once a week," he said, glancing at Bud, who glared and groaned.

"Good boy, Joe!" cried Humble, waving his glass excitedly. "You're shore all right, you are, and I'm your deputy, ain't I?"

"No, not my deputy, but my delirium," corrected Joe.

"Glory be!" cried Silent as his plate was passed to him. "Chicken, real chicken! Mashed potatoes, mashed turnips and dressing and gravy! And here comes stewed corn, boiled onions and jelly and mother's bread. And stewed tomatoes? Well, well! I guess we ain't going to be well fed, and real happy, eh, fellows? My stomach won't know what's the matter–it'll think it died and went to heaven by mistake. Holy smoke! It hurts my eyes. What, cranberry jam? Well, I'm just going to close my eyes for a minute if you don't mind; I want to recuperate from the shock. This is where I live again!"

Humble stared in rapture at the feast before him and finally heaved a long drawn sigh of doubt and content.

"Gee!" he cried softly, a far-away look in his eyes. "Look at it, just look at it! Just like I used to get when I was a little tad back in Connecticut–but that was shore a long time ago. Well," he exclaimed, bracing up and bravely forgetting his boyhood, "there's one thing I hope, and that is that Lee beats my dog. Then I can shoot him and get square for all these years of imitation grub what he's handed out to me!"

"Hey, Tom!" eagerly cried Charley, "why can't we handle a herd of chickens out on the ranch, and have a garden? Why, we could have eggs every day and chickens on holidays!"

"No wonder Tom likes to ride to town," laughed Silent. "Gee whiz, I'd walk it for pie and cake and real genuine coffee!"

"Walk it!" snorted Jim. "Huh, I'd crawl, and stand on my head, knock my feet together and crow every half mile! Walk it, huh!"

Merriment reigned supreme throughout the meal and when the bashfulness had worn off the conversation became fast and furious, abounding in terse wit, verbal attacks and clever counters, and in concentrated onslaughts against the unfortunate Humble, who soon found, however, a new and loyal champion in Miss Ritchie, who took his part. Her assistance was so doughty as to more than once put to rout his tormentors, and before the dessert had been reached he was her devoted slave and admirer and was henceforth to sing her praises at every opportunity, and even to make opportunities.

At The Orphan's end of the table all was serene. He, Helen, Blake and the sheriff found much to talk about, and all the while Mrs. Shields regarded the four in a motherly way, and tempered the keenness of her husband's wit, for he was prone to break lances with The Orphan and to tease his sister, much to her confusion. She was very happy, for here at her side were her husband and the man she had feared would harm him, laughing and joking and the best of friends; and down the table a crowd of big-hearted boys, her boys now, were having the time of their lives. They were good boys, too, she told herself; a trifle rough, but sterling at the heart, and every one of them a loyal friend. How good it was to see them eat and hear them laugh, all happy and mischievous. The welding of the units had been finished, and now the Star C and The Orphan were one in spirit.

CHAPTER XVIII PREPARATION

After the dinner at the sheriff's house, life meant much to The Orphan, for the dinner had done its work and done it well. Whatever had been missing to complete the good fellowship between him and the others had been supplied and by the time the outfit was ready to leave for home, all corners had been rounded and all rough edges smoothed down. With his outfit he was in hearty, loyal accord, and the spirit of the ranch had become his own. With the sheriff his already strong liking had been stripped of any undesirable qualities, and he felt that Shields was not only the whitest man he had ever met, but also his best friend. He had become more intimate with the sheriff's household, and for Mrs. Shields he had only love and respect.

With Helen his cup was full to overflowing, for he had managed to hold several long talks with her during the afternoon, and to his mind he had heard nothing detrimental to his hopes. His eyes had been opened as to what it was he had been hungering for, and the knowledge thrilled him to his finger-tips. He was a red-blooded, clean-limbed man, direct of words and purpose, reveling in a joyous, surging, vigorous health, in tune with his surroundings; he was dominant, fearless, and he had a saving grace in his humor. To him came visions of the future, golden as the sunrise, rich in promise and assurance as to a happiness such as he could only feebly feel. Himself he was sure of, for he feared no failure on his part; as far as he was concerned it was won. Helen, he believed from what the day had given him, would not refuse him when the time came for her to decide, and his effervescent spirits sent a song to his lips, which he hurled to the sky as a war-cry, a slogan of triumph and a defiance.

As yet he knew nothing of the sheriff's plans, and his thoughts concerning his future position in the community did not dare to soar above that of foreman of some ranch. To this end he would bend his energies with all the power of his splendid trinity–heart, mind and body. He was far too happy to think of failure, because there would be none; had the word passed through his mind he would have laughed it into oblivion. His experience gave him confidence, for he was no weakling sheltered and protected by any guiding angel; to the contrary, he was the survivor of a bitter war against conditions which would have destroyed a less strong man; he was victor over himself and his enemies, a conqueror of adverse conditions, a hewer of his own path; his enemies had been his best friends, and his long fight, his salvation. For ten years he had constantly fought a bitter fight against nature and man; hunger and thirst, plots and ambushes had all played their parts, and he had won out over all of them. He was young, hopeful and unafraid, and now that he was on the right trail he would bend every energy to stay there, and he would stay there, be the opposition what it might; and if the opposition should be man, and of a strength dangerous to him, he would destroy it as he had destroyed others before it. While now scorning to use his gun on every provocation he would depend upon it as on a court of last resort–and its decision would be final.

He held ill wishes against no man save one, and that one was the man who had placed the rope about the neck of his father. He did not know that man's name, and he did not know that he might not be among those who had already paid for that crime. But should he ever learn that he lived he would take payment in full be the cost what it might.

But he had no thoughts for strife, he only knew that the sun had never been so bright, the sky so blue and the plain so full of life and beauty as it was on this perfect day. Only one other day rivaled it–the day he had swayed weakly by the side of a dusty coach and had felt warm, soft fingers touching his forehead. But, he told himself with joy, there would be days to come which would eclipse even that.

He was aroused from his reverie by the approach of the foreman, who gave him a hearty hail and smiled at the happy expression on the puncher's face.

"Well, you look like you had struck it rich!" cried Blake. "What is it, gold or silver?"

"Gold or silver!" cried The Orphan in contempt at such cheapness. "By God, Blake, I wouldn't sell my claim for all the gold and silver in this fool earth! Gold or silver! Why, man, I know where there is plenty of both. Here," he cried, plunging his hand into his chaps pocket, "look at this!"

The foreman looked and whistled and took the object into his hand, where he examined it critically. "By George, it's the yellow metal, all right, and blamed near pure!" He returned it to its owner and added: "That's the real stuff, Orphan."

"Yes, it is," replied the other as he pocketed the nugget. "And I know where it came from. There's plenty left that's just like it, but I wouldn't go after it if it was diamonds."

"You wouldn't!" exclaimed Blake in surprise. "By George, I'd go to-morrow, to-night, if I knew. Gold like that ain't to be sneered at. It spells ranches, ease, plenty, anything you want. And you wouldn't go for it?"

"No, I wouldn't, and I won't," replied the puncher. "I'm going to stay right here on this range and make good with my hands and brains. I'm going to win the game with the cards I hold, and when I say win I mean it. There are times when gold is a dangerous thing to have, and this is one of them, as you'll understand when I disclose my hand. When I win I won't need gold bad enough to go through hell and hot water for it and risk not getting back to my claim, and it's one hundred to one that I wouldn't get back, too. And if I lose, mind you, if, I won't have any use for it. I picked that nugget up in the middle of the damnedest desert God ever made, and when I got off it I was loco for a week. I won't tell any friend of mine where it is because I want my friends to go on drawing their breath. I need my friends a whole lot, and that's why I don't tell you where it is. I was saving that for my enemies. Two have gone after it already, and haven't been heard of since."

"Well, you are the first man who ever told me that gold isn't worth going after, and you have convinced me that in your case you are right," laughed the foreman.

"You wouldn't have to be told if you knew that desert as I do," replied The Orphan.

"How was the sheriff last night?" asked Blake. "Or didn't you notice, being too much occupied in your claim?"

The Orphan looked at him and then laughed softly: "He was the same as ever–the best man I ever knew. But how in thunder do you know about my claim? How did you know what I meant? I thought that I had covered that trail pretty well."

Blake put his hand on his friend's shoulders and gravely looked at him: "Son, having eyes, I see; having ears, I hear; having brains, I think. If you have been fooling yourself that you are on a quiet trail, just listen to this: There ain't a man who knows you well that don't know what you're playing for, even Bill had it all mapped out the second time he saw you. And most of us wish you luck. You're not a man who needs help, but if you do need it, you know where to come for it."

"Thank you, Blake," replied The Orphan, eagerly filling his lungs with the crisp air. "That's why I ain't hankering for that gold–I'm too blamed busy making my own."

"Well, what I wanted to speak to you about is this," said the foreman, thinking quickly as to how to say it. "Old man Crawford got me to promise that I'd pick up a herd of cows for him before fall. Now, I would just as soon do it myself as not, but if you want to try your hand at it, go ahead. He wants about five thousand, to be delivered in five herds, a thousand each, at his corrals. He won't pay any more than the regular price for them, and the more you can drop the price the better he will like it, of course. They must be good, healthy cattle and be delivered to him before payment is made. What do you say?"

"I say that it's a go!" cried The Orphan. "I've had some great luck lately!" he exulted. "I'm ready to go after them whenever you say the word, to-night if you say so. And I'll get the right number and kind or know the reason why. And I'll take a hand in driving the last herd to him myself. Good Lord, what luck!"

Blake talked a while longer about the trip, giving necessary instructions about prices and where he would be likely to find the herd, and then rode off in the direction of Ford's Station for a consultation with his friend, the sheriff.

"Hullo, Tom!" came from the stage office as he rode past. He quickly turned his head and then stopped, smiling broadly.

"Why, hullo, Bill," he replied. "Glad to see you. How are things? Had any trouble lately?"

"Nope, times are real dull since that day in the defile," Bill answered with a grin. "I saw Tex once at Sagetown, but he ain't talking none these days, he's too busy thinking. You see, I've got a purty strong combination backing me and nobody feels like starting it a-going, because there ain't no telling just where it'll stop. The Orphant and the sheriff make a blamed good team, all right."

"None better at any game, Bill," replied Blake. "And you used the right word, too. They're going to pull together from now on, in fact, the Star C will be in harness with them."

"That's the way to talk!" cried Bill enthusiastically. "I always said that Orphant was a white man, even before I ever saw him," he said, forgetting much that he might be in hearty accord. "He can call on me any time he needs me, you bet. He cheated the devil twice with me, and I ain't a-going to forget it. But say, what do you think of the sheriff's sister, Helen? Ain't she a winner, hey? Finest girl these parts have ever seen, all right, and her friend ain't second by no length, neither."

"Why, Bill," exclaimed Blake, a twinkle coming to his eyes, "you are not allowing yourself to get captured, are you? That's a risky game, like starting up The Orphan and the sheriff, for there's no telling just where it will stop."

"No, I ain't letting myself get captured," sighed Bill. "I ain't no fool. Bill Howland knows a thing or two, which he learned not more than a thousand years ago. I've got it all sized up. And since then I've seen a certain bang-up puncher hitting the trail for the sheriff's house some regular twice a week. Nope, I'm a batchler now and forever, long may I wave."

"Say," he continued, suddenly remembering something. "What's the sheriff up to now? Is he going to have a picnic out on Crawford's ranch? He asked me if he could have the lend of the stage on an off day some time soon. Wants me to drive it for him out to the A-Y and back. I don't know what his game is, and I don't care none. I'll do it, all right. But what's he going to do out there, anyhow?"

Blake laughed: "Oh, nothing bad, I reckon. You'll probably learn all about it as soon as the rest of us. How do you expect me to know anything about it? Mebby he is going to have a picnic out there for all we know. The A-Y is a good place for one, ain't it?"

"You just bet it is," cried Bill. "Your ranch is all right, Blake, but I like the A-Y better. It's got windmills and everything. Finest grove near the ranch-house that I ever saw, and I've seen some fine groves in my time. Old man Crawford knew a good thing when he saw it, all right. Here comes Charley Winter like he had all day to go nowhere–he's got a good job with the Cross Bar-8, but I wouldn't have it for a gift–no, sir, money wouldn't tempt me to be one of that outfit. But I reckon it's some better out there than it once was since the sheriff and The Orphant amputated its inflamed fingers. Hullo, Charley," he cried as the newcomer drew rein. "I was just telling Blake what a good job you have got with Sneed."

"Hullo, you old one-hoss driver," grinned Charley. "Hullo, Tom," he cried. "Looking for the sheriff?"

"Hullo, Charley," said the foreman, shaking hands with Sneed's substitute puncher. "Yes, I am. Do you know where he is?"

"He's out at the Cross Bar-8, giving Sneed a talking to," Charley answered. "Bucknell went and got loaded again last night, raised h–l in town and out of it all the way home. He thought he wanted to shoot up The Orphan, so he was some primed. Jim is telling Sneed to hold him down to water and peace unless he wants to lose him. He'll be in soon, though. How's The Orphan getting on out at your place?"

"Fine!" answered Blake, his face wearing a frown. "But I'm some sorry about that fool Bucknell, though. He may get on a spree some day and find The Orphan. I don't want any more gunplay, and if that idiot does find him and gets ambitious to notch up his gun another hole, there'll shore be some loose lead. If he ever gets on Star C ground, and I catch him there, I'll shore enough wipe up the earth with him, and when you see him, just tell him what I said, will you? It ain't no joke, for I will."

"Shore I'll tell him," replied Charley. "When will that bunch of cattle be on hand–I'm anxious to swap jobs."

Blake flashed him a warning glance and tried to ignore the question by changing the subject, but it was too late, for Bill was curious.

"What cattle is that, Charley?" asked the driver in sudden interest.

"Oh, some cattle that I'm going to get of Blake for Sneed," lied Charley easily.

"What in all get out does Sneed want with any Star C cows?" Bill asked in surprise. "He's got plenty of cows of his own, unless The Orphant shot a whole lot more than I thought he did."

"I don't know, Bill," replied Charley. "I didn't ask him, it being plainly none of my business."

Bill scratched his head: "No, I reckon not," he replied doubtfully.

"Here comes Shields now," said Blake suddenly. "I reckon I'll ride off and meet him. So long, Bill."

"So long," replied Bill. "Be sure to tell The Orphan I was asking about him. So long, Charley." He turned abruptly and entered the stage office: "I don't understand it," he muttered. "There's something in the wind that I can't get onto nohow. He has shore got me guessing some, all right."

The clerk tossed aside the paper and stared: "Well, that's too d–d bad, now ain't it?" he asked sarcastically. "You ought to object, that's what you ought to do! What right has anybody to keep quiet about their own business when you want to know, hey? If I wanted to know everybody's business as bad as you do, I'd shore raise h–l, I would. Why don't you choke it out of him, wipe up the earth with him? Go out right now and give him a piece of your mind."

"Oh, you would, would you! You're blamed smart, now ain't you? You work too hard–your nerves are giving away," drawled Bill as he picked up the paper. "Sitting around all day with your feet on the table and a pipe in your mouth that you're too lazy to light, working like the very devil trying to find time to do the company's business, which there ain't none to do. Ain't you ashamed to go to bed?–it must take a lot of gall to hunt your rest at night after finding it and hugging it all day. What would you do for a living if I forgot to bring the paper with me some day, hey? You ain't got enough animation to want to know what is going on in this little world of ours, you—"

"You get out of here, right now, too!" yelled the clerk. "I don't want you hanging around bothering me, you pest! Get out of here right now, before I get up and throw you out! Do you hear me!"

Bill crossed his legs, pushed back his sombrero, turned the page carefully and then remarked, "I licked four husky cow-punchers, real bad men, last month. One right after the other, and I was purty near all in, too." He glanced at the next page disinterestedly, spat at a fly on the edge of the box cuspidor and then added wearily and with great deprecation, "I'm feeling fine to-day, never felt so good in my life, but I need more exercise–I'm two pounds over weight right now."

The clerk showed interest and awe: "Weight?" he asked. "What is your fighting weight?"

Bill looked up aggressively: "Fighting weight?" he asked, raising his eyebrows. "My fighting weight is something over nine hundred pounds, when I'm real mad. Ordinarily, one hundred and eighty. Why?"

"Oh, nothing," replied the clerk, staring out of the window.

CHAPTER XIX
THE ORPHAN GOES TO THE A-Y

The A-Y had been a very busy place for the past two weeks because of the cattle which had to be re-branded and taken care of, and of other things which had to be done about the ranch. The sheriff had taken title and had persuaded Crawford to remain in nominal charge for a month at the most so as to keep the sale a secret until the new owner would be ready to make it known. So word went around that Crawford had hired the sheriff to put things on a paying basis and that half of the old outfit had left, their places being filled by Charley, the two Larkin brothers and two men from a northern ranch.

Shields had been very much pleased with the cattle which The Orphan had bought for him and had asked Blake if he could borrow the new puncher to help him get things in good running shape. Blake had told The Orphan of the sheriff's request and had advised him to accept, which the puncher was very glad to do. So this is how the former outlaw became temporary foreman of the A-Y under the sheriff.

Only the sheriff's most intimate friends knew his plans, one of whom was Charley Winter, who found food for mirth in the unique position things had taken. The sheriff's deputies who had lain out-doors all night on the Cross Bar-8 waiting to capture or kill the outlaw were now working under him, and the best of feelings prevailed. The man who had hunted The Orphan now employed him as the bearer of the responsibilities of the new ranch. Truly, a change!

While The Orphan was busy with his duties on the A-Y the sheriff rode to the Star C and sought out the foreman, whom he finally found engaged in freeing a cow that had become mired in a quicksand. As the terror-stricken animal galloped wildly away from the scene of torture and indignities to its person Blake mopped his face and began to scrape the quicksand from him.

"Playing life-saver, eh?" laughed the sheriff.

The foreman looked up and smiled sheepishly: "Yes," he replied as he shook hands with the sheriff. "One cow more or less won't make nor break no ranch, but I just can't see 'em suffer. The boys and I were passing, so we stopped and got to work. But cows ain't got no gratitude, not nohow! That ornery beast will be all ready to charge me the first time he sees me afoot. Did you see him try to horn me when I let go?"

His friend laughed, and when they had ridden some distance from the others he turned in his saddle:

"Well, The Orphan is working like a horse, and he likes it, too," he said. "You ought to hear him giving orders–he just asks a man to do a thing, don't order it done. When he talks it sounds like the puncher would be doing him the greatest possible favor to do the work he is paid to do, but there is a suggestion that if any nastiness develops, hell will be a peaceful place compared to the near vicinity of the foreman of the A-Y. He sizes up a thing with one look, and then tells how it should be done. Everything has gone off so fine that I'm going to ask you to lose a good man, and real soon, too. What do you say, Tom?"

Blake laughed: "Why, we were a-plenty before he came and we'll be a-plenty after he goes. That's for your asking me to turn him over to you. The boys will be both sorry and glad to have him leave, because they like him a whole lot. But of course they want to see him land everything that he can, so they'll give him a good send-off. That reminds me to say that I know they will want to be on hand when you break the news to him. It'll be a circus for your Eastern friend, Miss Ritchie."

"Now you're talking!" enthused the sheriff. "I want to have as many fireworks at the ceremony as I can possibly get. Oh, it'll be a great day, all right. We are all going out and take a bang-up lunch, just like we're going on that picnic that Bill's been so worried about, and Bill is going to drive the women over in his coach. The first surprise will be the announcement of the new ownership of the A-Y, and right on top of it I'm going to fire the second gun. I hope none of your boys know anything about it," he added with anxiety.

"Not a thing," hastily replied the foreman. "You have your wife send a message to me by Joe when he rustles our mail to-morrow and ask us to come to the picnic at the A-Y on the day which you will decide on. They'll go, all right, no fear about that. Nothing more than your wife's cooking is needed to attract them," and he laughed heartily at how suddenly they would come to life at such a summons.

Shields thought intently for a few seconds and then slapped his thigh: "I've got it!" he exulted. "I'll ride over to your place with you and write a letter to my wife telling her just what to do. Joe can deliver it and bring back the invitation. You see, I won't be home to-night, but that will do the trick, all right. Now, what do you say to this coming Saturday?–this is, let me see: Wednesday. Will that be time enough for you to make any arrangements you may want to make?"

"Shore, plenty of time," Blake laughed. "It's good all the way. Joe will be delighted to have a real good excuse to call at your house. He's a bashful cuss, like all the rest. They talk big, but they're some bashful all the same. He's been worrying about it, for one day he came to me with a funny expression on his face and acted like he didn't know how to begin. So I asked him what was troubling him, and he blurted out like this, as near as I can remember:

"'Well, you know Mrs. Shields said we was to go to her house when any of us hit town?' he asked.

"'I shore do,' I answered, wondering what was up.

"'Well, I go to town a lot, and it takes a h–l of a lot of gall to do it,' he complained, looking so serious that it was funny.

"'Gall!' said I, surprised-like, and trying to keep my face straight. 'Gall! Well, I can't see that it takes such a brave man to call at a friend's house when he's been told to do it.'

"'Oh, that part of it is all right," he replied. 'But she'll think I only call to get my face fed, and it makes me feel like a–I don't know what. You see, I always get away quick.'

"'Well, stay longer, there ain't no use of being in a hurry,' I said. 'Stay and talk a while.'

"'Then they'll think I ain't got enough and push more pie at me, like they did once,' he complained.

"'Suppose I give Silent your terrible ordeal to do,' I suggested tentatively, 'or Bud, he's dead anxious for your job.'

"'Oh, it ain't as bad as that!' he cried quickly. 'I only thought that I'd speak to you about it. I thought you could suggest something.'

"'Well,' I replied, 'every time you call you say I sent you over to ask about the sheriff's health. How'll that do?'

"He grinned sheepishly and then swore: 'H–l, that would make a shore enough mess of it,' he cried. 'I'd be a royal American idiot to say a thing like that, now, wouldn't I?'"

The sheriff laughed heartily, and they talked about the picnic until they had reached the ranch-house, where he wrote the note to his wife. Bidding his friend good-by, he rode out past the corrals and headed for the A-Y.

When about half-way to his own ranch, and on A-Y ground, he surmounted a rise and saw a figure flit from sight behind a thicket, and his curiosity was immediately aroused. Not knowing who the man might be, he stalked his quarry and finally found Bucknell standing beside his horse.

"Well, what's the trouble now?" the sheriff asked as he came out into sight. He was dangerously near angry, for Bucknell was on forbidden ground and was flushed as if from liquor. "What's the trouble?" he repeated.

Bucknell looked confused: "Nothing, Sheriff. Why?" he asked, evading the searching gaze of the peace officer.

"Oh, I thought something might have gone wrong on the Cross Bar-8, and that you were looking for me," Shields coldly replied.

Bucknell looked at the ground and coughed nervously before he replied, which only made the sheriff all the more determined to get at the matter in a true light.

"No, nothing's wrong," replied the puncher. "I was just riding out this way–I was some nervous, that's all."

"That don't go with me!" the sheriff said sharply. "I've lived too long to bite on a yarn like that. Why, you can't look at me!"

The puncher did not reply and the sheriff continued:

"Now, look here, Bucknell, take some good advice from me–stay on your ranch, mind your own business and let liquor alone. As sure as you monkey around the Star C Blake will give you a d—n sound licking, and he's man enough to do it, too, make no error. And as for the A-Y, well, the temporary foreman of that ranch is the cleverest man with a gun that I ever saw, and I've seen some good ones in my time. If you go up against him you'll get shot, for he'd think you were about the easiest proposition he ever met. As sure as you drink you'll get drunk, and as sure as you get drunk you'll work up an appetite for a fight, and if you pick a fight with him you'll never know what hit you. You stick to water and the Cross Bar-8."

"Oh, I reckon I can take care of my own business," sullenly replied Bucknell. "I can come out here drunk or sober if I wants to, I reckon."

"You can do nothing of the kind," rejoined the sheriff. "And you certainly ought to be able to take care of your own business, as you say," he retorted, holding his temper with an effort. "But in the past you didn't, and you may not in the future. And when your business gets too big for you to handle it gets into my hands, and if you make any trouble I'll d—n soon convince you that I can handle your surplus. Now, get out of here and think it over."

Bucknell swung into his saddle and then turned, the liquor making him reckless.

"D—n it!" he cried. "The Orphant killed Jimmy and a whole lot more good cow-punchers! He's nothing but a murdering thief, a d––d rustler, that's what he is! And you are his best friend, it seems!"

The wan smile flickered across the sheriff's face, but still he refrained, for such is the foolish consideration given by brave men to liquor. A drunkard may do much with impunity, for the argument states he is not responsible, forgetting that in the beginning he was responsible enough to have left liquor alone, and that injury, whether unintentional or not, is still injury.

"There is no seem about it!" he retorted. "I am his best friend, and he needs friends bad enough, God knows. But speaking of murder, those four good cow-punchers that stopped me in the defile tried hard enough to qualify at it, and The Orphan not only saved me, but also some of them, for I'd a gotten some of them before I cashed. You're a h–l of a fine cub to talk about murders, you are!"

"That's all right," retorted Bucknell, "he's just what I said he was. And a side pardner of our brave sheriff, too!"

"D—n you!" shouted Shields, his face dark with passion. "You have said enough, any more from you and I'll break your dirty neck! Just because I felt sorry for you when you got half killed in the saloon and let you stay in the country don't think you are the boss of this section. When I saw what a pitiful, drunken wreck you were, I felt sorry for you, but not any more. You don't want decent treatment, you want to get clubbed, and you're right in line to get just what you need, too! Now, I'm not going to stand any more of your d—d foolishness–my patience is played out. And if you were half a man you wouldn't sit there like a bump on a log and swallow what I'm saying–you'd put up a fight if you died for it. You are no good, just a drunken, lawless fool of a puncher; just a bag of wind, and it's up to you to walk a chalk line or I'll give you a taste of what I carry around with me for bums of your kind. What in h–l do you think I am? No, you don't, you stay right where you are 'til I get good and ready to have you go! You've come d––d near the end of your rope and there is just one thing for you to do, and that is, get out of this country and do it quick! You stay on your own side of the Limping Water, for if I catch you riding off any nervousness off of Cross Bar-8 ground without word from your foreman, I'll shoot you down like I'd shoot a coyote! And for a dollar I'd wipe up the earth with you right now! You d—d, sneaking, cowardly cur, you tin-horn bully! Pull your stakes and get scarce and don't you open your mouth to me–come on, lively! Pull your freight!"

Bucknell slowly rode away, his eyes to the ground and not daring to say what seethed in his heart. He swore to himself that he would get square some day on both, not realizing in his anger that when sober he feared them both.

The sheriff stared after him and then returned to the point where he had left his horse. As he mounted he shook his head savagely and swore. Glancing again after the puncher he struck into a canter and rode toward the ranch.

CHAPTER XX
BILL ATTENDS THE PICNIC

The picnic aroused quite a stir for so frivolous a thing. When Blake read Mrs. Shields' invitation to the outfit they acted like schoolboys dismissed for a vacation. Grins of delight were the style on the Star C, and the overflow of bubbling happiness took the form of practical joking against Humble, whose life suddenly held much anxiety. In Ford's Station there was an air of expectancy, and Bill spent all of Saturday morning from daylight until time to start in cleaning his stage and grooming the horses, whose astonishment quickly passed into prohibitive indignation. After narrowly escaping broken bones and chewed arms Bill decided that the sextet could go as it was.

"Serves 'em right!" he yelled to his friendly enemy, the clerk, after he had barely dodged a vicious kick, wildly waving a curry comb. "Let the ignoramuses go like they are! Let 'em show how cheap and common they are! They never was any good for anything, anyhow, eating their heads off and kicking their best friend!"

"How about the time they beat out them Apaches?" asked the clerk, settling back comfortably against the coach.

"You get out!" yelled Bill pugnaciously. "Who asked you for talk, hey? And get away from that coach, you idiot, you'll dirty it all up!"

"Sic 'em, Tige!" jeered the clerk pleasantly. "Chew 'em up!"

"What!" yelled Bill, swiftly grabbing up the pail of water which stood near him. "Sic 'em, is it!" he cried, running forward. "Chew 'em up, hey!" he continued, heaving the contents of the pail at the clerk, who nimbly sprang inside the vehicle and slammed the door shut behind him as the water struck it. He leaped out of the other door and was safely away before Bill realized what had happened. Then the driver said things when he saw the mess he had made of the coach, upon which he had spent two hard hours in polishing.

"Suffering dogs!" he shouted, dancing first on one foot and then on the other. "Now look what you've done! You're a h–l of a feller, you are! After me rubbing the skin off'n my hands and breaking my arms a-polishing it up! You good for nothing, mangy half-breed! Wait till I get a hold of you, you long pair of legs, you! Just wait! I'll show you, all right!"

The clerk twiddled his fingers from afar and jeered in his laughter: "Serves you right! Sic 'em, Towser! Eat 'em up, Fido! Sic 'em, sic 'em!" he shouted joyously, and forthwith ran for his life.

Bill returned to the coach and worked like mad to undo the evil effects he had wrought and finally succeeded in bringing a phantom glow to the time-battered wood. Then he hitched up and drove to the sheriff's house, where he saw huge baskets on the porch.

"Good morning, Mrs. Shields," he said as he stamped to the door. "Good morning, ladies."

"Good morning William," replied the sheriff's wife as she hurried to collect shawls and blankets. "Will you mind putting those baskets on the coach, William? We will soon be ready."

"Why, certainly not, ma'am," he answered, recklessly grabbing up the two largest. "Jimminee!" he exulted. "These are shore heavy, all right, all right! Must be plumb full of good things! To-day is where your Uncle Bill Halloway gets square for the dinner the company froze him out of. Wonder if there's apricot pie in this one?" he mused curiously. He gingerly raised the cover and a grin distorted his face. "Must be six, yes, eight–mebby ten!" he soliloquized as he placed it on the stage. "Hullo, bottles of some kind," he whispered as he picked up another basket. "Hear the little devils clink, eh? Must be coffee and tea, hey? Yes, shore enough it is. Good Lord, how hungry I am–wish I had eaten that breakfast this morning–how in thunder did I know we was going to be so late? I'll be the strong man at this picnic, all right!"

"Here are some blankets, William," called Mrs. Shields. "Helen, would you mind showing him how to carry that box?–he's sure to turn it upside down if you don't."

"Next!" he cried, returning from the trip with the blankets. "I put them blankets up on top, Mrs. Shields, is it all right? How do you do, Miss Helen, any more freight?"

"How do you do," she replied. "This box is to go, please. Now, do be very careful not to turn it up, or jar it!" she warned. "And put it on the seat inside the coach where we can steady it."

"Gee, what's in it?" asked Bill, nearly dying from his curiosity. "Must be the joker of the feast, eh?"

"Three layer cakes," she laughingly replied. "Chocolate, coconut and lemon."

"Um!" he said. "I'll carry this one high up, it deserves it."

"Oh, do be careful!" she cried as he swooped it up to his shoulder. "Oh!" she screamed as it thumped against the top of the door frame.

"Whoa! Back up!" cried Bill, executing the order. "Easy, boy–all right, off we go!"

"Grace, Mary," cried Helen, "we are all ready to go!"

"Ain't there any more boxes?" asked Bill from the coach.

"Come, girls," cried Mrs. Shields as she stepped into the coach. "Close the door after you, and lock it, dear."

Bill gallantly helped the ladies into the coach, grinned at the cake box and started toward the front wheel when he was called back.

"Now, William," cautioned Mrs. Shields, laughing. "We will not be pursued by Apaches to-day, and this cake must not be shaken!"

"You won't know you're riding, ma'am, you shore won't," he assured her as he danced toward the front wheel again.

"Wake up there, you!" he yelled from the box. "Come on, Jerry, think you're glued to the earth? Come on, Tom! Easy there, you fool jackrabbit! –haven't you learned that you can't reach this high!"

When they had arrived at the A-Y the baskets were carried into the ranch-house and the women became very busy getting things ready for the feast. Bill took care of his team and then carried the blankets to the grove.

While the picnic was being prepared there arose a series of blood-curdling whoops off to the south where the outfit of the Star C made the air blue with powder smoke. As they came nearer something peculiar was noticed by Helen. It appeared to be a sort of drag drawn by a horse and supported by two long, springy poles, one end of which rested on the ground, and the other fastened to the saddle. While she wondered Bill came up and she turned to him for light.

"What have they got fastened to that horse?" she asked him.

He looked and then smiled: "Why, it is a travois," he said. "But what under the sun have they got on it? They must be bringing their own grub!"

The travois dragged and bumped over the uneven plain and soon came near enough for its burden to be made out. A man and a dog were strapped to it.

At this point Blake joined Helen and Bill, and as he did so he espied the travois.

"Thunder!" he cried, running forward. "Somebody is hurt! What's the matter, Silent?" he shouted.

"Matter?" asked Silent, in surprise as the outfit drew near. "There ain't nothing the matter. Why?"

"What's that travois doing with you, then?" Blake demanded.

Silent's face was as grave as that of an owl. "Travois?" he asked. Then his face cleared: "Oh, yes–I near forgot about it," he added, apologetically. "You see, Humble he shore wanted his dog to come to the picnic, so we reckoned we'd let it come along. Bud and Jim was for slinging it at the end of a rope and dragging it over, but I said no. We ain't got any ropes to have all frayed out and cut a-dragging dogs to picnics, and I said so, too. So we built the travois and strapped Lightning to it. When Humble saw what we had done he acted real unpolite. He said as how he wasn't going to have no dog of his'n toted twenty miles in a fool travois. Said that he'd make it stay home first, which was some mean after inviting the dog to come along. He said that he'd go in a travois himself first before he'd let the setter be made a fool of. Well, we simply had to subdue him, and he got so unreasonable that we just had to tie him with his dog. He shore does get awful pig-headed at times."

"Take off the gag, Jim," requested Silent, turning to the grinning cow-puncher. "Let him loose now, we've arrived."

Jim leaned over and whispered in Humble's ear, the information being that there were ladies about, and that all swearing must be thought and not yelled. Then he slipped the gag, and untied the ropes. Gales of laughter met the angry and indignant puncher when he had leaped to his feet, and he flashed one quick glance at the women and then, boiling with wrath and suppressed profanity, fled toward the corrals as swiftly as cramped muscles would allow. The dog snarled at its tormentors and then set off in hot pursuit of its discomfited master, whose waving arms kept time with his speeding legs.

"That's all the thanks we get," grumbled Bud, "but then, he don't know any better anyhow."

Blake laughed and regarded his grinning and expectant outfit, and the longer he looked at them the more he laughed. They had paid their respects to the women while Silent explained about the travois and now they cast many longing glances at the blankets and cloths spread out on the grass and at the baskets which Bill was busy over. They had tried to coax the driver to them to give information as to what they might expect in the way of edibles, but he had haughtily and disdainfully refused to enlighten them, taking care, however, to arouse their curiosity by looking fondly at the box and the baskets and even showed his elation by taking several fancy steps for their benefit.

"Well, get rid of the cayuses," said Blake, "and square things with Humble. Bring him back with you or you don't get any pie. You're such a darn fool crowd that I can't get mad this time, but don't ever drag a man in a travois again."

"Did he come, or was he kidnapped?" murmured Bud. "What we did once we can do again, and Humble will be on hand when the feast begins."

Jim had been scowling at Bill, whose manners were most aggravating. "You just wait, you heathen," threatened Jim. "You're ace high with the grub, all right, but just you wait 'til we get you alone!"

"Yah!" laughed the driver. "I shore can handle the best cow-wrastler that ever lived."

"Bill seems to be running this here festival," Bud complained to Helen.

"Oh, he is our right-hand man," she replied with enthusiasm. "We couldn't possibly get along without him, now. He has charge of the pie and cake."

Bill's chest expanded: "I'm foreman of the pie and cake herd," he exclaimed proudly. "You can't get ahead of me."

Bud looked at the driver and then significantly waved his hand at the travois: "And you'll shore travel in style, just like a real pie foreman, too, when we gets a chance to honor you like we wants to."

"You'll get no pie if you acts smart, little boy," retorted the driver. "Run along and play till lunch is ready, and don't dirty your hands and face."

"Well, we've got fine memories," Bud suggested as he led the way to the corrals, where he found The Orphan.

"Hullo, Orphan!" he cried enthusiastically as he gripped the outstretched hand. "Plumb glad to see you. How's things?"

"Glad to see you, boys," cried the temporary foreman, who was all smiles. "One at a time!" he laughed as they crowded about him. "Make yourselves right at home–that smallest corral is for your cayuses. And you'll find plenty of soap and water and towels by the bunk-house, and there's a box of good cigars, a tin of tobacco, and a jug on the table inside. Help yourself to anything you want, the place is all yours."

"Gee, this is a good game, all right," Bud laughed as he turned to put his horse in the corral. "The sheriff shore knows how to deal."

"Leave a cigar for me, Silent," jokingly warned Jim as his friend turned toward the bunk-house. "Too many smokes will make you sick."

"Well, you've got a gall, all right!" retorted Silent. "You better let me bring yours out to you and keep away from the box, for I'm always plumb suspicious of these goody-goody, it's-for-your-own-good people."

A crafty look came to Jack Lawson's face and he turned to The Orphan: "Has Bill Howland got his cigars yet?" he asked, winking at his friends.

"Why, I don't know whether he has or not," replied The Orphan. "But I don't believe that he has been out of sight of the pies since he came. They've got him in a trance."

"Guess I'll take him one," continued Jack, grinning broadly. "He likes to smoke."

"Shore enough, go ahead," endorsed the foreman of the A-Y as he turned toward the grove. Then he stopped, and with a knowing look added: "If you want to see Humble, he just went in the bunk-house."

A yell of dismay arose as the outfit started pell-mell for the house. Silent entered it first and his profanity informed his companions that their fears were well grounded. Neither Humble, cigars, tobacco nor jug were to be seen, and a search was forthwith instituted. Jack looked at a distant corral and saw Lightning as the dog disappeared from sight into it.

"Hey!" he cried. "He's in the big corral–I just saw his dog go in, and it was wagging its tail a whole lot. Come on, we'll surround it and show that frisky gent a thing or two!"

No more words were wasted, and in a very short time figures were creeping around the corral. Then there was a scramble as most of the searchers scaled the wall at different points while two of them ran in through the gate. The first thing they saw was the dog, and his tail was still wagging as he curiously followed, nose to the ground, a huge horned toad. He looked up at the sudden disturbance and backed off suspiciously, looking for a way to escape.

"— —!" chorused the fooled punchers, who discovered that deductions don't always deduct, and then they returned to the bunk-house to "slick up." When finally satisfied about their appearance they made their way to the grove and the sight which greeted their eyes as they entered it almost made them drop in their tracks.

Humble and Bill sat cross-legged on a blanket, which was surrounded with guns. The jug, tobacco and cigars were flanked by pies and a cake, while each of the conspirators held a lighted cigar in one hand while they took turns at the jug. A huge piece of pie rested in a plate at Humble's side, while Bill's knee held a piece of cake.

"Hands up!" shouted Humble, grabbing a gun. "Don't you dare to raid the gallery! You stay right where you are!"

Bill's blacksnake whip leaped from point to point experimentally, picking up twigs and leaves with disturbing accuracy.

The invaders halted just beyond the range of the whip and consulted uneasily, not noticing that the driver had shortened his weapon by twice the length of its handle. Finally Jim and Docile ran back toward the corral while their friends waited impatiently for their return, grinning at the enemy with an I-told-you-so air.

Bill suddenly leaned forward, the whip slid down into his hand to the end of the handle and cracked viciously. Joe Haines, who had grown a little careless, leaped into the air and yelled, grabbing at his leg.

"Keep your distance, you!" warned the driver, trying to look ferocious. "Twenty feet is the dead-line, children."

Jim and Docile returned apace and brought with them half a dozen lariats, which ranged in length from thirty to forty feet.

"Hey, you!" cried Humble in alarm. "That ain't fair!"

Grim silence was the only reply as the invaders each took his rope and surrounded the two. Then, suddenly, the air was full of darting ropes and in less time than it takes to tell of it the pair were hopelessly and helplessly trussed. Silent ran in and hurled the whip away and then squatted before the prisoners, throwing their cigars after the whip as he took up the pie and cake, which he tantalizingly munched before their eyes.

"I like a hog, all right, but you suit me too blamed well!" asserted Bud, grabbing at Silent's pie.

"Gimme some of that," demanded Jim, trying for the cake. And when the disturbance had ceased there were no signs of either pie or cake.

"It's the travois for you, Humble dear!" softly hummed Charley Bailey. "And to the ranch, by the way of town!"

"And Bill will be pleased to explore the Limping Water on the bottom," amended Jim. "One of us can drive the women home!"

CHAPTER XXI
THE ANNOUNCEMENT

About thirty people sat in a circle on the grass in the grove on the A-Y, engaged in taking viands from the well-filled plates which made the rounds. Keen humor from all sides kept them in roars of laughter, Humble and Bill provoking the greater part of it. Humble sat next to Miss Ritchie, while The Orphan and Bill flanked Helen, the sheriff next to his new foreman. Humble's face had a look of benign condescension when he allowed himself to bestow perfunctory attentions on the members of his outfit, whom he graciously called "purty fair punchers in a way."

Crawford, the former owner of the A-Y, sat next to Shields, and when the lunch had reached the cigar stage he arose and cleared his throat.

"Ladies and Gentlemen, Bill and Humble," he began amid laughter. "I have been regarded as the host of this picnic, and the false position embarrasses me. But any such momentary feeling is compensated by the importance of what I have to tell you.

"When I took up the A-Y it was with a determination to keep it and to spend the rest of my days on it in peace. This I have found to be impossible, and in consequence I have turned it over to a better man. The energy which I have seen applied in the right way for the last few weeks has assured me that the A-Y will soon be second in importance and wealth to no ranch in this country. I have seen order, system, emerge from chaos; I have seen five thousand cattle re-branded and taken care of in such dispatch as to astonish me and be almost beyond my belief. The sheriff has been as economical in the use of his energy as he can be in the use of his words. By that I don't mean in the way that is causing you to smile, but simply that he knows how to accomplish the most work with the least possible expenditure of effort and time, as witnessed by the condition of this ranch to-day. But while he has been the guiding spirit in the work of putting the ranch on its proper footing, he has had as good assistants as it is possible to find.

"I don't wish to tire you with any long speech, for brevity is the soul of more than wit, so I will close by telling you that the A-Y is in new and better hands–our sheriff is now its owner, and I extend to him my heartiest wishes for his success in his new venture. I must thank him and all of you for a very pleasant day and a memory to take East with me."

For an instant there was intense silence, and then a small battle seemed to be taking place. The noise of the shooting and cheering was deafening and smoke rolled down like a heavy fog. The sheriff met the rush toward him and put in a very busy few minutes in shaking hands and replying to the hearty congratulations which poured in upon him from all sides. Everybody was happy and all were talking at once, and Bill could be heard reeling off an unbroken string of words at high speed.

The Orphan fought his way to his best friend and gripped both hands in his own.

"By God, Sheriff!" he cried. "This is great news, and I'm plumb glad to hear it! I hope you have the very best of luck and that your returns, both in pleasure and money, far exceed your fondest expectations. Anything I can do is yours for the asking."

"Thank you, son," replied the sheriff, looking fondly into his friend's eyes. "I'm going to call on you just as soon as I can make myself heard in all this hellabaloo. Just listen to that!" he exclaimed as Silent let loose again.

"Glory be!" yelled he of the misleading name, slapping Humble across the back. "For this you ride home like a white man, Humble–all your sins are forgiven! Hurrah for the sheriff, his family and the A-Y!" he shouted at the top of his lungs, and his cheer was supported unanimously with true cowboy enthusiasm and vim.

"Hurray for me, too!" shouted Bill in laughter. Then he fled, with Silent in hot pursuit.

The sheriff tried to speak, and after several attempts was finally given silence.

"Thank you, everybody!" he cried, his face beaming. "I am happy for many reasons to-day, but foremost among them is the fact that I have so many warm and loyal friends. The A-Y is always open to all of you, and I'll be some disappointed if you don't put in a lot of your spare time over here."

He paused for a few seconds and then looked at The Orphan, who stood at Helen's side.

"Mr. Crawford did his part a whole lot better than I can do mine, I'm afraid, but I'm going to do my best, anyhow. The news has only been half told–the name of the new foreman of the A-Y henceforth will be The Orphan! Whoop her up, boys!" he shouted, leading a cheer which was not one whit less a cheer than those which had gone before.

The Orphan stared in astonishment, for once in his life he had been surprised. The sheriff at last had the drop on him. He looked from one to another, started to step forward and then changed his mind and looked appealingly at Helen, who smiled in a way to double the speed of his heart-beats.

Her eyes were moist, and the sudden consciousness that she formed half of the objective of all eyes caused her cheeks to go crimson. Her hand impulsively went to his shoulder and without thought on her part, and his incredulous questioning was answered by her.

"It's all true," she said earnestly. "I've known of it for a whole week now. You are the real foreman of the A-Y, and I most earnestly hope for your success."

He suddenly seemed to be above the earth and his voice broke in his stammered reply. For a fraction of a second her eyes had told him what he had dreamed of, what he had hoped for above all things, and he grasped her hand for a second as he stepped forward toward his new employer, whose hand met his with a man's grasp.

"Thank you, Sheriff," he said, his head whirling from the surprises of a minute. "You've been squarer and fairer with me than any man I've ever known, and hell will look nice to me if I don't make good with you.

"Thank you, boys; thank you, Bill: you're all right, every one of you!" he cried as his friends crowded about him. "What the sheriff said about warm friends was the truth–thank you, Bud and Jim! Thank you, Blake–you're another brick! Good God, what I have gained in two months! I can scarcely believe it, it seems so like a dream. That's a real warm grip, all right, though," he exclaimed as he shook hands with Humble, "so I reckon it's all true. Two months!" he marveled. "Two glorious, glorious months! A new start in life, a loyal crowd of friends, a–and all in two months! And there is the man I owe it all to," he suddenly cried, pointing to the sheriff. "There's the whitest man God ever made, and I'll kill the man who says I lie!"

"Good boy!" shouted Bill in enthusiastic endorsement. "You two make a pair of aces what can beat any full-house ever got together, and I'll lick the man who says I lie!" he yelled pugnaciously. "The Orphant may be an orphant, all right, but he's got a whole lot of brothers."

Mrs. Shields walked over to The Orphan and placed a motherly hand on his shoulder as he recovered.

"You won't be an orphan any longer, my boy," she said, smiling up at him. "You're one of us now–I always wanted a son, and God has given me one in you."

CHAPTER XXII
TEX WILLIARD'S MISTAKE

During the month which followed the picnic things ran smoothly on the A-Y, and the rejuvenated ranch was the pride of the whole contingent, from the sheriff down to the cook. The Orphan had taken charge with a determination which grew firmer with each passing day and the new owner was delighted at the outcome of his plans. The foreman, elated and happy at his sudden shift in fortune, radiated cheerfulness and consideration. His men knew that he would not ask them to do anything which he himself feared to do, which would not have been much consolation to a timid man, since he feared nothing; but to them it meant that they had a foreman who would stick by them through fire and water, and a foreman who commands respect from his outfit is a man whose life is made easy for him. He had known too much of unkindness, harshness, to become angry at mistakes; instead, he set diligently at work to undo them, and mistakes were rare. The very men who had once wished for his life would now fight instantly to save it. They were proud of him, of the owner, the ranch and themselves; and proudest of all was Bill, once driver of the stage, but now a cowboy working hard and loyally under the man who had once held him up for a smoke.

Visitors were numerous, and every man who called became enthusiastic about the ranch, and after he had departed marveled at the complete change in the man who was its foreman, and felt confidence in the good judgment of the sheriff. Ford's Station was openly jubilant, for the town exulted in the discomfiture of the Cross Bar-8 and in the proof that their sheriff was right. And Ford's Station chuckled at the news it heard, for the foreman of the Cross Bar-8 had called twice at the A-Y and was fast losing his prejudice against The Orphan. Sneed had found a quiet, optimistic foreman in the place of his former enemy, and the laughter which lurked in The Orphan's eyes closed the breach.

He had seen the man in a new light, and when he had said his farewell at the close of his second visit the grip of his hand was strong. As for the Star C, a trail had been worn between the two ranches and hardly a day passed but one or more of its punchers dropped in to say a few words to their former bunkmate, and to stir up Bill. The Star C, no less than his own men, swore by The Orphan.

One bright morning the sheriff left for a trip to Chicago and other packing cities to arrange for future cattle shipments, and announced that he would be away for a week or two. On the night following his departure trouble began. The ranch and bunk houses of the Cross Bar-8 were fired into, and when Sneed and his men had returned after a fruitless search in the dark the foreman stared at the wall and swore. Was it The Orphan again? In the absence of the sheriff had he renewed the war? First thought cried that he had, but gradually the idea became untenable. Why should The Orphan risk his splendid berth on the A-Y, his prospects now rich in promise, to work off any lingering hatred? When Sneed had shaken hands with him he found apparent sincerity in the warm clasp. He would ride over at daylight and have the matter settled once and for all. And if satisfied that The Orphan was guiltless of the outrage he would turn his whole attention to the imitator of the former outlaw.

The Orphan was mending his saddle girth when he saw Sneed cantering past the farthest corral. The latter's horse bore all the signs of hard riding and he looked up inquiringly at the visitor.

"Good morning, Sneed," he said pleasantly, arising and laying aside the saddle. "What's up, anything?"

"Yes, and I came over to find out about it," Sneed answered. "I hardly know how to begin–but here, I'll tell it from the beginning," and he related what had occurred, much to the wonder of The Orphan.

"Now," finished the visitor, "I want to ask you a question, although I may be a d—n fool for doing it. But I want to get this thing thrashed out. Do you know who did it?"

The foreman of the A-Y straightened up, his eyes flashing, and then he realized that Sneed had some right to question him after what had occurred in the past.

"No, Sneed, I do not," he answered, "but in two guesses I can name the man!"

"Good!" cried Sneed. "Go ahead!"

"Bucknell?"

"No, he was with me in the bunk-house," replied the foreman of the Cross Bar-8. "It wasn't him–go on."

"Tex Williard," said The Orphan with decision.

"Tex?" cried Sneed. "Why?"

"It's plain as day, Sneed," The Orphan answered. "He's sore at me, but lacks nerve."

"But, thunderation, how would he hurt you by shooting at us?" Sneed demanded, impatiently.

"Oh, he would scare up a war during the sheriff's absence by throwing your suspicions on me. He reckoned you would think that I did it, get good and mad, fly off the handle and raise h–l generally. He figured that I, according to the past, would meet you half way and that you or some of your men might kill me. If you didn't, he reckoned that the sheriff would kick me out of this berth, and that one or both of us might get killed in the argument. He could sit back and laugh to himself at how easy it was to square up old scores from a distance. It's Tex as sure as I am here, and unless Tex changes his plans and gets out of this country d—n soon he won't be long in getting what he seems to ache for."

Sneed pushed back his sombrero and smiled grimly: "I reckon that you're right," he replied. "But you ain't sore at the way I asked, are you? I had to begin somewhere, you know."

"Sore?" rejoined his companion, angrily. "Sore? I'm so sore that I'm going out after Tex right now. And I'll get him or know the reason why, too. You go back and post your men about this–and tell them on no account to ride over my range for a few days, for they might get hurt before they are known. Put a couple of them to bed as soon as you get back–you need them to keep watch nights."

He turned toward the corral and called to a man who was busy near it: "Charley, you take anybody that you want and get in a good sleep before nightfall. I will want both of you to work to-night."

"All right, after dinner will be time enough," Charley replied. "I'll take Lefty Lukins."

The Orphan went into the ranch house and returned at once with his rifle, a canteen of water and a package of food. As he threw a saddle on his horse Bill galloped up, waving his arms and very much excited.

"Hey, Orphant!" he shouted. "Somebody's shore enough plugged some of our cows near the creek! I lost his trail at the Cottonwoods!"

"All right, Bill," replied the foreman, "I'll go out and look them over. You take another horse and ride to the Star C. Tell Blake to keep watch for Tex Williard, and tell him to hold Tex for me if he sees him. Lively, Bill!"

Bill stared, leaped from his horse, took the saddle from its back and was soon lost to sight in the corral. In a few minutes he galloped past his foreman and Sneed swearing heartily. His quirt arose and fell and soon he was lost to sight over a rise near the ranch-house.

The foreman of the A-Y rode over to Charley: "Charley, in case I don't get back to-night, you and Lefty keep guard somewhere out here, and shoot any man who don't halt at your hail. If I return in the dark I'll whistle Dixie as soon as I see the lights in the bunk house, and I'll keep it up so you won't mistake me. So long."

Sneed and he cantered away together and soon they parted, the former to ride toward his ranch, the latter toward the Cottonwoods near the Limping Water and along the trail left by Bill.

When near the grove The Orphan saw five dead cows and he quickly dismounted to examine them.

"Not dead for long," he muttered as he examined the blood on them. He leaped into his saddle and galloped through the grove. "Now, by God, somebody pays for them!" he muttered.

Here was a sudden change in things, positions had been reversed, and now he could appreciate the feelings which he had, more than once, aroused in the hearts of numerous foremen. He emerged from the grove and rode rapidly along the trail left by the perpetrator, alert, grim and angry. Soon the trail dipped beneath the waters of the creek and he stopped and thought for a few seconds. If it was Tex, he would not have ridden toward the Cross Bar-8 and the town, and neither would he have ridden south toward the Star C, nor north in the direction of the A-Y. He would seek cover for the day if he was still determined to carry on his game, and would not emerge until night covered his movements. That left him only the west along the creek, and more than that, the creek turned to the south again about five miles farther on and flowed far too close to the ranch-houses of the Star C for safety. He must have left the water at the turn, and toward the turn rode The Orphan, watching intently for the trail to emerge on either bank. His deductions were sound, for when he had rounded the bend of the stream he picked up the trail where it left the water and followed it westward.

The country around the bend was very wild and rough, for ravines between the hills cut seams and gashes in the plain. The underbrush was shoulder high, and he did not know how soon he might become a target. The trail was very fresh in the soft loam of the ravines and the broken branches and trampled leaves were still wet with sap. Soon he hobbled his horse and proceeded on foot, but to one side of and parallel with the trail. He had spent an hour in his advance and had begun to regret having left his horse so early, when he heard the report of a gun near at hand and a bullet hissed viciously over his head as he stooped to go under a low branch.

He threw up his arms, the rifle falling from his hands, pitched forward and rolled down the side of the hill and behind a fallen tree trunk which lay against a thicket. As soon as he had gained this position he glanced in the direction from whence the shot had come and, finding himself screened from sight on that side, quickly jerked off his boots and planted them among the bushes, where they looked as if he had crawled in almost out of sight. That done, he crawled along the ground under the protection of the tree trunk and then squirmed under it, when he pushed himself, feet first, deep into a tangled thicket and waited, Colt in hand, for a sign of his enemy's approach.

A quarter of an hour had passed in silence when a shot, followed by another, sounded from the hillside. After the lapse of a like interval another shot was fired, this time from the opposite direction. He saw a twig fall by the boots and heard the spat! of the bullet as it hit a stone. Two more shots sounded in rapid succession, and then another long interval of silence. Half an hour passed, but he was not impatient. He most firmly believed that his man would, sooner or later, come out to examine the boots, and time was of no consequence: he wanted the man.

Whoever he was, he was certainly cautious, he did not believe in taking any chances. It was almost certain that he would not leave until he had been assured that he had accomplished his purpose, for it would be most disconcerting at some future time to unexpectedly meet the man he thought he had murdered. Another shot whizzed into the place where the body should have been, according to the silent testimony of the boots. It sounded much closer to the thicket, but in the same direction of the last few shots. Then, after ten minutes of silence, a twig snapped, and directly behind the thicket in which The Orphan was hidden! The foreman's nerves were tense now, his every sense was alert, for his was a most dangerous position. He quickly glanced over his shoulder into the thicket and found that he could not penetrate the mass of leaves and branches, which reassured him. He was very glad that he had forced himself well into the cover, for soon the leaves rustled and a pebble rolled not more than four feet off, and in front of him, slightly at his right. More rustling and then a head and shoulder slowly pushed past him into view. The man moved very slowly and cautiously and was crouched, his head far in advance of his waist. The Orphan could see only one side of the face, the angle of the man's jaw and an ear, but that was enough, for he knew the owner. Slowly and without a sound the foreman's right hand turned at the wrist until the Colt gleamed on a line with the other's heart. The searcher leaned forward and to one side, that he might better see the boots, when a sound met his ears.

"Don't move," whispered the foreman.

The prowler stiffened in his tracks, frozen to rigidity by the command. Then he slowly turned his head and looked squarely into the gun of the man he thought he had killed.

"Christ!" he cried hoarsely, starting back.

"I don't reckon you'll ever know Him," said The Orphan, his voice very low and monotonous. "Stand just as you are–don't move–I want to talk with you."

Tex simply stared at him in pitiful helplessness and could not speak, beads of perspiration standing out on his face, testifying to the agony of fear he was in.

"You're on the wrong side of the game again, Tex," The Orphan said slowly, watching the puncher narrowly, his gun steady as a rock. "You still want to kill me, it seems. I've given you your life twice, once to your knowledge, and I told you with the sheriff that I would shoot you if you ever returned; and still you have come back to have me do it. You were not satisfied to let things rest as they were."

Tex did not reply, and The Orphan continued, a flicker of contempt about his lips.

"You were never cast for an outlaw, Tex. If I do say it myself, it takes a clever man to live at that game, and I know, for I've been all through it. As you see, Sneed and I didn't shoot each other, for the play was too plain, too transparent. You should have ambushed one of his men, burned his corrals and slaughtered his cattle, for then he might have shot and talked later. And he might have gotten me, too, for I was unsuspecting. I don't say that I would kill an innocent man to arouse his anger if I had been in your place, I'm only showing you where you made the mistake, where you blundered. Had you killed one of his men it is very probable that his rage would have known no bounds, but as it was the provocation was not great enough."

Tex remained silent and unconsciously toyed at his ear. The Orphan looked keenly at the movement and wondered where he had seen it before, for it was familiar. His face darkened as memory urged something forward to him out of the dark catacombs of the past, and he stilled his breathing to catch a clue to it. He saw the little ranch his father had worked so hard over to improve, and had fought hard to save, and then the picture of his dying mother came vividly before him; but still something avoided his searching thoughts, something barely eluded him, trembling on the edge of the Then and Now. He saw his father's body slowly swinging and turning in the light breeze of a perfect day, and he quivered at the nearness of what he was seeking, its proximity was tantalizing. The rope!–the rope about his father's neck had been of manila fiber; he could never forget the soiled, bleached-yellow streak which had led upward to Eternity. And manila ropes were, at that time, a rarity in that part of the country, for rawhide and braided-hair lariats had been the rule. And on the day when he had given Tex his life in the defile he had noticed the faded yellow rope which had swung at the puncher's saddle horn. As he strained with renewed hope to catch the elusive impression another scene came before him. It was of three men bent over a cow, engaged in blotting out his father's brand, and instantly the face of one of them sprang into sharp definition on his mental canvas.

"D—n you!" he cried, his finger tightening on the trigger of the Colt which for so many years had been his best friend. "I know you now, changed as you are! Now I know why you have been so determined for my death. On the day that I cut my father down I swore that I would kill the man who had lynched him if kind fate let me find him, and I have found him. You have just five minutes to live, so make the most of it, you cowardly murderer!"

Tex's face went suddenly white again and his nerve deserted him. His Colt was in his hand, but oh, so useless! Should he fight to the end? A shudder ran through him at the thought, for life was so good, so precious; far too precious to waste a minute of it by dying before his time was up. Perhaps the foreman would relent, perhaps he would become so wrapped up in the memories of the years gone by as to forget, just for half a second, where he was. The watch in The

Orphan's hand gave him hope, for he would wait until the other glanced at it–that would be his only hope of life.

The foreman's watch ticked loudly in the palm of his left hand and the Colt in his right never quivered. The first minute passed in terrifying silence, then the second, then the third, but all the time The Orphan's eyes stared steadily at the man before him, gray, cruel, unblinking.

"They told me to do it! They told me to do it!" shrieked the pitiful, unnerved wreck of a man as he convulsively opened and shut his hand. "I didn't want to do it! I swear I didn't want to do it! As God is above, I didn't want to! They made me, they made me!" he cried, his words swiftly becoming an unintelligible jumble of meaningless sounds. He stared at the black muzzle of the Colt, frozen by terror, fascinated by horror and deadened by despair. The watch ticked on in maddening noise, for his every sense was now most acute, beating in upon his brain like the strokes of a hammer. Then the foreman glanced quickly at it. The gun in Tex's hand leaped up, but not quickly enough, and a spurt of smoke enveloped his face as he fell. The Orphan stepped back, dropping the Colt into its holster.

"The courage of despair!" he whispered. "But I'm glad he died game," he slowly added. Then he suddenly buried his face in his hands: "Helen!" he cried. "Helen–forgive me!"

CHAPTER XXIII
THE GREAT HAPPINESS

The town was rapidly losing sharpness of detail, for the straggling buildings were becoming more and more blurred and were growing into sharp silhouettes in the increasing dusk, and the sickly yellow lights were growing more numerous in the scattered windows.

Helen moved about the dining-room engaged in setting the table and she had just placed fresh flowers in the vase, when she suddenly stopped and listened. Faintly to her ears came the pounding hoofbeats of a galloping horse on the well-packed street, growing rapidly nearer with portentous speed. It could not be Miss Ritchie, for there was a vast difference between the comparatively lazy gallop of her horse and the pulse-stirring tattoo which she now heard. The hoofbeats passed the corner without slackening pace, and whirled up the street, stopping in front of the house with a suddenness which she had long since learned to attribute to cowboys. She stood still, afraid to go to the door, numbed with a nameless fear–something terrible must have happened, perhaps to The Orphan. The rider ran up the path, his spurs jingling sharply, leaped to the porch, and the door was dashed open to show him standing before her, sombrero in hand, his quirt dangling from his left wrist. He was dusty and tired, but the expression on his face terrified her, held her speechless.

"Helen!" he cried hoarsely, driving her fear deeper into her heart by his altered voice. "Helen!" She trembled, and he made a gesture of hopelessness and involuntarily stepped toward her, letting the door swing shut behind him. He stood just within the room, rigidly erect, his eyes meeting hers in the silence of strong emotion. Breathlessly she retreated as he advanced, as if instinct warned her of what he had to tell her, until the table was between them; and a spasm of pain flickered across his face as he noticed it, leaving him hard and stern again, but in his eyes was a look of despair, a keen misery which softened her and drew her toward him even while she feared him.

The silence became unbearable and at last she could endure it no longer. "What is it?" she breathed, tensely. "What have you to tell me?"

His eyes never wavered from her face, fascinated in despair of what he must read there, much as he dreaded it, and he answered her from between set lips, much as a man would pronounce his own death sentence. "I have broken my word," he said, harshly.

"Broken your word–to me?" she asked.

"Yes."

Her face brightened and was softened by a child-like wonder, for she felt relieved in a degree, and unconsciously she moved nearer to him. "What is it–what have you done?"

He regarded her without appraising the change in her expression and his reply was as harsh and stern as his first statement, accompanied by no excuses nor words of extenuation. "I have killed a man," he said.

A shiver passed over her and her eyes went closed for a moment. The great choice was at hand now, and in her heart a fierce, short battle raged; on one side was arrayed her early training, all her teachings, all regard for the ideas of law and order which she had absorbed in the East, where human life was safeguarded as the first necessity; and on the other was the Unwritten Law of the range as exemplified by The Orphan. Blood, and human blood, was precious, and her early environment fought bitterly against this regime of direct justice, so startlingly driven into her mind by his bold, cold admission. And then, he had sinned in this way again after he had promised her not to do so. The last thought dominated her and she opened her eyes and looked at him hopefully.

"Perhaps," she said, eagerly, "perhaps you could not avoid it–perhaps you were forced to do it."

"No."

"Oh!" she cried. "You did not–you did not shoot him down without warning! I know you didn't!"

"No, not that," he said slowly. "And, besides, this was his third offense. Twice I have given him his life, and I would have done so again but for what I discovered after I faced him." He paused for a moment and then continued, with more feeling in his voice, a ring of victory and an irrepressible elation. "I found that he was the man for whom I have been looking for fifteen years, and whom I had sworn to kill. He killed my father, killed him like a dog and without a chance for life, hung him to a tree on his own land. And when I learned that, when he had confessed to me, I forgot the new game, I forgot everything but the watch in my hand slowly ticking away his life, the time I had given him to make his peace with God–and I hated the slow seconds, I begrudged him every movement of the hands. Then I shot him, and I was glad, so glad–but oh, dear! If you–if you—"

His voice wavered and broke and he dropped to his knees before her with bowed head as she came slowly toward him and seized the hem of her gown in both hands, kissing it passionately, burying his face in its folds like a tired boy at his mother's knee.

Her eyes were filled with tears and they rimmed her lashes as she looked down on the man at her feet. Bending, she touched him and then placed her hands on his head, tenderly kissing the tangled hair in loving forgiveness.

"Dear, dear boy," she murmured softly. "Don't, dear heart. Don't, you must not–oh, you must not! Please–come with me; get up, dear, and sit with me over here in the corner; then you shall tell me all about it. I am sure you have not done wrong–and if you have–don't you know I love you, boy? Don't you know I love you?"

He stirred slightly, as if awakening from a troubled sleep, and slowly raised his head and looked at her with doubt in his eyes, for it was so much like a dream–perhaps it was one. But he saw a light on her face, a light which a man sees only on the face of one woman and which blinds him against all other lights forever. Then it was true, all true–he had heard aright! "Helen!" he cried, "Helen!" and the ring in his voice brought new tears to her eyes. He sprang to his feet, tense, eager, all his nerves tingling, and his quirt hissed through the air and snapped a defiance, a warning to the world as he clasped her to him. "I knew, I knew!" he cried passionately. "In my heart I knew you were a thoroughbred!"

He tilted her head back, but she laughed low with delight and eluded him, leading him to a chair, the chair he had occupied on the occasion of his first visit, and then drew a low, rough footrest beside him and seated herself at his feet, her elbows resting on his knees and her chin in her hands. He looked down into the upturned face and then glanced swiftly about the homelike room and back to her face again. She snuggled tightly against his knees and waited patiently for his story.

He sighed contentedly and touched her cheek reverently and then told her all of the story of Tex Williard, from the very beginning to the very end, from the time he had seen Tex bending over one of his father's cows to the last scene in the thicket. When he had finished, Helen took his head between her hands, pressing it warmly as she nodded wisely to show that she understood. He looked deep into her eyes and then suddenly bent his head until his lips touched her ear: "Helen, darling," he whispered, "how long must I wait?"

"Why, you scamp!" she exclaimed, teasingly, threatening to draw away from him. "You haven't even told me that you love me!"

He pressed her hands tightly and laughed aloud, joyously, filled with an elated, effervescent gladness which surged over him in waves of delight: "Haven't I? Oh, but you know better, dear. Many and many times I have told you that, and in many ways, and you knew it and understood. You never doubted it, and I hope," he added seriously, "that you never will."

"I never will, dear."

They did not hear Grace Ritchie in the kitchen, did not hear her quiet step as it crossed the threshold and stopped, and then tiptoed to the rear door and sped lightly around the house to the street, and down it to where Mrs. Shields and Mary were walking toward the house. They did not know that half an hour had passed since the coming of the quiet step and the three women, and that the supper was hopelessly ruined. They knew nothing–and Everything: they had learned the Great Happiness.

THE END

Also by Clarence E. Mulford

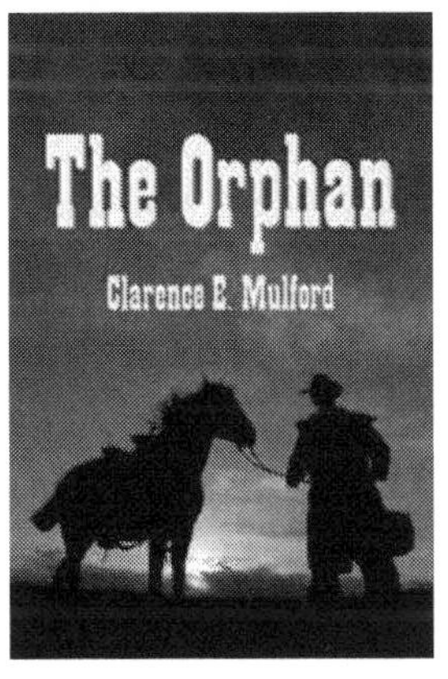

1835593R00100

Made in the USA
San Bernardino, CA
07 February 2013